SET CONTROLS FOR THE HEART OF THE SUN

Exordium

Imagine if you were able to see every person in the world that happened to be defecating at a given moment, altogether at the same time. You would look up at a huge cavernous canopy of assholes excreting into a void above you. And the sight of countless sphincters quivering and palpitating overhead would be combined with the collective, grisly stench of human effluent and the squelching rasps of half a billion dilating anuses. Although you think your situation is not real, you just cannot be sure. Escape would be impossible. Close your eyes and you risk drowning in putrid, reeking faeces; run for the door and there may be something even worse on the other side. Your need to leave the real world has been expropriated by your out of control subconscious, and you are being punished for your own suppressed, incoherent wants and desires.

The trip had begun well. Within thirty minutes of taking a hit I watched the artex-patterned ceiling develop into a vast rolling ocean above me, and sensed the sofa shift lightly so as to drift a small distance above the floor. The gentle drone of viola and mellotron from the hi-fi washed around the room and created a haze of ambient sound about me. Before long the music formed into visible waves that broke against the walls and floor with a gentle tidal ebb. The window glass sparkled with the crystallised points of orange light from the street lamps outside, some breaking free from the window frame and floating past me on currents of whispering, solidifying air. I settled down and began to luxuriate in the thick, cloying sumptuousness of a trip out of the real world and beyond my saturated ego.

It was probably the sound of screeching car tyres, crunching metal and the ensuing argument caused by the accident outside that shifted the course of the trip for the worse. I moved unsteadily over to the window and squinted to the street four storeys below. The concrete walkway and parapet prevented me seeing what was happening but I could make out the sound of inarticulate abuse being exchanged between the parties involved in whatever collision had taken place. The angry voices vibrated in the coloured night air and immediately I felt threatened.

I stumbled back to the sofa and attempted to filter out the fracas beyond, but already the ocean on the ceiling was becoming a dreary hue of brown and the music had lost its harmonious ambience and gained a repetitious, grating discordance. The sofa now felt hard and uncomfortable and I could not escape the suspicion that there were other people in the room, hiding from me: an undisclosed presence. My body prickled with sweat and my heart raced wildly. Gingerly, I leant over the arm of the sofa to check in the corner for whoever had entered the room. They were there, I knew, but the shadows hid them from me. They must have been Lilliputian in stature, but that didn't mean they couldn't grow larger whenever they desired. In fact, they had probably crept in through cracks and crevices as tiny creatures, and were about to expand into their monstrous bodies.

I huddled back into the middle of the sofa and listened to the shouting and yelling getting louder and closer. Then, suddenly, I realised that the beings hiding in my room had stolen the angry voices from outside and appropriated them for their own. They first whispered then yelled from their hiding places, each word diffusing from one end of the room to the other in succession and then above me, like an early stereo recording swapping sounds between speakers:

'Fuckin' arsehole... stupid bastard... twat...'

I looked upwards, from where the voices now seemed to come. The artex waves of the ceiling had turned into an unending expanse of dilating anuses. The scene was fascinating in its massive, grotesque obscenity. I could not look away despite a retching disgust at the sight, the all-

SET CONTROLS FOR THE HEART OF THE SUN

Neil Rushton

Bright Pen

Visit us online at www.authorsonline.co.uk

A Bright Pen Book

ISBN 978-07552-1147-0

Authors OnLine Ltd
19 The Cinques
Gamlingay, Sandy
Bedfordshire SG19 3NU
England

This book is also available in e-book format, details of which are
available at www.authorsonline.co.uk

For Chris... dead but dreaming

embracing acrid smell and the insinuated – but at the same time real – juicy splatter of excrement on my face.

Then, finally, I saw the beings that had invaded the flat. My weirdly extended vision compelled me to range close up to the quivering sea of sphincters, where every now and then a Gollum-like head and torso would duck down below its own disembodied alimentary canal, cackle insanely and hurl a stream of broken invective at me: 'Fackin' arsehole, heh heh heh... shit arse, shit arse... splatter it, splatter it.'

The timeless horror of the night ahead stretched before me.

But then these are the risks you take when you allow LSD to take your mind down the neural rabbit hole.

I

I don't really know how it happened to me. After their deaths, a year ago, it crept up on me when my defences were down and then burrowed deep inside like a neurological parasite intent on causing a pathological condition. But I didn't notice the signs when they first appeared. There was probably a gestation period of several months as it slowly infiltrated me and imperceptibly changed my every thought, action and decision without me realising. I was just too overwhelmed dealing with my grief and guilt to see it getting a grip on me. The thousand shitty accoutrements of living alone on the blocks distracted the remainder of my energy until I was almost completely under its power. It was not as though I had it as bad as so many of the social refugees that inhabited the blocks: the single mothers on welfare and Valium, the junkies spiralling into oblivion, the isolated, hopeless elderly. Compared to them I would have said that I was quite low on the list of latent psychosis-timebombs. And yet within six months I was almost a prisoner in my own home, with only the flat and the walkway outside my front door offering safe refuge.

I should have been on medication during that time, but I never seemed to get around to going to the doctor. The fear of the crowded waiting room was one thing, but the dread of having to articulate my condition to a stranger was even worst. And despite the trauma no one from the Health Services ever got in touch to offer help of any kind. I now know that was an administrative mistake, I had slipped through the system, but at the time I had just thought that was how the system worked.

So I grew into myself, alone in the flat day after day, constantly thinking about *them* and what I had done but at the same time, without knowing it, gradually repressing each emotive image, each sensual memory of what we had been. As the months passed my neuro-parasite appended itself to the repression of my memories and I began sinking into a pit. It was a dank pit of despair and lethargy, both vying for precedence amidst the nameless days. All I was left with was an emotionless image of *them* turning round and round inside my head and a crippling dread of the world that had beaten me into a corner.

There were no friends or family to help me through. They had always seemed unnecessary when it was the three of us. They had drifted away over the years. So I found myself interacting with no-one, talking only to myself and the few people who it was necessary to talk to in order to function. One was my cannabis dealer, a slicked-back nameless pouter on the ground floor of my block who had taken pity on me and supplied me with decent grade stuff at cost. He even delivered it to my door. And I needed it. Cannabis got me through that first six months. It allowed me to make it to the shops without being overcome by sweating palpitations and it allowed me to hold a conversation with another person without stammering my words into an embarrassing meaninglessness. I had replaced my GP with my dealer.

But still I had been confined to the flat for most of the time. It was my harbour from the brutality that I could sense as a predator outside. The beast sometimes took the form of people, but just as often it was simply buildings, traffic, noise, the never-ending maelstrom of the city. The flat was a refuge and a prison. I voluntarily incarcerated myself amidst the concrete blocks that so oppressed me, because even that was better than being outside.

Then, six months ago, my parasite got tired of its attritional neurological war and burst out like a mental cluster bomb. On one of my rare trips to the shops I found myself in a crowded aisle being jostled by all and sundry. After the usual sweating, shaking and flushing I began to feel a surge of uncontrollable anger breaking down all my internal barricades. But the anger was not contained or directed in any way or at anything. It unleashed itself from God knows where and splattered itself in every direction. It was mixed up with visceral panic and a confusion that attempted to ricochet itself off every cerebral wall in my brain. All I remember is shouting and screaming, lashing out wildly at the people around me, and then passing out. Actually that's not quite true. During a fleeting lucid moment I *do* remember landing a particularly satisfactory thwack onto the jowls of one old woman, who had been zealously pushing me to one side in her belligerent pursuit of the last half-priced can of black beans in front of me. *Then* I passed out. But I've never told anyone that I remember this.

Either way, I was hospitalised, sectioned for twenty-eight days and assigned to a psychiatrist. And now I'm taking LSD as the main constituent medication of my treatment.

I wandered outside onto the walkway for a constitutional joint after another unproductive day. It had been two days since my scatological trip and I had done nothing since. As usual, the days were made up of lying in bed or trying to read, the evenings of listening to music and observing the monotonous, rancorous routine of the blocks at night. The previous night I had not felt safe even on the walkway, because there was so much shouting and insidious movement everywhere.

I leant on the concrete and fibreglass parapet, carefully avoiding the weakened section where rusty iron rods poked out of two cracks that had been widening and contracting with the seasons for as long as I could remember. My view was a close trajectory of tenement blocks, some rising no higher than the five-storey block I lived in, but others eliminating the sky and imposing their grim cementious aspects over the relentless asphalt plan. In summer the front window of the flat was granted about twenty minutes per day direct sunlight as the sun moved between the two highest monoliths during the late afternoon. The rest of the time I lived in a constant shadow. It was as if the shade cast over the flat contained all the misery, sorrow and disappointed aspirations of the tenants in the tower blocks. A residue of their pitiful lives had become captured in the gloom that spread out from their concrete dwellings and embraced my home.

Reinforced-concrete tower blocks. They seemed imbued with a malady, a symbol of the urban underclass that had become a *real* sickness. The malaise was contained within the concrete itself, infecting us, unceasingly polluting our existence until it had gained control of every thought and action. The concrete oppression kept us in our place, opiated and disenfranchised from society, never able to clean off the grey qualm that signalled us out and which would never leave us. It reached deep down into our subconscious filling our dreams up like liquid cement in a foundation trench. Everyone knew this. At some level it seemed that we were collectively aware of each other's depression. There was a subliminal recognition of our hopeless, stunted lives. Sometimes, in my claustrophobic, dimly lit dreams, I would see people from the blocks that I knew only by sight. They would be weeping and running their fingernails down endless lengths of concrete walls and running through dank underground tunnels beneath the blocks, always looking over their shoulders, afraid of where they were but without any ideas for finding a way out. And I knew that I was in their dream, their collective somnambulant confirmation of despair. I would be there. I had always been there. But I only realised it since I accepted the blame for necessitating the deaths of the only two people I had ever loved.

The sound of two exasperated voices pulled me from my thoughts and drew my gaze to the third storey walkway of the block across the road about fifty metres away. A girl and boy, neither over eighteen, were making their way to the den at number thirty-three. It took them about five minutes to cover the short distance from the dilapidated stairwell to the front door due to interminable arguing, frequent finger pointing and backward stepping. Finally they reached their destination, knocked the door with furtive, unseeing glances around them, and were let in to the darkened interior. Two minutes later they sidled out of the half opened door, bickering and looking about nervously as though trying to conform to a stereotype of guileless junkies inexperienced in the world into which they had fallen. They disappeared into the stairwell and on to whatever version of reality they would find that night.

Their little act fed the grim inevitability of another evening in the blocks. Before long there was a stream of society's toe-end on the way to the den and other lesser outlets. Singles, couples, gangs, young, old(ish), white, black, hooded and secretive, t-shirted and brash, talkative, silent, laughing like clowns, trying not to cry – but all of them, every last one, desperate and lost.

I stubbed out my third joint, went inside and double-locked the door.

II

Another day passed as useless as the previous two. But in the evening there was an unusual stillness about the blocks as though the red dusk held everything in its suppressive thrall. I leant over the safe parapet and scanned the walkways. Not a body in sight. The only sound was the invariable rumble of traffic from the unseen main road behind my block. But there were no cars on the road below and nothing moved except the clothes hanging out on balcony washing lines, flapping in the gentle warm breeze, tinged magenta by the dusk light.

Twilight was the only time of day that I was ever marginally comfortable with myself, especially when it was like this. The world, even this graffiti-strewn asphalt world, suddenly began to resonate with a quiet torpor – a torpor that was often mimicked by the altered states brought on by LSD and, to a lesser extent cannabis. The edges of everything became softened and I was able to put some distance between the moment and all the things that were usually wrong with me. The depression became a wistful melancholia; the anxiety disorders became dulled memories. The reddened world somehow suppressed the usual exasperation that inhabited the everyday and replaced it with something liminal, something on the edge of normality, something better. I could never properly grasp the link between this twilight ambience and the fathomless experience of an altered state, but it existed. They were both touching the same hidden parts of my subconscious and allowing me to glimpse the otherness that dwelt there. The dusk and LSD used the same coded language.

The twilight ambience washed over me and allowed me to approach the memories of my LSD trips over the past six months. Not the last few trips, they had drifted towards the malicious and nasty, especially the canopy of pube-matted assholes three nights ago. But previous to that they had given me access to perceptions so austere, so unimaginable, that they had changed everything fundamentally. I had realised that all I'd known of life previous to taking acid was at best partial and at worst a lie. And the memories lived in a strange place. They were beyond the normal recall of events and feelings. They had their own special whereabouts and only came back when they had a reason to. And as my gaze coasted beyond the tower blocks I recognised the first glinting insinuation of the acid-memory tapping into the languid atmosphere. Or was it the other way round? Either way I knew what was coming and my grip tightened on the parapet.

My gaze became fixed as I stared out to the west. The endless expanse of rooflines beyond the blocks were schemed in deepening shadows, interrupted by the vaguely glistening patches of greenery in distant parks and gardens. It was a view that usually subdued me and sapped my energy, but the dusky stillness of the blocks had begun to lend lucidness to it and I squinted a little to take it in. The roofs seemed uncertain, transitory. There was something about them that evoked a remembrance – a remembrance that belonged to someone else... or something else.

I closed my eyes and visualised the drug slip slyly into my nerve cells and fool my brain into shooting it across the synaptic cleft. After this the flashback was inevitable. The constant backdrop of traffic noise started to warp and come nearer before funnelling off into a void. But the void remained open and filled, and so could not be a void...

...My gaze is fixed as I stare out to the west. The endless expanse of rooflines beyond the blocks no longer exists and a church bell tolls deep and resonant across a broad, wooded valley. A blue mist hangs over the canopy of trees infused with the scent of wood smoke. The drifting molecules of the chiming bell are visible as scattered iron particles, each wave dancing to its own key. The wood is obsidian and alive with movement. It suddenly seems full of animals, unseen but infiltrating every part of the forest with their sinuous, ever-moving presence. I put myself there with them. I stand amidst the austere beech groves and listen to their imaginations making sense of the all-embracing world in which we think we live. Looking up I feel a film of pollen filling the air with its sumptuous, embodied presence. It makes the trees seem indistinct and flat, like blurred images on a screen. In another instance they are gone altogether and I feel myself gravitating to the ground amidst the thick, perfumed air. I lower my heavy, tired head until it touches the leaf mould and fungi-infested bark of the forest floor. It gradually turns into the cold hard concrete of the parapet...

I blinked hard and drew a gulping, unsteady breath. I was back on the walkway. The grey blocks resonated with their usual clamour, invigorated by its previous, temporary absence, and the dusk had darkened into a deep, velvety purple. I cleared my watery eyes and rubbed my temples. My heart was still thumping away. I was not surprised to find myself back on the walkway, but the dissociation of the flashback brought with it an aching, mournful longing when replaced with the mundane scope of my reality. This longing to be back in my altered state, the realm of otherness, was always the same, was always overwhelming. But this time it included a sense that something had changed, or that something was about to happen, or both. The flashback had come loaded with an awareness of impending transformation and I was not sure whether I should be afraid or delighted.

I straightened up and moved back inside, keen to remove myself from the noise and movement of the outside world. Ober was sitting in the old leather armchair; his aquiline features dusted violet with the deepening twilight. I wondered how long I had been burrowing my head into the parapet and how long he had been there.

'What's going on my friend?' he said, inspecting me with his customary air of edited concern. 'I thought I'd caught you communing with the concrete, so I let you be.'

I half-laughed to mask my embarrassment, but Ober was looking at my shifty hands and absorbing my awkwardness. I attempted to slow my breathing and keep control of my speech but my stutter was inevitable.

'N-n-no. I had a bit of a hard trip a few nights ago and I think that now it's t-t-trying to make it up to me.'

'With *my* LSD?'

'Yes. You said I was ok to t-take it without you if I felt comfortable.'

'But you evidently didn't feel comfortable,' he said, his languid public school accent imposing itself on me. 'You had better tell me about it.'

I slumped into the sofa and started to go over the remembered details of my scatological trip three evenings previous. But as usual it sounded awkward. Attempting to describe and express the essence of a psychedelic experience within the limitations of language was just not possible. And, for once, I didn't blame my own intellectual inadequacies. It was down to the experience, the somehow non-human emotional qualities of participating in an existence that had no reference to what the brain usually processed in everyday reality. I attempted to tell Ober what it felt like to be there, but, as always, the description sounded hollow and contrived.

Not that it mattered too much. Ober was my psychiatrist. He understood.

'Entheogens, such as LSD, are not always predictable when taken in high doses in an uncontrolled environment,' he said, after listening to my account. 'We have discussed this at length.'

I nodded and lost eye contact.

'But as therapeutic tools entheogens are unrivalled... providing the environment is right and that the taker is properly monitored.' He drew my eyes back to him. 'I'm not just another bored clinician going through the psychiatric motions with you my friend. We've found ways into and out of consciousness with these substances and you must take my word for it that they are here to help you. Their purpose is to help you.'

'Help me,' I found myself saying, as if repeating a mantra.

'Everything will change for the better.'

'Everything... everything.'

'Now sit back and relax for a moment. You need to dampen the anxiety I can feel welling up.'

Ober started to take deep, controlled breaths. It was a tried and tested magical trick he had of making me calm down. Almost immediately I found myself following his composed, even breathing. It infected me. It was almost like a drug. The bubbling anxiety caused by the recall of the trip was suppressed. All my muscles relaxed and I sunk deeper into the sofa. I closed my eyes and allowed my concentration to focus on steady breaths: four in, hold for two, four out, hold for two.... Within moments my inner imagery became more sharp-focussed, more real. It was often like this with Ober – it was almost as if he carried in his presence an aspect of the drugs with which he was treating me. He set my breathing right, defined my internal imagery and allowed me to think straight. Perhaps he was even putting thoughts into my mind. It was a bit of a ridiculous concept, but his influence over me was more complete than with anyone else I'd ever known. Why shouldn't I confer supernatural abilities on him? The drugs had certainly made it very clear that supernatural was actually quite ordinary.

I found myself mentally scanning over my patient-psychiatrist relationship with Ober. When I came round in the hospital ward from my psychotic episode in the shop he was one of the first people at my bedside. I think it was only three days later, after a couple of token sessions of CBT, that he was explaining to me the treatment he would be taking me through over the coming months: supervised sessions involving the administration of ever-increasing doses of LSD. Why not? I'd never taken it before and at the time I had no idea just how many thousands of miles it was off the scale of medical ethics.

Nothing happened at the hospital. Ober got me released from my section and we started the very next day in the flat. He injected my first dose – 100 micrograms – and I was up in five seconds. The initial visuals were startling, but I supposed they were just the usual things: billowing walls, tracers in the air, congealing colours. I didn't know they were just the forebears to a comprehensive overhaul of what I had come to think of as everyday reality. Ten hours later I was back down again, sure that nothing was ever going to be the same. Everything in my life I had learnt, believed and experienced before that point was like a record cover – the LSD-state was the recording.

Six months down the line I was taking the LSD orally on blotters laced with one milligram – 1000 micrograms – of Ober's pure samples. Twice a week usually, sometimes three. I'd never taken it without him being present before the asshole-trip, primarily because I was too scared. Just lately the trips had been turning in on themselves, becoming recurrent meditations on a theme of death and decay. And, although I was not really able to contemplate it, I knew why.

'I'm not going to bore you with any tedious psychoanalyses of why your subconscious got itself hooked up on anuses,' he said, bringing me out of my thoughts and back into the room. He was grinning slyly and eyeing me up with a diagnostic squint. 'Let's just see it as a bit of a joke.'

'A joke?'

'Or perhaps a parting shot from LSD. A farewell gesture'

I tightened up. Was Ober thinking of suspending my treatment? I started to think of arguments against this course of action.

'Because when the LSD-experience begins to turn in on itself it usually signifies a change is needed in the treatment. I'm not really interested in your subconscious' proclivity towards anal analogy.'

'But—'

Ober held up his hand. 'When was the last time *they* formed a fundamental part of one of your entheogenic sessions?'

My heart flitted and my mouth stuttered. 'I d-d-don't

know... it's probably been three or four since they were last th-there.'

'It was session forty eight, nine sessions ago.'

'Oh.'

'After that session it was the first time you had been able to talk about them or what had happened in any detail. In fact that's probably the reason for the downturn in the LSD-experience. The main root of your anxieties has been flushed out. It's done its job.'

'So why is it that I still can't bring myself to step outside until I've smoked a j-j-joint?'

Ober shrugged. 'These things take time. Six months isn't that long to make a recovery from what happened to you... even with as many LSD-sessions as you've had. If I were diagnosing you from the DSM you'd have a list of anxiety disorders as long as my arm, all compounded by or associated with depressive episodes.'

'But—'

'But, as you know, I'm not diagnosing you from DSM. You are not mentally ill. You are reacting in a very normal way to very traumatic events. Plus you had six months without any help before you were sectioned to cultivate a set of debilitating syndromes.'

'You told me no-one is really mentally ill.'

'No, I told you that either very few people are really mentally ill or that nearly everyone is. It's just a question of who controls the diagnoses and the definition of "mental illness".'

I clammed up, nervous, as unsure as always of my ability to engage with Ober. I glanced to the bookshelves to one side of him to avert eye contact. But he followed my look and came back with his eyes smiling.

'Your library's growing,' he said, narrowing his eyes just enough to let me know he was coaxing a reaction out of me. But I just nodded. A *library* – one bookcase, half of which was filled with introductions to this or that. I turned red.

Ober got up and plucked a book from the shelf. '*The Secret Heresy of the Cathars*,' he read out. 'Have you read it?'

'Not yet.'

'Interesting beliefs, Cathars. Probably pretty close to the truth. Certainly closer than the maniacs who persecuted them. But imagine how they'd be treated today. They would be diagnosed with every type of delusion under the DSM sun.'

I was never quite sure whether Ober did benevolent condescension on purpose or not. It didn't really matter; the tendrils of anxiety were beginning to grab hold of me. Ober, as always, noticed. He replaced the book and sat back down.

'Will I not be taking LSD again then?' I asked, after a pause, attempting to sound as if I didn't care too much.

'Probably not,' replied Ober. 'We'll move you on to something new.'

'Another psychedelic?'

'Another entheogen, yes.'

I relaxed.

'We need you to start bringing some things back with you. The LSD's been breaking up your repression, but you're not consolidating enough of what you find in your altered states.' He paused and seemed to zone out for a moment. '... And now that I've assessed you we need to pin you down...'

'Pin me down?'

He snapped back into the conversation. 'We know where the new entheogens will take you. We'll be able to monitor you in a more... satisfactory way.'

'Monitor me?'

'Follow your entheogenic movements more closely.'

'Will we not be having sessions then?'

'Sort of. I'll explain it later this week when I bring over the material.'

I wanted to pursue Ober on this but he made a gesture that clearly signified that was all there was to be said on the matter. He got up again and pointed to the pouch of skunk on the table.

'Shall we?' he said.

I put something ambient onto the hi-fi and rolled a nice big cannon for us to share. We relocated to the walkway outside and leant on the safe parapet, smoking the joint in silence and watching the regathered momentum of block-life taking place amidst the last vestiges of dusk. Across at number thirty-three the den was receiving its first visitors of the evening. Two hooded guys, one black one white, were shoulder-strutting their way along the striplit walkway as if they owned the block. One of them whistled once outside the door and they were let in.

'Paper boys,' I said, 'every Wednesday and Saturday at eight without fail.'

'Right,' replied Ober, taking the joint from me. 'Crack and heroin?'

'What else would it be?'

Ober curled his lip into a sneer and raised an eyebrow as though to express his repugnance at everything around him. It was such a familiar expression that it was how I always pictured him whenever he came into my thoughts. I could never be sure whether it was an affectation or an involuntary reaction to the blocks. I didn't know him well enough to be sure.

'It can be more. Why do you think I've been treating you with LSD and not...' he gestured towards the den, 'that stuff?'

I smiled, relighting the faltering joint. 'Are you saying you'd like all these people to be on acid instead of heroin?'

Ober recoiled at 'acid' – he never liked me using the term – but then fixed his gaze on me again and took the joint.

'Sort of. Eventually.'

'Eventually?'

His eyes shimmered in the half-light and his lips twitched into a parodied smile. It was always his expression of superiority – at least, that is, it made me feel inferior. But, as with most things about Ober, I was never sure if it was simply his natural character filtering through his professional psychiatrists' poise or a set of postures designed especially for me as part of my treatment. He leaned a bit further into the parapet and impregnated the moment with a pause.

'Have you ever thought about how society might work as a collective intelligence?' he asked, enunciating each word clearly as though to ensure the meaning hit home.

'Um...'

'With a collective intelligence so much of humanity is superfluous; individuals are expendable. These addicted, useless, depressed people could be shed from the main body

15

of society in the way a living being can shed a certain number of cells without any harm coming to it. In fact it's probably preferable for them to be cast out, allowed to be non-participants in the collective.'

'Jeez Ober, that sounds a bit like an application of the Final Solution.'

'There's *a* final solution,' he said, sounding unusually earnest. 'Not what you're thinking though. And besides, take a look at the world my friend. Junkies are hardly the biggest problem.'

I waited for him to continue but he didn't. I was reluctant to engage – even under the influence of the weed I was afraid of highlighting my ignorance and my poor use of language. But what the hell, this was only one of Ober's theories wasn't it?

'So couldn't they be brought into the collective?' I asked, unconvinced I knew what I really wanted to say. 'I may not take heroin but I'm one of them aren't I? I'm underclass, not economically productive... not of much use to society. But am I part of this collective intelligence when I take LSD?'

Ober's smirk turned into a more genuine smile. 'That's very prescient my friend. Does it feel like you're part of something bigger when you're on it?'

'You know it does.'

'Yes I do don't I.' He took a long draw on the joint and passed it over to me indicating that I should finish it off. 'Do you think it would affect them in the same way?' he said, averting his eyes to the den. Rhetorical questions were Ober's speciality.

'I don't know. Wouldn't they need to be weaned off their opiates first?'

'Well, if, let's just say, the collective intelligence – if we accept there is such a thing – had a core of people at its centre, controlling the furtherance of a civilisation based on such a concept. Then they would have to make the decision as to whether the section of humanity, or society, which was fulfilling no social role, was worth the time and endeavour needed to bring them to a stage where they were able to contribute to such a furtherance. There is actually a large body of evidence that entheogenic drugs, when used as part of a systematic programme of psychiatric treatment, are extremely successful in helping people to overcome opiate and alcohol addictions. But a collective intelligence, by its own definition, may not think it worthwhile to invest resources on individuals whose loss will not affect the whole. In fact, their wastage may strengthen the collective.'

I took in the last of the smoke and flicked the stub over the parapet. I'd rolled it strong. I'd also smoked the majority of it, which left me struggling to keep up with Ober's line. The cannabis surge was getting in the way of thinking straight.

'Wastage?'

'The future holds many social developments that would seem inconceivable at the moment.'

'Does it?'

'One of them is the evolution of humanity. There'll be no place left for the individual. The Collectivity of the entheogenic experience will be transferred to all.'

My vision was tunnelling into the night, dragging in the concrete blocks and layering Ober's words with a lacquer of cannabis weediness. I was having difficulty differentiating statement of fact from theoretical concept. What was he talking about?

'I think we can help you to be ready for the revolution though my friend.'

God, I was monumentally stoned. 'Revolution?'

'Revolutions... evolutions: social, cultural, political,' he continued, his voice now slightly terse and distant. 'But personal evolutions need to come first. And consciousness is where it begins.'

It wasn't often I regretted how much I'd smoked, but this was one such occasion. Ober was trying to infiltrate me with an idea but I was too monged to take anything on board. I couldn't even work out if he was only saying these things *because* I was stoned.

'So is this... is this collective intelligence the same as the collective unconscious? What do you call it... ?'

Even in my stoned state I recognised Ober's marginal drift away from me – his slight loss of patience.

'I call it the Phylogenic Memory, but you can call it

whatever you like my friend. I'm not a big fan of excessive terminology for concepts that don't need words.'

'So are they the same?'

'In some ways.'

'The repository of all human knowledge past and future, existing for anyone to access should they be in the right state of consciousness.' I was pleased with being able to pull that one up through the cannabis smog in my brain. Ober just nodded slowly. 'So how can it... how can we...' I'd lost my thread.

Ober filled in the thought: 'How can we utilise a psychoanalytical conceptual theory to bring about revolutions?'

'Yeah.'

'Well, the answer to that most likely depends on the validity of the theory. If the theory of a Phylogenic Memory is valid then it can be utilised to change everything.'

'Everything?'

Ober took a prolonged breath. 'Try to imagine a society that had access – if it exists of course – to a Phylogenic Memory. That society would potentially know everything at a collective level. And if you know everything then you have the ability to always make the right decisions.'

'Socrates!' I exclaimed, triumphantly, inordinately proud of extracting the correct reference from my cannabis-steeped brain.

'Socrates indeed. But whereas he thought such knowledge could be utilised by individuals within the prevailing political and social conditions, a real understanding of *everything* will actually turn us into something else. And it will require a collective intelligence to harness the new state.'

'But who'd be in charge?' I was starting to feel a bit sick.

Ober grinned and started to roll another, smaller joint. 'Quis custodiet ipsos custodes?'

'Eh?'

'No one will need to be in charge.'

He sealed the joint and lit it up. Despite my queasiness I accepted it when he passed it over. The first drag made me feel marginally better, but when I closed my eyes for a second I saw her. My heart billowed and my stomach moved in an upward direction. Her sunlit face was startlingly clear and I thought that I was heading for another flashback. But I felt Ober's hand on my back and immediately her image began to fade.

'Are you all right?' He said, removing his hand.

'Yeah... yes.' But I wasn't. I pulled back the sudden choking in my throat, my eyes welling up. A single uninvited tear rolled down my cheek and fell with a surprisingly loud plop on the concrete. Ober was silent, but when I looked at him again through my watery eyes he was evidently making mental notes. It was a tactic to which I had become accustomed during our sessions. It was as if he were able to assess me remotely, without asking any questions. Sometimes it disturbed me but at that moment I was glad for the silence.

'It's hard you know,' I said after a minute, my voice unsteady but free of stutter. 'I still can't believe I'm here and they're not. I wish they were here. I'd do anything to hold them... to...'

Ober seemed about to say something but pulled back and leant on the parapet again, toking on the joint as if to express his tacit, unspoken understanding.

We watched the two paper boys swagger out from number thirty-three and along the walkway, where below their hoods their strained grins were briefly illuminated by the garish striplights for a few seconds before they vanished down the stairwell.

III

The first day of May. Even the concrete blocks couldn't completely check the diffusion of spring air; the palpable sense of change and renewal that thickened the atmosphere, seeping through the cement morning.

Through the window I watched the watery blue sky, only disturbed by a couple of jet streams. I sat at one end of the couch so that all I could see was a patch of sky, mostly unencumbered by the blocks. There were memories locked in that sky. It was the same spring sky of my seventies childhood, a hazily perceived past invoked not so much by the sky itself but by the essence of its existence. Somewhere in that atmosphere were my ancient diluted thoughts and perceptions of reality, my interactions with the changing seasons and the presentiments of spring optimism. My childish reception of life had been infused there and was now able to communicate with me by a mutual agreement that was somehow triggered by the specific ambience of that spring sky. It was a type of time travel, dependent on living memory.

I closed my eyes and pictured a seaside holiday long ago. A week in April that had taken on Elysian proportions from my nostalgic viewpoint. The sense of spring allowed me to touch it, allowed me to restore the fragments of childhood memory into a coherent whole. I was using the sixth sense of memory to link my past to my present, to allow deeply stored perceptions to resurface and inform the person I had become from the person I once was. The innocence, the optimism, the thought that everything would always keep getting better. The locked in remembrance would always be there, waiting for me to tap into it whenever some external agency sanctioned its temporary release. I dwelt on my childish existence, visualised my previous conceptions of reality. It was deeply satisfying. It was my only means of escape from what I had become.

But, as always, it didn't last long. The recalled sea and sky from another decade retreated back to wherever it exists when I wasn't thinking about it and I began to lose the easy, flowing relationship with my past. The suppressed agitation of the present and the anxious fear of the future replaced it. I opened my eyes and remembered where I was and what I had to do.

Deadline. I had a deadline. I slumped back into the sofa, my head starting to ache with the enforced return to the here and now. The sky became just another anonymous pale blue backdrop and the living room's dated interior, with encrusted carpet and dust-filled furniture, recaptured my attention and imposed its authority on me. I closed my eyes again and tried to relax, but my moment of communion with the spring morning was ended and the buoyancy of my mood retreated to a familiar despondency.

And yet, the seed had been sown. However completely my fleeting optimism had dissipated I felt there was now, in some ill-defined way connected to the past, the possibility of escape and recovery, of getting beyond this festering life that kept me drained, exhausted and afraid to set foot outside the front door. For the first time I thought that perhaps my treatment really was beginning to work.

But for now I had a deadline to think about, brought to an uncompromising crisis by my lethargic indolence over the past three days since my cannabis-infused discussion with Ober. The temptation to put off the work for another couple of hours was strong but I knew that Ober would be coming along early evening with his new drugs and unless I got under way before noon I would not get the product out today. The dread feeling that I wouldn't get paid – electronic money transfer on delivery, providing the deadline was met – spurred me from the sofa and into the bedroom, to the spongy old chair in front of the computer. Five minutes later I was using the only skill I had managed to garner in life that had the remotest chance of earning me enough money to live on beyond the Incapacity Benefit that barely covered the bills: designing crappy websites for crappy clients. It wasn't even something at which I was particularly good, but in a world where every two-bit business has to have a website, and yet where so few people have the slightest idea how the technology works, there were always 'clients' willing to pay someone to design their website and set them up with a host. My design skills were pretty rudimentary, learnt from a half-hearted college course a few years ago, but with a decent piece of (pirated) software I was able to put together fairly professional looking sites and earn just enough to keep my cannabis stock topped up and to avoid living on thin air.

But I hated it. I hated having to spend so many hours in front of a computer struggling with a design, wrestling with software that I wasn't trained to use and always having to meet deadlines that had crept up on me amidst my natural lack of inertia. And always alone. I worked from a CD of images and text and a few ideas in e-mails or telephone conversations, but ultimately I sat alone day after day, putting designs together for people who wanted a lot of product for very little money. It was usually dull small business, cheap porn or some moneymaking rubbish involving self-help CDs and courses. The momentary recall of some of the dross that I had produced over the past few years made me squirm in the chair.

I took a deep breath and stared at the ceiling. Why didn't I just get an easy, unskilled part-time job that would allow me to supplement or replace my benefit legitimately? Well, I knew why. I knew how the terror of mingling amongst people incessantly while serving in a shop, or mixing it up with the lumpen proletariat working in a factory would be simply too much for me. It was still hard enough queuing up once a week in the co-op, feeling the sweat break out on my back and the blood rush to my head as people closed in all around me. I certainly was not at the stage yet where I could guarantee not to have another violent panic attack. Jesus, I still couldn't even make it past the stairwell of my block without first toking off two or three joints. I might be on the verge of clinical depression sitting in my flat alone day after day, but at least I didn't have to deal with people and the outside world on a daily basis.

Ober arrived at six o'clock. I had spent the last seven hours dragging and dropping pictures into galleries, pasting text together and trying to get my head around the database coding. It was not going well. I had, as usual, not allowed myself enough time to complete the job, which had been started a couple of weeks before. Occasionally I would be able to extend deadlines, but this client had a particularly uncompromising attitude and had already been e-mailing me to ask where his product was, telling me how important it was that it was delivered on time.

'So what is it?' asked Ober, after setting his briefcase down on the table beside the computer and hearing about my self-imposed situation.

'*The Gloop Shop,*' I replied, realising that what I now considered normal web behaviour was probably going to sound a trifle outrageous to someone, even a psychiatrist, who might have limited knowledge of the more bizarre types of fetish sites.

'The Gloop Shop?'

I braced myself for the synopsis, feeling the first prongs of embarrassment. 'It's a site for people who want to... who want to swap their c-c-cum.' Ober's face remained impassive. I controlled my breathing. 'Basically they appear to want to set up a network of people who can swap, buy or sell their... well, their gloop.'

Ober's lip quivered into his measured impromptu snarl.

'Do you want to see some pics?'

He cocked his head and I opened the home page. A large picture of the hairy Mr Gloop, grimacing at his orgasm and cumming into a sealable plastic bag adorned the page, which then scrolled down to smaller images of various men and women gleefully dribbling jizz into their, or their partners', mouths from bags. All this was set against a deliberately garish all-page background of a medley of penises delivering their ejaculations in a variety of poses and locations. I opened the 'swap shop' page but Ober had already removed himself a couple of steps. He took his chin between his thumb and forefinger.

'Well... there is an eastern Tantrik tradition of magical Kalas... one of which includes the ingestion of semen. A woman is supposed to lick it off a bay leaf to gain precognitive powers. But I'm reasonably confident that Mr Gloop and his compatriots aren't following any Tantrik teaching. It's more like an internet dependent semenophilia... although that doesn't quite do it justice does it.'

I smiled and shrugged. 'Not really, although this site does have something about... "A select group of discerning gloop-eaters who have been active for some time in the south of England."'

There was a pregnant pause before we both laughed. I couldn't remember having seen Ober laugh out loud before.

'And you say this character is threatening to not pay you if you can't deliver the product today?' he said, quickly losing the laughter.

'Well, I can deliver it as it is, so he can see the main design, and try to explain that I need another day or so to finish the coding and sort out a host. But the main problem is that there's no written contract. He won't pay before he receives the goods, and then there's a real possibility that he'll just take the designed site and find someone else to finish it off and host it. People like me are two-a-penny and without any written agreement I don't really have a leg to stand on. And from my contact with him to date I don't think he'd have any compunction about turning me over.'

'Compunction.' Ober sounded pleased with himself as he repeated the word and moved to open his briefcase on the table. He turned and examined me for a moment. 'What if I were to make you an offer that would absolve you from the need to peddle your wares for people like Mr Gloop?'

'An offer?'

'Yes. A... research position.'

Ober explicated his words carefully, allowing me to interact without him having to spell things out.

'A research position doing what?' I obliged.

'Well, let's call it a programme of psycho-pharmacological research, attached to my consultancy. It would also, of course, be the next stage in your course of therapy, as we discussed the other day. So you would be able to retain some of your incapacity benefits.'

He took a couple of padded envelopes out of his briefcase, slipped a sheet of headed paper from one and handed it to me. 'Those would be your obligations and that's how much you'll be paid,' he said, pointing at the paper.

I scanned the page and lingered on the terms for a moment before flipping the paper over to see if there was something on the other side. There wasn't. I realised the terms must have been drawn up specifically for me with the expectation of me accepting them and I suddenly I felt a familiar anxiety, as though in the presence of a complete stranger.

'You'll see that the project lasts for a year,' he continued, 'depending on results.'

I still couldn't make my eyes meet his. 'So this research position entails me...'

'...It entails an exploration-based therapy. The derealisation and reciprocal inhibition treatment we have been carrying out under the LSD will be taken to another... phase,' he said, sounding slightly unhappy with his choice of words. 'You'll be supplied with a variety of entheogenic drugs and you will take them in controlled sessions with me, allowing a reasonable interval between each trip. Much the same as your treatment with LSD, only with a different type of monitoring. Unfortunately, I can't offer you a written contract any more than Gloop, but I think you probably know that you'll always be paid as per the terms of the agreement.'

'Is anybody else going to be part of the project?' I asked, still not on top of the situation, but starting to feel the first tremors of something that felt like relief, maybe even excitement.

'You'll be part of a research team. You'll probably never meet the other members, but your experiences will be assessed alongside theirs.' Ober lifted his finger to his mouth in a gesture of correction that looked as if it might have been premeditated. 'Actually, you probably will meet some of them. In certain ways. Depending on... conditions. But I don't think you need to worry about it now. Let's just say that we need an articulate member of the underclass with some well-developed neuroses.'

I raised my eyebrows. 'Oh, thanks.'

But I wasn't bothered about being socially and psychologically tagged by my psychiatrist. I was starting to ruminate on the *we*. However, that could wait. I didn't want to ask too many questions about the offer or who else was doing the offering. I was being given the chance of extended treatment by my psychiatrist and getting paid for it. It may not have been legal, or even ethically acceptable, but that wasn't my problem. Ober seemed to know exactly what he was doing, and that was good enough for me.

'Do I have to sign in blood?'

'You don't sign anything. But if your brain isn't too fried by dealing with the exploits of Mr Gloop and friends all afternoon I'd like to show you the materials you'll be working with, and what you might be likely to expect from them.'

We moved into the living room and Ober emptied half a dozen small vials from the second envelope onto a thin, polished wooden board that he'd extracted from his briefcase and placed on the sofa. Suddenly there was a businesslike air about him. He had manoeuvred the situation back to

25

psychiatrist and patient and I realised that I was beginning to sweat a little, as though I were out in public, amongst people.

'Do you know what phenethylamines are?'

'No.'

'Well, they are different but similar to the LSD you've been taking for the last few months. A synthetic substituted phenethylamine is taken in larger doses than LSD but it affects the neurotransmitters serotonin and dopamine and enables a psychedelic, or entheogenic, experience in a comparable way.'

Ober spread out the vials, each marked with printed labels. He picked up one, marked in large letters "2C-E: 100mg", and looked at me for a moment, either gauging me or measuring his words before they were spoken.

'This, for instance, is a synthetic phenethylamine called 2, 5-Dimethoxy-4-Ethylphenethylamine.'

I balked at his enunciation. 'Right...'

'To you and me, 2C-E,' he continued, handing me the vial, quarter filled with two units of an off-white powder. 'Most of the substituted phenethylamines don't have pet names as yet – they're too new and too obscure. Ecstasy is one, but that doesn't really count as an entheogen. Most of *these* were developed during the late seventies and eighties, but they've only really been synthesised and made available widely since the late nineties.'

I picked up a second vial marked "2C-T-7" and another "2C-P", with their full chemical names printed below in smaller type. All the vials were marked as containing 100mg in two 50mg doses.

'We'll start with this, 2C-C. It's amongst the most relaxed of the new entheogens; it will be kind to you. But a relatively large dosage, 50mg, has a chance of giving you a Plus Four... a peak experience. We don't want to be messing around with small doses.'

'And these are all illegal, like LSD right?' I asked, ruing the question immediately. It had always been a prickly subject with Ober. His left eye twitched and he smiled his laconic smile.

'They are mostly controlled substances, but we shall be working under a special licence, as with the LSD.'

That was about as much as he ever said on the subject. He moved the vials about on the board and picked up the 2C-C.

'We can try this out tomorrow night. As before, I'll be here during the entire session.' He motioned towards me with the vial. 'You need to know that this has the potential to take you further than the LSD you've been taking. You will almost certainly experience contact with your mother and sister.'

'Oh.' My stomach lurched. Their faces glanced in front of me for a moment, then faded into the early evening gloom of the flat.

Ober looked at the door as if assessing the location, then got up and walked over to the window. He contemplated the grey cement and leaden sky for a minute or so before turning back to me. 'This *isn't* the ideal environment of course. But these places will be a part of the evolution.'

His face had clouded over and his gaze diverted into the middle distance. This time I didn't quite understand what he meant by "evolution". Personal? Social? Something else? But at that moment I didn't care too much. My inquisitiveness was submerged beneath a burgeoning, quickened excitement that I was about to escape. I was about to be freed from the relentless servitude of supplementing my benefits by the execution of meaningless work, and I was going to do so by taking exotic psychedelic drugs. Not just as a treatment but as research. For the moment my last, unmonitored, acid experience and the cumulative paranoia of recent trips were forgotten and the precious transcendental states I had achieved during my first trips came back to me as if they were beautiful memories I had appropriated from another, better person.

'Do you want me to record what happens in a journal like before?' I asked, trying to mask my excitement.

'That would be good, yes. Anything supplemental beyond the session can be useful, in words and pictures. Although, with the new entheogens, I want to move you on to a type of therapy called Anaclitic Therapy. It can be rather... intrusive, but the results can be outstanding. I'll explain further before our first session.'

He sat back down on the sofa. I noticed for the first time

that his eyes seemed to be two slightly different colours, grey and deep blue. How had I missed that in six months of knowing him? He ran them over me for a few seconds, evidently formulating his words.

'This does represent a change in approach to your treatment,' he said, extracting a small bag of skunk from his jacket pocket. I handed some papers and a pouch of tobacco to him from the coffee table and he proceeded to roll one up. 'But all I can do is ask you to trust me.'

I nodded, thinking that I'd have done what he told me even if I didn't trust him.

He squinted at me again creating a segue in the conversation.

'When was the last time you went out?'

'Earlier in the week.'

'Why?'

To do the shopping.'

'Where?'

'The co-op down the street, it has everything I need.'

'And when was the last time you went anywhere else?'

My back began to prickle with sweat. 'I'm n-n-not sure. A couple of weeks ago, to the p-p-park,' I lied.

The stutter was a warning sign, brought on by the close proximity of an anxiety that seemed suddenly palpable in the room – outside of me, existing of its own accord. I attempted to control my breathing and take the tension from my shoulders. Ober noticed and held back whatever else he was going to say. He finished rolling the joint and lit up, handing it to me after a single draw. I breathed in the pungent vegetative smoke and allowed it to fill my lungs with a deep inhalation. Three more drags and I could feel myself turning back.

'Anxiety disorders are much more common than people imagine,' he said. 'And depression... well, places like this are designed to cause it. There are millions of people strapped with every kind of diathetic mental illness known, and they don't really believe it could be any different.'

I breathed the smoke out of my nose, feeling calmer but still slightly put upon. Deliberately, I slowed my speech to avoid stuttering.

'But I think they do. They just have no way to express it. I can feel the tension of other people in the blocks all the time, people who *just* get by on a daily basis. They do want something better to believe in but they're shackled. And maybe they are all depressed but what are they supposed to do, take Prozac for the rest of their lives?'

'If their lives are made slightly less miserable then yes. But an anti-depressant just staves off external and internal influences. Entheogens provide chemical gateways that...' Again, he drew himself back from what he was about to say. Instead he gestured to the vials. 'I had hoped the LSD would have had more far-reaching results by now, but you have a certain resistance to it. It's not that uncommon, even at relatively high doses. The new phenethylamines will break down that resistance. They act in a slightly different way on the brain's neurotransmitters, most specifically serotonin and dopamine. I would rather you did not take any of them outside of our sessions.'

I nodded, wondering with how many other patients Ober had had this conversation and whether they had a better understanding than me of what was being done to them.

'Shall we start tomorrow night?' he said.

'Ok. Tomorrow night.' Automatically I glanced at my watch. 'What about Gloop? He'll be bombarding me with e-mail threats unless he gets something tonight.'

Ober's upper lip curved into a snarl again and he moved his hand as though to dismiss my concerns. 'Send what you've done, tell him he can have it for nothing and that he's not to bother you again.'

My pulse lurched. 'I can't really afford to do that.'

'Yes you can,' said Ober turning his sneer to a smile, 'your research is paid in monthly instalments, in advance.'

To my surprise he took a wad of banknotes from his briefcase and handed it to me. Then, in a lowered tone I had never heard him use before: 'You have not been chosen at random for this. You have complex anxiety disorders and depression, much of which is generated from a deeply embedded repression of the events of twelve months ago. But I'm confident that this treatment will help you as much as us.'

I smiled nervously and tried to remember if anyone had ever told me that I had been specially *chosen* to do anything. I concluded that they had not. Then, once again, I wondered who, or what, Ober meant by *us*.

IV

I spent most of the next afternoon searching the web for information on the phenethylamines that Ober had left with me. There was more information than I had imagined, mostly consisting of descriptions of the chemical composition of the drugs and experience reports from those who had taken them. These experiences seemed to me similar to LSD trips, although how could I be sure that the person describing the experience was doing so adequately? I wouldn't have been able to do so. But there did seem to be a high proportion of people writing about having 'brought something back' from the trip, often something of spiritual or emotional value, though usually ill defined. One American girl described how she had been buried in the earth, which then became the Mother Goddess' womb. When she returned reconciliation with her own long-estranged mother was made possible, she wrote, because the trip had made her understand her maternal needs and actions at a deep, fundamental level. I thought of my own dead mother. The drugs could mediate no reconciliation with her.

However, I couldn't find anything to suggest the drugs were being used as a treatment for mental illness. No research programmes either. Some were scheduled as class-A drugs but the illegality of others was slightly equivocal, largely resting on their chemically analogous relation to scheduled drugs. The drug enforcement agencies had simply not been able to keep up with the chemists, who were constantly synthesising new versions. But the classification of the drugs as phenethylamines seemed enough to prevent any new research being carried out with them, either on humans or animals from what I could tell.

It was early evening before I gave up the search and went into the living room to roll one up. There had been no word from Ober all day so when the phone rang, I broke my usual habit of filtering calls through the voicemail and answered it. He couldn't make it. Something about a hastily arranged meeting that he was unable to avoid.

'*But don't worry, I'm sending round someone to sit with you.*'

I got up and paced through the flat on edge, taking short, sharp drags on the joint. 'I'd rather it were you,' I said, attempting to calm my breathing to avoid a stutter.

'*Don't worry, she's very experienced... and very unique. Actually she should be with you any minute.*'

I went out onto the walkway. The usual suspects were milling around the blocks and, as I made my customary check of the cracked concrete and fibreglass in the parapet, I saw a young girl emerge from number thirty-three. There was something unusual about her bearing that I couldn't quite put my finger on, something that I never associated with anybody using the den. The nearest I could get to it was *pity*. She seemed to carry it in her posture as she made her way along the walkway towards the stairwell, looking back once, not in fear, but in commiseration.

'What does she look like?' I asked, noticing by the backdrop of voices that Ober was in company.

'*Blonde hair, thin, a bit new-agey.*'

That described the girl I was watching, but she was much too young for Ober's experienced stand-in. 'How old is she? I asked, watching the girl's blonde head disappear down the stairs and starting to feel the first click of apprehension.

'*Fourteen.*'

'What!'

'*Fourteen in years, much older in wisdom. You'll see. You must trust me on this... oh, and her name's Alice I'm afraid.*'

Before I could say anything else Ober made a hurried farewell amidst a few platitudes and reassurances, which were difficult to make out over the raised volume of his companions' voices. With my stomach in my mouth I instinctively rushed back inside the flat and closed the door on the outside world. I was shaking and my heart raced ridiculously. A fourteen year old girl. Ober was trusting my therapy to a fourteen year old girl. And her name was Alice.

Was it a joke? Was it some cunning psychoanalytical ruse to overwhelm my disabling anxieties? If so, it was certainly bringing out all the sweaty, shaky symptoms of my phobic existence. I couldn't even get a curse out without stuttering wildly.

'J-J-Jesus C-Christ.'

By the time she knocked at the door, five minutes later, I had managed to calm myself down a bit, using the deep breathing techniques that I had learnt were my best defence against the onset of panic attacks. And, of course, smoking the remainder of the joint.

I took a last toke, stubbed out the joint, calmed my breathing and opened the door. Half of me was still expecting to see someone else, someone older, someone more *appropriate*. But there she was, looking older than fourteen, but not by much.

'Hiya. I'm Alice, Alice Liddell. Ober sent me as your sitter. I'm guessing he's already told you.'

Her Received Pronunciation was like liquid. I stared at her like an idiot. The pity I had sensed from afar was still present, lingering about her like an aura. She was also sickeningly pretty. In the two seconds I had to take in her physical presence before being required -- in order to prevent her thinking me an utter dimwit -- to speak, I took in the delicate proportions of her face and decided that her bloodline belonged in Scandinavia. But there was something almost cartoonish about her cuteness. It made her age somehow irrelevant.

'Y-y-yes. But I haven't really been used to strangers... I've only been t-t-treated by Ober since I came out of hospital.'

I silently cursed my galvanised priggishness and my incompetent stuttering. Why could I never just take a grip on things?

'Can I come in?' she asked, bypassing my awkwardness with a knowing smile. 'Then we can talk about it.'

Without waiting for a reply she moved past me and drifted around the living room, looking around the place and then back at me like a particularly laconic social worker. She had shaken off her age. She'd somehow pulled off being a woman in a young girl's body.

'I'm afraid I don't know too much about you,' she said, sitting on the sofa and beckoning me to join her. 'Ober only gave me a sketchy outline of your conditions. But he's been using me for first time Anaclitic Therapy just lately.'

'Right. And are you really only fourteen?' I asked, wondering whether Ober had always planned to send her in his stead.

'And a half', she said, with a semi-smile that seemed as if it may have been mimicking Ober's. 'The half's important mind – I've only been with Ober for the last six months.'

'Same here,' I said, taking a seat on the sofa but maintaining maximum distance from her. I made another conscious effort to control my breathing. 'But I presume you're not a patient.'

'No, I'm not a patient. In as much as anyone else is not a patient that is. Everyone's ill to some extent.' She looked at me quizzically. 'Have you had this conversation with Ober?'

'Yes, I guess... sort of.'

She pulled her trainers off and sat cross-legged on the sofa facing me, close enough to make me uncomfortable. 'I'm a facilitator, a monitor, a helper. There are a few of us.'

'How many of you does he need?'

'More every day,' she said, scrutinising my reaction with her turquoise eyes. 'The drugs need us for them to be properly effective. Phenethylamines take you places... places where you may need help.'

She had stumbled on 'phenethylamines', but her cut-glass articulation was starting to intimidate me. As was her worldliness. I was on the defensive, and I had the worrying feeling that was where she wanted me.

'And are *you* helping the *patients* in the d-d-den over the road?' I said, hearing the question stumble out of my mouth in an explicit admission of my agitation. She sensed it and drew her body back into the sofa.

'No. I'm just quite good at talking to people in that sort of situation. They don't feel threatened by a posh schoolgirl.' We smiled together for the first time.

'But did Ober send you there?'

'Sort of... but I'm under strict instructions to concentrate your mind on the therapy session. You're not to worry about anything else.'

I nodded, unwilling to pursue it further. Our shared smile had relaxed me a little and I didn't want to spoil it. I felt obliged to overturn the impression I was giving of a foolish nerd unable to adjust to the situation.

'What do you know about me?' I asked, still not happy with my strained tone.

'I know about your mum and your sister and the basics of your phobias and depression since.'

'How much do you know about my... sister?'

'As much as I need to know. I'm sorry I have the same name.'

'Well, you can't help that. At least you don't look like her.'

But didn't she? There *was* something Alice-like about her. The features were all different, but she had a resonance, a supernal quality that hung about her and shaped her face and body. And now that I'd relaxed with her a little bit, I began to notice her waifish, slight curves and the way her hair fell loosely on her bare shoulders. For a fraction of a second I felt she was *my* Alice sitting there and I wanted to reach out and hold her. I wanted to feel her face against mine. But the moment passed and I closed my eyes and turned my head away.

'What about you,' I said, still averting my eyes and attempting to divert the conversation to safer ground, 'how come you're doing this at fourteen?'

'I feel much older.'

'You seem it.'

'I had to grow up quickly... lots of death and separation. I cared for my mother for years before she died. MS.'

'I'm sorry.'

'Don't' be. It's made me see life and death differently. More clearly. This is why I'm here... I like to help people.'

I made eye contact again as she looked at me from a slight angle. Once again I thought that I could sense an aura of commiseration about her, a collection of pity being thrown my way. It was as if she knew something about me that I thought was hidden. Or perhaps it was more like something that was about to happen to me. Yes, that was it. She had a gallows look – the sympathy of one who accompanies the condemned to their last exit. It should have put me on edge, should have made me suspicious of the new drugs. But it was more than that. It was like she knew what the future must hold, had precognition of events to come and was unable to hide completely her sorrow at their outcome. For a fleeting moment I had an image of me in a cell and her sweeping in from the free outside world. Things that were undisclosed to me in my prison were well known to her and no matter how hard she might try she could not fully conceal her condolences for my inevitable and unavoidable fate. The image in my head gained vividness so quickly that I had to look away from her as if that might counter the disturbing impression, an impression that seemed to flag up my own ignorance and her superiority.

I had to move away. I got up to retrieve my pouch of tobacco and weed but Alice shook her head, smiling out the corner of her mouth. 'No smokes I'm afraid. We need to have a pure chemical session from here onwards. But you'd better take these first.' She handed me two travel sickness pills from her pocket and took two herself. 'For the nausea.'

'And so why are you taking them?'

'Ah. Ober hasn't explained exactly what Anaclitic Therapy is has he?'

'No.'

'Or I should say *his* version of Anaclitic Therapy. It's the only way for it to work properly.'

She looked around and spotted the vial of 2C-C I had left on the coffee table. 'Why do you think there are two doses in each vial?' she asked, picking up the vial.

'I hadn't really thought...'

'We take this trip together. And we take it in close physical contact.'

She began taking a few things from her small rucksack: some incense sticks, a CD, some rose petals.

'Physical contact?'

'Fusion. Body, mind and spirit.'

Just for a moment she sounded like a young girl saying the words. I watched in silence as she lit and dispersed the incense about the room and put the CD in the player, looking for all the world as if she'd lived there as long as I had.

'We don't need too many more words,' she said, sitting back down beside me. 'We just need to take this journey together. Do you trust me?'

I looked back into her eyes. They seemed colder now, but I knew she was doing this for me, giving a part of herself to me. Maybe I'd misinterpreted the pity. Perhaps she just wanted to help me, as simple as that. 'Yes, I think I do.'

'Good, then let's start. We should come up on this in less than half an hour.'

Alice carefully emptied the two 50mg doses onto Ober's polished wooden board on the coffee table. I leant forward to mop up my dose, but she took hold of me and gently manoeuvred me back onto the sofa. It was the first time we had touched and a sinuous vibration alerted my body. She took a handful of the rose petals and, standing above me, let them fall on me. I felt their feathery touch on my face and caught the faintest of aromas piercing, just for a moment, the heavy scent of the sandalwood incense.

'*Scar os mo chionn do bhrat fionn dom anacal.*'

Her words were mumbled but they immediately changed the atmosphere of the room. The curtains billowed slightly with a soft breeze and evening seemed to envelop the place in an instant. The incense smoke now filled the room and I settled back in the sofa, shrouded in the opulent muskiness. I felt half-drugged already.

She wetted her finger and collected one of the doses, spooning it into her mouth, never losing eye contact. She did the same for me, holding her finger out for me to suck. I sucked. She left her finger in my mouth a second longer than she needed to and then pulled it out putting it to her own lips to gesture quiet. We washed down the metallic-tasting powder with a bottle of water.

'These are the rules,' she said, starting the CD and coming to stand over me. In a single quick movement she carefully straddled me, her lithe body wrapping itself around me. 'No ass, no tits and definitely no cunt. I'm fourteen years old remember.'

She winked, smiled and buried her head into my neck, her thyme scented hair falling across my face.

'But otherwise, we need to stay close throughout.'

Her whispered voice melded into the brooding, synthesised pipes of *Shine on You Crazy Diamond*, which now eased itself into the room. I held her tight. I held her as tight as I used to hold my Alice.

V

Flying is exhilarating. I can't quite think why it is I don't allow myself to do it more often. The frozen air particles clinging to my protective aura, the wind swishing from one side to another in multicolours, the thermals allowing me to drift along on their deep timbre. Why don't I just live like this all the time? It probably has something to do with the matchbox houses far below me. They are grey and ugly and there is someone in there who is a little like me. But I can't be bothered with them or him. What futility to be trapped like that when all you have to do is fly away.

And yet, I can't take my eyes from the grey houses. If I'm not careful they are going to come closer and impede my flightpath. There is music as well. It's like distant pipes and very beautiful, but it is connected to the grey houses in a way that I just don't understand and so I try to ignore it. But it keeps drawing me back in huge swirling circular movements that sweep me downwards as if within an airy whirlpool. It's not an unpleasant sensation at all, quite the opposite. But I feel as if I've only been flying for a short time and I am unsure how the greyness will fit into my aerial world. It makes me slightly afraid. I turn on to my back so that all I see is the maroon sky supporting towering, multi-textured cumuli, moving and transforming above me as I carry on my spiralling descent.

Then, abruptly, there is a change. Four equally spaced musical notes in a minor chord fill the air, mournful and pensive, but at the same time filled with a muted expectancy. I twist my head around and see the notes drifting up towards me, their tails still attached to one of the big grey houses. They engulf me. They take hold of me and lead me to another sky, a sky of crystalline turquoise, undisturbed by clouds. I look down and the grey houses are gone. There is an ocean, but I'm not ready to go there yet. Going there would mean dispersal. I wouldn't be me anymore. And I'm happy being me for the moment. Instead, I kiss the notes, one by one, their jellyish forms quivering playfully before fading into the sea below. And now that I've done that I can drift back into the turquoise. It's like a colour I've never seen before, a colour from another world where everything is different. Perhaps the sky is that of another world.

But below things are changing. No ocean anymore, just a vast patchwork of hedgerowed fields stretching to a green and brown vanishing point. I am thinking that I am too high to be able to see the contours of the land, but I can, and there is a hill rising up abruptly from the fields, its grassy slopes a luminous green. Its conical shape makes me laugh. It is absurd and wondrous and I decide that I want to land on it so that I can hold it in my arms and be a part of it. As my amorphous body begins to make a silky contact with the grass on the hill I look up once more into the turquoise sky. But the colour is no longer filling the sky. It is filling the eyes of my companion.

'I thought I'd lost you,' she says, smiling and slightly breathless. 'I didn't think I'd given you a head start.'

'A head start? I don't understand.'

'You don't need to. Just follow me.'

She takes my hand and leads me up the hill. The soft breeze seems to scale up and down the octave range, fitting in with our gentle footfalls on the winding path to the top of the hill. Sandalwood and thyme scent the air and somewhere far away a blood red rose sends its visible perfume on a wave of nothingness.

I sit down with my back to a large stone, partly melding into it. She sits between my legs and I hold on tight. I can still hear the music, but it seems more like a reverberating memory, and I know that she is thinking the same. I bury my head into her hair and see the landscape below through the blonde strands that blow across my face with the breeze. The scent of thyme shows itself as a smoky mist settling over both of us.

'Hold me tighter,' she says, pushing her body back into mine. 'This can last for as long as you want it to. You haven't touched anyone for so long have you?'

I am not sure what she means. But I want to hold her tighter so I do. And I hold her for a long time. Beneath us the landscape changes with the seasons: full and yellow in high summer, stark and ivory in midwinter. But everything is diffused through her hair and modified by the pressure of her body against mine.

When the sky turns violet with the dawn of some forgotten day decades ago, there is a new sound that joins the wind and the pipes. It is a regular beat, like the shunting of a steam train, but it is so far away as to be ridiculous. And yet, it is coming closer, at an indefinable pace.

'So that's the road,' she says, and immediately I see that the shunting comes from two huge hammerhead, piston-driven machines, way out across the landscape where the air is filled with the misty grey of falling rain. They seem to be creating a road behind them, but I can never see whether it is straight or sinuous because as soon as a section is created it becomes obscured by surface water sprayed up by the machines.

'Where is it going?' I say, feeling marginally disturbed by the intrusion into our landscape.

'The road to recovery. The road to nowhere. A dead-end road. The long and winding road. You tell me.'

But the hammerhead machines are already beginning to slow and they are becoming more difficult to make out across the distant fields. There seems to be a single car coming out of the spray behind the machines, but it is a long way away and I can't be sure. Before the day ends the roadbuilding has stopped and there is no sign of the car.

'You're not quite ready yet are you,' she says, looking round at me with that air of pity lingering on her face.

'For what?'

She shakes her head and manoeuvres herself around so that she sits on top of me with our faces close.

'Whatever has happened to me, or happens to me, just remember that it doesn't really matter too much. Human bodies are only machines to be used for a short while. Things only seem to matter when you are using them. Don't mourn me. I am here, but I'm not here. I am in Time and out of Time.'

I don't feel as if I need to say anything. What she says

seems to have come from somewhere far away... in the past, future or in space I can't quite tell. They are words from a Void.

I look into her eyes and see that her pity has turned to sorrow. A tear escapes from her eye and rolls down to her chin, drops off and then streams down my bare chest, for we are now both naked.

'Love me like Alice,' she says, her long black hair cascading over me as she pushes me onto my back and sinks my psychedelic erection deep into her wet tightness. Her bucking rhythm builds and builds then thrusts over me, pressing me into the soft ground.

'I want to know everything between you both,' she whispers. 'I want to feel you inside me as a brother. I want to know the moments in time when you were joined... like this.'

She comes down, touching me with as much of her body as she can, all the while grinding herself on me. I catch glimpses of the midsummer sun high in the sky between her frantic kisses and feel the sweat from our bodies mingle.

'It's ok you know,' she breathes, still kissing me. 'You did nothing wrong. You just loved me. We just loved each other. We do love each other'

'Alice?'

She pulls herself up on me, fondling her breasts with one hand and feeding me the fingers of the other, just as she always used to. Her cunt is excruciatingly tight and I feel the first waves of an entheogenic orgasm. But she knows this and stops for a moment. From her hair she pulls out a long pin and in a single movement draws it across her wrist creating a hairline cut from which the blood slowly oozes out and down her arm. She holds my wrist and does the same to me. The sharp sensation of pain is electrifying. We hold our bloody wrists together as she regains her momentum, bucking and writhing in time to a cacophony of drums reverberating through the hill. I cum ferociously, a frightening sensation that takes over my nervous system as though it means to destroy it. I realise that the drumming is my heart, beating harder than is possible, and I faint away to a vision of red blood cells swirling through arteries, pumped there by my all-pervading life force.

VI

I woke up on the sofa with Alice. She was still asleep nestling her body against mine. I carefully extracted myself from her and made for my morning spliff, waiting to be rolled on the coffee table. But the instant I stood up an enormous throbbing in the back of my head forced me onto the leather armchair instead, my vision swaying in a burst of spangled lights. I usually got headaches the morning after a trip, but this was something else. All I could do for the moment was sit as still as possible and watch her in the grey morning light. But it hurt to have my eyes open, so I closed them and attempted to piece together the sequence of events during the trip.

The details were already fading, like the contents of a dream, but the embrace of emotions was still there, folded into every thought and feeling. Just like an LSD experience it was rendered as direct contact with something that did not translate into linguistic metaphors. I could recall the imagery and the sensations to a certain degree, but the experiential heart remained an abstraction not able to lodge itself anywhere within my brain or find description. But unlike an LSD experience I had felt that there were consciousnesses there with me, observing me. In fact that feeling was one I could understand and translate. They had been everywhere, diffused in every atom of the sky and earth, watching and understanding. And at the same time they had somehow also been me. My own consciousness was the same as theirs. That's as close as I could get to characterising it.

I opened my eyes with the singular thought that I was still being observed – they hadn't gone away yet. But the pulsing pain of the headache forced them close again. My memory migrated to Alice in the trip. I lingered on the sex, the abandonment of control and the sensation of orgasm that had felt like being fired from out of an atomic cannon. After that the plus-four trip fizzled out. I had simply started to come down, probably about six or seven hours after taking the drug, gently and with no negative effects. Alice and I had talked during that time, her voice slightly warped and echoing with the residual effects of the drug, but very definitely in the real world. Well, at least this world.

'Morning.'

Her voice brought me round, but even the marginal movement of my head to face her caused another rupturing pain in my skull.

'Hi. Is the headache part and parcel?'

'You're probably just dehydrated. I'll get some water.'

She returned from the kitchen with a full bottle and once I had finished half of it the headache began to dull.

'Do you remember us talking last night?' She asked.

I could sense a reserve in her that I had not noticed before. It was probably just the early morning, but I couldn't help thinking that she had purposely shifted to a more distant position. But I was still comfortable enough with her to avoid stuttering.

'Yes, some of it. We talked about what happened at the peak didn't we? About me and Alice... my Alice. Though it was you to begin with. Did I tell you that?'

'Mmm.'

'So you were really there?'

'*I* was on the sofa, as were you.'

'But were you on the hill with me?'

She smiled indulgently. She seemed more forty than fourteen.

'Kind of.' She sat up on the edge of the sofa gesturing with her hands. 'The drug allows you to access the collective unconscious. Has Ober explained this to you?'

I nodded. 'Sort of. He calls it the Phylogenic Memory.'

'Yes, he does doesn't he.' She smiled an uninterpretable smile and seemed to drift away.

'But how could you be there with me? It's not a real place. You can't just turn up.'

She still seemed zoned out. Perhaps the residual of the drug was still dictating its terms to her. 'Not a real place,' she whispered, mimicking my voice. 'But it is a real place. It's the most real place you'll ever be. Everything is there: past, present, future, hidden, disclosed, thought, done, human, non-human. And I can be there with you because... well, just because.'

Getting used to her talking like this was still difficult. I nodded my head again as if I understood. She refocused on me.

'That's why these drugs can offer such powerful therapy. You have someone to guide you through the root causes of all your deep-seated anxieties.'

'But how can you be a guide when you're as off your head as the patient?'

She shrugged. 'Maybe I wasn't all that 'off my head' last night.'

'You took the same dose as me, fifty milligrams.'

'Did I?' Again, she zoned out, apparently losing interest in me.

'Well, yes you did.'

She ran her fingers through her hair and breathed in deeply. She was evidently formulating a simplified explanation, much as a mother would with a child who was engaged with an idea but not quite getting it.

'I was only here last night to provide support for you,' she said in a low voice as though concerned about being overheard. 'Anaclitic Therapy is about lending physical, tactile comfort for you whilst you trip. It ensures you stay rooted in a safe, loving environment whilst your mind is elsewhere. But I didn't need to be with you last night in order to be with you in your altered state.'

'No?'

'There's no Time in the Phylogenic Memory. I could have taken the drug months ago and participated in the experience you had last night. I might even know about all your drug-induced experiences, however far in the future they are for you.'

'Are you saying that you took a drug months ago and experienced then what happened to us last night?'

'I don't think you need to worry about it too much.'

'Don't I?'

'No. Sometimes you just need acceptance.'

I could feel my headache returning with a purposeful numb thudding. I had thought Ober's Phylogenic Memory made perfect sense to me, at least at an abstract level, or at least when I had the benefit of large amounts of psychedelic drugs inside me. But sitting in the flat in the grainy light of morning with my brain feeling as if it were too big for my skull, Alice's conceptual abstract was just too much for me. The otherworldly resonance of the trip was still strong, but I was, at that moment, unable to see Time as anything but a relentless forward progression imposed on the physical world. I just couldn't quite understand what she was telling me and it was starting to make me feel a bit thick. She was fourteen for Christ's sake.

I drank the rest of the water and massaged the back of my neck. I didn't want this to develop into a debate where I would be the inevitable loser. I needed to get things back on home ground. 'Well, am I on the research project because I'm particularly amenable to this treatment? I mean, does it work for everyone?'

'Mmm, you seem to respond well to treatment with entheogens. Do you see how contact with your sister exposes the guilt you have felt and allows you to come to terms with it... to normalise it? Screwing your sister in such a positive way dispels the need for you to feel bad about it.'

I recoiled from her words. But she was right. I was remembering feelings that had been put beyond recall, feelings that had been suppressed and incarcerated. For the first time since her death I was starting to think about what we had done without remorse, and it felt very liberating. What was the point of my ceaseless round of regret?

'But there's much more isn't there?' she asked, that forbearing look of pity springing up again.

I nodded my head expecting her to continue, but instead she sank back into the sofa and closed her eyes in meditative poise. I suddenly remembered the blood-brother ritual in my altered state and took the opportunity to look closely at her wrists. But they were covered with bead-bracelets. What did I expect anyway? We weren't really there. Our flesh and bones were on the sofa all night. And yet the image nagged at me. I pulled up my sleeve and looked at my own wrist but the act of bending my head brought on an abrupt and overwhelming wave of tiredness. My head lolled and jolted.

Slit. Blood. Snake. Arteries. Turquoise blood. Dead. Dying. Refugees from another world. They're making their arterial way through my body and into our world. Grab throat. Slit.

I started violently, my hypnagogic vision instantly recoiling back into its lair. Alice was looking at me queerly. My heart was pounding in my ears.

'Don't think you've properly woken up yet,' she said, sitting up slightly. She suddenly looked much younger, like a proper fourteen year old. 'Come here.'

The queerness in her tone and the sunken hypnagogic imagery set me on edge. I looked again at my wrists, feeling my eyes grow wide. They were unmarked, but I was suddenly starting to feel as if perhaps my trip was unfinished. There was a cardboard cut-out quality to the room and Alice's presence was now intrusive. I looked at her and shook my head.

'It's ok, no harm's going to come to you,' she said, cold and flat. I just want you to fuck me once before I die. I think we still have time... though it's always difficult to tell.'

I dug my nails into the palms of my hands and my abdominal muscles tensed up.

'D-d-don't do this to me Alice, this can't be part of the treatment. You're making me paranoid.'

She just smiled, stood up and started taking her clothes off. In a few seconds she was naked, rubbing her cunt with three fingers and looking at me like she was going to kill me. Her thin, taut body sidled from one side to another, her nipples standing erect on her small breasts. After a moment of paralysis I jumped up and away from her.

'Please Alice.'

'All I'm asking is this one little thing.'

And she was beneath me. But we were in the bedroom. Moments were becoming mixed up. It was like a real-life skipping CD. She kissed me wildly, biting my lips and tongue like a savage little animal. I pulled up, looked down and saw my cock buried into her sparsely haired cunt, the swollen lips enfolding me as if in an exaggerated cartoon. I went to pull out but she wrapped her legs round me and forced me into her. I yanked myself out violently.

'We can't do this Alice. This isn't how it should be.'

'Isn't it?'

I lunged off the bed and stood looking at her lying with her legs wide apart, her virginal blood, smeared over her thighs. I instinctively looked down at my erection. It was covered in blood and dripping the last drops of semen from an ejaculation. I jerked my head back to the bed and saw there my sister in the last moments of childbirth, blood everywhere and the baby's head just appearing.

'Jesus. Can't you stop this!?'

Then I was in the living room sitting in the armchair and holding onto it like it was the only thing preventing me taking off.

'It's ok. I'm here.' Alice was kneeling at my feet, fully clothed and looking confused or concerned, I couldn't quite tell.

'Then tell me who the *we* is,' I said, hearing the words as if spoken by another person.

'We?'

'The *we* and the *us* that I keep hearing from Ober and you.'

Then she was sucking my cock, looking up at me from her kneeling position like a fake-lascivious porn star.

'Try to pull away and I'll bite it... hard.'

I watched her move up and down on my enormous erection. It certainly wasn't that big in real life, but real life was being scuttled into a cartoon world. I closed my eyes and told myself that this was just part of the trip. But it didn't feel like it. This felt like my version of reality was sliding all over the place. This was nothing to do with the drug.

I looked back down. On the road four storeys below the morning was just getting under way. The old man with the trilby from number fifty-seven was taking his dog for a walk and I could hear two women on the walkway above exchanging pleasantries. Normality. Thank God. I looked at my wrists again and then back through the door. Alice, fully clothed, was watching me.

'Are you alright now?' She asked, apparently reluctant to come out and join me.

'I think so.'

But I wasn't. The substance of everything was flitting around at the periphery of my vision. And the heavy, subdued atmosphere wasn't right. The concrete around me had become a presence, holding secrets about the past and future. I was locked into time but it was not and it was trying to communicate to me everything that it had witnessed and would witness. It creaked and groaned as a sliver of sunlight passed over it.

And then there were steps. They were determined steps, making their way up the dirty concrete stairs of my block. I turned to the stairwell entrance and waited. I counted the steps up each storey, coming closer and getting louder. I tried to imagine the person to whom they belonged, but all I could think of was the concrete, soaking up each footfall as it had a million before and would do a million again. And what would get locked into its cementious memory this time? What moment in time were these steps about to represent?

They were at the third storey now. They stopped. Perhaps I'd never know why they were here and why I had been listening to them. They would be just another abstract moment without meaning, because they were part of someone else, another individual to whom I had no connection. I touched my hand to the concrete and felt its cold presence.

The steps continued again, up the stairs to my storey, speeding up as they came to the top. I glanced into the flat. Alice was standing with her head in her hands. I looked back to the stairwell and waited, my vision blurred. For a moment there was a silence and I thought that the steps might have belonged to no one, that I was just tapping into the concrete's remembrance. The footfalls were simply something that had happened on another spring morning in the past or in the future. But then, in a jerky slow motion, first the arms then the head, legs and body of a person came round the corner. He was young, a stranger, not from the blocks. He saw me and shouted something. It also came out in slow motion, the words rebounding off each other so as to become incomprehensible. I laughed. This fellow was the most ridiculous person I'd ever seen as he came lurching up the walkway towards me bellowing inarticulate words that he seemed to leave behind him.

Then, in a snapshot, everything changed. Alice was out the door running towards him and the slow-motion action in front of me flipped into normal, or maybe even quicker than normal, speed. The youth was big, breathless and sweating. He gripped Alice by the throat and pushed her back against the wall. I made to help her but I couldn't move a muscle. I was frozen to the spot, goggling at the spectacle. He turned his contorted face to me. There was an instant of eye contact – turquoise eyes – then he let go of Alice, took one bounding movement towards me and punched me hard in the stomach. I crumpled to the ground immediately, doubling up winded from the pain, but still able to shuffle away from his menacing boots.

'No! Don't do this, it's not what you think,' Alice cried, lunging at him as he started to pull his leg back to kick me. He caught her by the arms and swung her round like a ragdoll, his fury now rendering him all but mute. With her feet off the ground he let her go and her body crashed up against the broken piece of parapet fibreglass with an exaggerated violence. For an extended moment it seemed to bend with her weight and I somehow expected it to spring back like a piece of elastic. But it did not bend. It splintered into shards, the concrete top collapsed in two and she fell through.

She didn't make a sound. All I saw was her upside-down body disappear amidst the shards of fibreglass, the two detached sections of concrete and the rusted iron rods. Four long seconds later there was a quick succession of dispassionate thuds below.

The man had become completely rigid, his posture that of his last action. His face was caught between the contorted rage, which was all I had known of him, and open-mouthed shock. The silence of the moment was exquisite. There was just one long, stretched out heartbeat that I presumed could be heard for miles.

I looked down at my stomach, which felt as if it were being twisted in a knot. An ever-broadening blob of blood stained my top. I lifted it up to see a gash that was spurting thick globules of blood. Bile formed in my gullet. I looked back at the man and through my teary eyes saw the reddened blade in his hand.

Then, from either side of my vision, a pair of draped curtains, like those of a theatre stage, began to close into the middle. They swished together causing a velvety, purple darkness, but then inched open at their join to reveal a chink of bright white light. From out of the chink a large solid block of concrete with arms, legs a bowler hat and cane slipped between the curtains. It doffed its hat to me, wiggled its cane and smiled with its beaky mouth.

'Th-th-that's all folks,' it announced.

Blackout.

VII

The English countryside was in its June splendour. I watched it pass with one eye open and my head propped against a sweater on the car window. Everything seemed green and gold: sun-drenched hills dotted with sheep and patchwork fields, some with solitary oaks standing sentinel-like in their centre. Hedgerows disappeared into secret corners and every now and then tracts of woodland took over the landscape, shimmering with summer life. We travelled through rural backwaters with few villages and where towns of any size didn't seem to exist.

It had been over two years since I had been in the countryside proper. Alice and I had caught a random train out of the city, stayed on it for an hour and then got off when we came into a station that looked like it had a lot of green around it. We had ended up in a soft meadowland at the end of a steep wooded valley, and we stayed there all day, our bodies wrapped together, blissed out on being able to be together outdoors without other people around. The landscape outside the car reminded me of that day and my eyes began to well. It seemed so very long ago.

I fell asleep when we came onto a straight section of road and spent the last hour of the journey in a half-waking state, getting my dreams of dead people and half-remembered conversations with them mixed up with the grass, corn and woodland that sifted into my consciousness whenever I opened my eyes. The last time I dozed off I found myself back in the hospital with dozens of drips feeding into my veins. Ober was having an argument with a doctor at the end of my bed, something about unnecessary amounts of drugs, but they spoke mostly in an unknown foreign language. Just as I began to nestle down into the comfort of the blankets I was awoken suddenly as the car negotiated a speed bump in the road. I instinctively put my hand over the bandage on my stomach and then pulled myself up into a sitting position to look around.

'Where are we?' I asked, rubbing my eyes.

'Nearly there,' replied Ober. 'This is the village closest to the house.'

I squinted out the window at the soft-coloured stone cottages running along a single street that was lined with a canalised brook on one side, punctuated with little footbridges leading into the front gardens. As I opened the window the scent of unknown flowers and herbs drifted into the car. I closed my eyes and savoured it. After the blocks and the hospital it was like being on a different planet.

A couple of minutes after passing the last cottage we pulled off the road, along a short unmetalled track and into an enclosed courtyard with a brick gateway and two ranges of single-storey barns. The sense of being in an alien place was beginning to overwhelm me, not in the usual agoraphobic way, but as a child might be awed by something so large as to be incomprehensible. We parked, got out and walked through a gate that led into another courtyard, this one fronted with the house. It was a timber-framed pastiche of a building. Black wood and white panels, leaded windows, jetties everywhere and a wooden door that looked like it belonged on a cathedral.

'It was originally an H-shaped hall house with an open hearth,' Ober announced as we stood for a moment looking at the frontage. 'Of course they floored over the hall in the sixteenth century and put fireplaces in, but apart from that it probably looks essentially as it did in about 1450.' He glanced sideways at me, smiled and winked. 'Don't worry, it's been modernised inside.'

It certainly had. The interior dripped with moneyed taste. The ancient mellowness of the place had been allowed to survive and breathe beneath the modern accoutrements of a very wealthy owner. Ober gave me a quick tour of the house and we ended up in the living room, which, he informed me, used to be the open hall.

'I'm not sure I belong here really,' I said, running my hand over the gnarled timber lintel above the large fireplace. 'I'll get lost in it.'

'Oh, you'll get used to it soon enough. Within a week you'll be wondering how you ever lived without the peace and quiet of this place.'

'But I think it'll be *too* quiet. And I feel... well, to be honest, I feel as if I'm just not good enough to be living in a place like this.'

'And do you think that most people who live in places like this are *good enough*? The majority either inherited their wealth or acquired it through the exploitation of others. Their sole interest is in maintaining equilibrium in order for them to hold on to their privileged position.'

'And so who owns this?' I asked, slightly taken aback by Ober's tone. 'You've only called it the house in the country.'

Ober looked at me sideways. 'It is owned by a collective. There is no individual ownership.'

'So where are they?'

'We only use it as a retreat and as a place for convalescence. And you my friend, after what you've been through, are a prime candidate for convalescence. It's not a case of being good enough, it's a case of needing it enough. That's why you're here... and also so we can carry on your treatment in a more conducive environment.'

I nodded diplomatically, but I was unsure about my situation. During my stay in hospital Ober had been, apart from an initial visit from the police, my only visitor. He had come in almost every day and, when my physical condition began to improve, he had once again assumed the role of my psychiatrist. For several weeks he had been telling me about the *house in the country* and the ways in which he intended to carry on my course of treatment, made all the more urgent because of what had happened to Alice and the circumstances surrounding her death. But in my morphinic state I was disengaged. Time, policemen, doctors, pain, nurses, boredom, consultants, dreams, memory, ward cleaners, machinery – they all became amalgamated into a chaotic, delirious whole. And reigning over the chaos was Ober: arguing with the consultants treating me, exerting some kind of pre-emptive authority over my treatment and generally moulding my restricted world into a shape that suited him. I was little more than a passive receptacle of instructions and decisions. I had been denuded of the ability to make any kind of choice, and I had just let it happen to me because I had neither the energy nor the clarity of thought to do otherwise. Ober acted on a set of presumptions that involved me doing exactly what he wanted me to do once I was out of hospital and I allowed him to do so. In truth I didn't want to make any choices of my own. I felt hollowed out, at an end of things. The physical effect of the painkillers mimicked that of my mental state: numb and dull. It was easier and rather comforting to have someone else direct my life from out of the traumas with which it had become riddled.

But now that I was at the house I felt uncomfortable, out of control somehow. The chaotic perceptions of my time in hospital had been replaced by misgivings, by a lucid negativity. I'd never been in a house like this in my life and its manorial ambience was tapping into my fears and phobias of unknown places.

'I'll be staying the night,' said Ober, breaking a short silence, 'and so we can talk some more about the programme of treatment this evening. But for now I need to organise your provisions. I have a... a colleague in the village who will arrange everything for you. If you're lucky she might even cook for you.

'Here.' He gave me a bag of nice looking juicy weed with a pouch of tobacco and some papers. 'That should keep you going for a few days.'

A few minutes later he had left to go into the village (I was not invited) and I was left alone in the house. The quiet was overwhelming. I rolled a joint and lit up then stretched out in a window-seat overlooking the garden that extended from the back of the house down into a sinuous glade of trees that I presumed followed a stream. There was birdsong and the light rustle of a birch tree outside the window, but they were in league with the silence. They didn't seem like real noises. I had spent all my life in the blocks, had become inured to the constant reverberations of sound filtering through the concrete warrens. And, apart from my occasional excursions with Alice, I hardly ever left the city, never escaped from its interminable clamour. This new soundless environment was something to which I was not sure I could ever adjust. It held that same undertone of sinister uneasiness that populated the atmospheres of even the best of my dreams. It was like a surface calm that disguised a riptide.

But the calm was beguiling. I spent about an hour just staring out into the garden, allowing the drift of clouds and the sway of trees to join with the silence and distil the tranquillity of the place. I could feel it soften me. Even when my dead people began to claim places in my thoughts there was something greater overriding them, something that soothed the attritional feelings and allowed me to be calm, almost meditative. I wondered if everyone were given the opportunity of living in such a place, would there be any social or political problems in the world? I smiled at my naivety.

Another hour passed and the garden was beginning to take on the bluish tints of an early summer evening. Ober had still not returned and so I decided to take a look around the house whilst there was still some natural light. Wood everywhere. The house was trussed and beamed in dark oak that took over every aspect of the place. It gave the rooms a heavy, ponderous feel, and I tried to think what it would be like taking a psychedelic there. I imagined the knotty, creaking beams and uprights would take me into a medieval world. Perhaps I'd get to see the hall as it was originally, open to the roof and smoke filled from a central hearth. I closed my eyes and touched my palms and cheek against the rough wood of a supporting column. It allowed me to tap a deeply sunken memory. It was a story, an ancient story, Anglo-Saxon or something, which I must have heard in school or maybe read about in my brief, aborted foray into medieval history. It was about an open hall house of a great lord, whose bard pointed out a bird, that had, during a great feast, flown in from one end of the hall, rested on a beam for a moment and then carried on its way out the far end. The bard suggested that the bird's entrance, existence and exit was an analogy for human life: we come from an unknown place, spend a short time in the known world amidst familiar things and then we disappear once more into the unrevealed beyond. I opened my eyes feeling a strange contentment for having successfully dredged up such an arcane, buried memory.

In the south range of the house I came to the library, which seemed to take up most of the entire ground floor. Ober hadn't taken me there on the tour and I wondered for a moment whether I was supposed to have access. He hadn't said anything about restricted areas in the house, but there was a sense of privacy about the place and it felt as if I might be intruding. I hesitated at the threshold but decided I was being oversensitive and went in, although I could not help myself treading extra daintily on the floorboards as if that might nullify any perceived violation of space.

The walls by the windows were panelled in sumptuously carved oak, but everywhere else the walls were loaded with books from floor to ceiling. I took a thin volume at random from a row of brown leather-bound books, which threw up a scent of dust as they shifted on the shelf. *De Consolatione Philosophiae*. I flicked through the pages but it was in Latin without a translation. A cursory examination of the other ancient-looking tomes in that part of the library suggested they were all unreadable, so I moved to some more accessible looking brightly coloured spines on the next range. I picked out a thick book from the middle: *Paradise Engineering: A Blueprint for Humanity*, O. Liddel. The chapter headings looked interesting: *Brave New World?*, *A Short History of Psychedelic Drug Use*, *Biotechnology and Post-Genomic Medicine*, *Entheogenic Drugs and Serotonin*, *A Post Darwinian Evolutionary Model*.... I replaced it, making a mental note to take a better look later, and pulled out a familiar looking book from the bottom shelf: *Alice's Adventures in Wonderland*.

I turned some pages, stopping momentarily on the engraved illustrations of the little girl in Wonderland until I found the one I was looking for: Alice peering over the top of a mushroom at the hookah-smoking caterpillar. I read the text aloud:

'Who are you?' said the Caterpillar.

This was not an encouraging opening for a conversation. Alice replied, rather shyly. 'I-I hardly know, Sir, just at present – at least I know who I *was* when I got up this morning, but I think I must have been changed several times since then.'

The association of the words caught me unaware and without warning I found myself crying. I sat down in an armchair shaking and trembling. I attempted to calm myself with steady breaths but within moments I was heaving sobs – the type of sobs that take over every faculty in the body. I knew that if I attempted to stand up my legs would give way, and even sitting down seemed an effort. Everything was devolved to my tears. And all I could think about amidst the shuddering was my Alice. I began to extract memories that had been hidden since her death, the deeply buried moments that signified a brother's love for his sister, all that were left of what once was. It was as if a closet of remembrance had been opened and its contents were covering me, overwhelming me. There was more inside than I had ever reckoned on. I so desperately wanted to hold on to her again, to tell her how sorry I was, to just feel her humanity next to mine. But I couldn't. She was gone and at that moment I didn't believe in the psychedelic world where I had been led to think that I could still contact her. All I had were tears caused by the past, which now infected every moment of the present and future. Grief, sorrow, guilt, self-loathing – they were piled up on top of me, battering me down into submission. How was I ever going to deal with it? At the back of my mind there was a realisation that the physical and mental traumas of the last month and my removal into an alien world of timber-framed houses and dusty libraries were suddenly finding an outlet and were flooding my senses. But that didn't matter. What mattered was my convulsive present, which was existing on an explosion of memories.

I'm not sure how long I sat there crying. Each time I thought I had exhausted myself I became racked with another bout of sobbing as I punished myself with a further round of remembrance. By the time it finally stopped I was utterly drained. I sat staring into the nothing, still shaking, but with all my energy dissipated. There were no memories now, just a dull, grey fog.

Eventually I looked down at the book in my hands. It had flipped onto a page with the illustration of Alice accidentally tipping over the jury box of animal jurors. The page was soaked with my tears, which I tried to wipe off in vain. But the picture of Alice drew me to new thoughts, of Alice Liddell, of her death, and of my own failure to prevent it. I found it difficult to picture her face and so she became a version of the illustrated Alice. It suited what I remembered of her pretty cartoonish looks. I closed my eyes and lingered on her body wrapped around mine and then onto her last act, crashing through the parapet, an unintended victim of her own brother's out of control vengeance. He had come to stick a knife into me, as Alice's presumed agent of corruption, but ended her life instead. I wondered whether he was any more guilty of killing his sister than I had been of killing mine. But in my emptied out, exhausted state the question seemed almost rhetorical. I placed the book on the arm of the chair and sank back into the cushions.

'Liddell.' I spoke the name out loud and sat up in the chair, suddenly lifted out of my thrall. I got up and went to the book I had looked at earlier: *Paradise Engineering*, O. Liddell. There was no information on the author, just an address and website for more information. I started to scan the other book spines on the adjacent shelves, newly energised by something that was like a crossroads of anxiety and excitement. There were no more Liddells, but I now realised that there were at least a dozen long shelves put over to volumes that covered an eclectic subject base but which still managed to retain an autonomy: biotechnology, mysticism, the bicameral mind, shamanism, chemistry, quantum physics. They seemed to be deliberately separated from the heaving shelves of psychiatry/psychology volumes opposite. I pulled some out, but I had too much nervous tension to look at any in detail. I came back to *Paradise Engineering* and took it over to the armchair. I tried to recall if I'd ever heard Ober's surname. I must have at some point, but couldn't remember. I opened the book at random and read a few sentences from the summing up of a chapter on "Designed Compounds and Quantum Consciousness":

The recent developments of new phenethylamine and tryptamine compounds have opened up different exploratory pathways into quantum consciousness. We are no longer reliant on the impenetrable theoretical concepts of quantum physicists and what they tell us about the skewed exotic realities of the sub-atomic world – we can experience them ourselves. These compounds are the starting point to an evolution in consciousness, and thereby a revolution in our civilisation.

That certainly sounded like Ober. And if it was did that mean he was related to Alice Liddell? It spun my mind round. My bout of sobbing suddenly felt as though it had happened days ago. Ober had barely said a word about Alice's death; he seemed almost totally unaffected by it. He had told me about the arrest of her brother and some scanty details about her funeral when I had first come out of intensive care, but in my medicated state I couldn't remember too much about that. And later it became almost a taboo subject. Imperceptibly, as my physical condition improved, we had come to a mutual agreement not to talk about Alice Liddell or what had happened. Even the police had seemed to lose interest and had stopped visiting me in hospital after the first week.

Agitation was starting to make my ears throb. I had to ask Ober about this when he returned. Perhaps he was just trying to spare me the trauma of remembering and dwelling on what had happened. But that was not his way. As a psychiatrist he was always nailing home the need for the cathartic techniques of flooding and reciprocal inhibition therapy, where I was to dredge up all of my anxieties whilst in an altered state in order to come to terms with whatever was inducing them. Perhaps he was just waiting until he administered my next drug to talk it through.

Or maybe Alice Liddell had not been killed at all. My pulse skipped. I had probably still been tripping when she went through the parapet; had any of what I remembered from that morning really happened? Certainly, it had been a morning of weirdness. Ober might just have been going along with me, acquiescing to my version of events for his own reasons. Perhaps he needed me to construct this narrative of events as part of my treatment; allowing me to invent characters that would enable me to accept my own sister's death and my own part in it. He would need only minimum input, by way of an occasional suggestion, to ensure that the story was made into remembered reality. In fact, how could I be sure that Alice Liddell had been with me at all? My memory of her was like it came from a dream... or a trip. I had not been able to visualise her face properly since waking up in hospital.

This was not good. I was starting to feel the dirty claws of paranoia. I tried to think back to that night and reconstruct the line of events in chronological order, but I kept getting things mixed up. And whenever I attempted to picture Alice Liddell beyond her Wonderland likeness I ended up with my own sister. Was that the product of Ober's new psychedelics? They created an alternative story to my own traumatic events, which involved the confusion of people and experiences. If both Alices were my sister then the knife wielding, apoplectic brother might represent... I don't know: fate, or the general brutality of the world. The whole thing belonged as an episode in a psychedelically induced altered state.

But if that were the case why did I have a stab wound that had kept me in hospital for so long? I gently prodded the location of the still-bandaged wound, feeling a residual ache that seemed to move between my stomach and my kidneys. Or did it? I had never actually seen the wound. My natural squeamishness had prevented me looking whilst nurses had changed the dressings, and all I had to go on was the dull ache and the doctor's assurance that the wound had never been life threatening due to it missing my organs. But who were those doctors and nurses? I couldn't bring any of them clearly into my mind's eye. They were just part of the chaotic whole.

I started to tap the wound, then to scratch it through my top and bandage. The aching pain was going away. I stood up and quickly rolled up my top to reveal the bandage. My hands were shaking with the threat of my imagination. I took out the two safety pins and started to unwrap the thin gauze layers of bandage around my abdomen. The bandage held in place a padded rectangle of material, which had additional adhesive tape for support. When the bandage was off I ran my fingers over the pad. One by one I took off the strips of adhesive tape, wincing at the sharp tinge of pain each time one took a microscopic layer of my skin with it. When the last one was off I held the pad in place myself. I pressed the pad once or twice but there was no pain. With my pulse pumping in my neck and my hands trembling more every moment I peeled back the pad to reveal what was underneath.

VIII

'And how does that make you feel?'
The words reverberate around my head. I am sure they are solid objects, or perhaps a liquid, actually moving between the right and left hemispheres of my brain. Eventually they seem to get tangled up in the nerve fibres of the corpus callosum and slowly fade to nothing and silence.

A gentle evening breeze replaces the faded words. It contours over my face and through my hair bringing with it the scent of thyme and the warmth of a Neolithic summer. In front of me two biers are laid out at the entrance to the barrow, where huge sarsen stones guard the dark interior of the burial mound. On the biers are the disarticulated remains of two people, and around me are those who have come to inter them. They stand, swaying in trance, their faces lit by the flaming torches that surround us in the gathering dusk. Every now and then the breeze eddies around the stones and brings back to me the musky smell of the barrow's interior. It is the smell of a mother, of a giver and taker of life. I look down at the skeletal parts on the biers. I think of their death and of my new life. I am to be born again inside the barrow womb, just as they are to find an end there.

'Do you feel at one with the others?'
The voice in my head travels between right and left brain hemispheres again. I glance to the others but they are enjoined in their trance over the bodies. I look up to the sky where a cleft between dusk-tinged clouds seems to hold the voice. But I realise that the voice is part of my mind and that my mind is part of the sky.

'*Do you feel at one with the landscape?*'

I opened my eyes, immediately half closing one again against the light. 'Such a harsh light here,' I said, as the silhouette of Ober swayed slightly in front of me. 'Are you real?'

I'm real,' he replied, but his words echoed all over the place. I was dizzy and nauseous.

'Am I coming down?'

'It would seem so.'

I closed my eyes again.

I am supposed to be inside the barrow but there is nothing under my feet. I fall in darkness, out of control but safe. As I approach something, unseen but big, I open my eyes. But I am still falling. Ober seems a tiny figure disappearing at the far end of a vast expanse of space, enclosed within range after range of gloomy monoliths spanning up to a roof made up of the night sky.

'Let's see if we can take this a little further shall we.'

The voice is female, but I know it must be Ober speaking. He is somehow taking hold of my arm, even though he seems to be at the far end of the immense space. Then he whispers in my ear and this time the words stick in the right cerebral hemisphere of my brain, filling it up like helium in a balloon.

'I'm injecting you with 45mg of DMT. Just allow yourself to go and don't be afraid.'

I no longer know whether my eyes are open or closed. I feel the prick of the needle in my arm but it seems to be happening to another person. I slump back in the couch and wait for it to hit me.

'One, two, three...'

IX

There was no wound, not even a scar. The skin beneath the padding had discoloured slightly but it was unbroken. I had no idea how long a knife wound should take to heal, but I was sure that one month was too soon for it to disappear without trace. I ran my fingers over where the wound should have been. Soft, unbroken skin. Slightly wrinkled from the humidity caused by the bandage, but certainly no stab wound. I was uninjured.

I pulled my top back down and fell back into the armchair. This was exhausting. I was emptied out. I tried once again to think back to the flat and what had happened to Alice, but my concentration would not allow it. My memory could only manage a grainy set of images, like a half-remembered film. Maybe I had made a mistake about the nature of the wound. Perhaps it hadn't been a knife. But I had been told that was why I was in hospital. That was what I had been recovering from. And I had suffered pain around my abdomen every day since I had come round in the hospital.

I allowed my heavy head to slump against the back of the chair and loll to one side. Immediately a wash of tiredness ebbed over me and took me away towards sleep via the garbled episodes of hypnagogic visions and sounds.

I woke up to the sound of birdsong, a repetitive chugging report somewhere behind me. I pulled the throw away from my chest and sat up wiping my eyes.

'Morning. Well, just.'

A woman was sitting in a chair next to the couch, looking at her watch with one eyebrow arched as though in mock disapproval of me. I pulled the throw up around me as a protection.

'Where am I? I said, squinting at her blurry outline and looking round the unfamiliar room.

'Where do you think you are?' she said, placing the book she'd been reading on to the foot of the couch. The suppressed hostility colouring her words immediately set me on edge.

'Ober's place?'

'That's right.'

I sat up fully and began to recognise the room as the one I'd sat in looking out over the garden – the old main open hall of the house. I looked around in an attempt to gauge my surroundings and the passage of time, but I found it difficult to meet the woman's eyes. I was embarrassed. I was also starting to measure the disquiet that seemed to be hanging about me as if it were a living presence.

'What do you remember about last night?' she asked, without inflection. Her face matched her words: cold and white, with dark eyes that would never give anything away. She was probably older than me, in her forties maybe, but it was difficult to tell.

'I was in the library. I was—' I suddenly remembered taking the bandage off. I felt the surge of a big heartbeat thumping through me but resisted the urge to lift up my top to check for the wound. '... I was looking at my knife wound.'

'Yes. Do you remember thinking it wasn't there?'

I looked her hard in the eye and thought I saw a challenge there. I drew up my top and saw the bandaged pad. I pressed it hard. It hurt, a lot.

'It's a very interesting form of symbolisation,' she continued, as if talking to a child. 'You made the healed wound a symbol for your own psychological recovery. And even in an entheogenic state you were surprised.'

I was caged. I started to feel the first signifiers of a panic attack. I was desperate to be alone. But I was also annoyed at her presumptions. I didn't know who she was or what she was doing there, and I wanted to take hold of her and shake her smug disposition until she was out of my personal space.

'Would you m-m-mind telling me who you are,' I stuttered.

'Oh, this is interesting,' she said, sounding as if she might have genuinely meant it. 'You really don't remember who I am?'

'No I don't.'

'Do you not remember meeting me before starting the session last night?'

'I was on my own l-l-last night.'

She nodded her head slowly as people do when they realise for the first time that they are interacting with someone who has a mental impairment.

'No, you were taking part in a psychotherapeutic session that involved the administration of a very large dose of 2, 5-Dimethoxy-4-Ethylphenethylamine. Ober and I spent quite a long time talking it through with you beforehand.'

'What's your name?'

'Titania.'

I ran my fingers through my hair. I wanted to be alone to think about this, to work through my memory and see what mistakes I was making. But she did not show any signs of being about to leave and I was conscious that I had nothing on except my top and underpants so I was not able to escape from beneath the throw. She watched my exasperation with a potent grin.

'Phenethylamines can affect the Hippocampus region of the brain.'

I frowned.

'It's where new memories are stored and processed before being consolidated and transferred to other parts of the brain. Do you not remember us finding you in the library? Ober had spent a few hours at my place in the village and we came back here just as it was getting dark. You were sitting in the old armchair. You'd been... crying. We talked it through. We decided to carry on with the treatment straight away.'

My heart was pumping hard again. I had never seen this woman before. I would have sworn it. All I could remember was falling asleep in the library. I looked away from her, closed my eyes and tried to bring back the moments before sleep. But all I could do was dredge up the vestige of a hypnagogic hallucination.

'And can you not recall anything from the session?' she asked, sounding as if she were intrigued. 'The burial mound. The bodies. Your... *clan*.'

'No.'

'And as you started to come down you returned to the library and saw your healed wound.'

I shook my head. But I was starting to think of the morning after with Alice Liddell, of the chaotic confusion that precipitated her death and my injury. I blinked hard and squinted at Titania.

'We have... *recorded* your experiences. We have a good idea of what happened. But these substances can alter temporal perceptions. Maybe our record is from something that happens to you in an entheogenic future.'

She looked serious. I wanted to laugh out loud but the residual memory of my morning with Alice and my morphinic month in hospital stopped me from confronting the absurd with derision. I pulled my head back to rest on the couch.

'What do you mean, *recorded*?'

'Mmm. Ober has been a naughty boy hasn't he. Has he not told you about the synergetic possibilities of these drugs?'

'Well, I don't know what "synergetic" means, and no, he hasn't told me.'

She smiled out one side of her mouth and leant forward in her chair. 'I'm guessing he thought that perhaps your experience with Alice would be enough to let you know how it works,' she said, her eyes twitching. 'You do remember Alice Liddell?'

I sunk back as far as I could into the couch and pulled a face that I hoped would dissuade her from pursuing me on this. But she didn't move. She was pressing me for an answer by hovering on the boundaries of my personal space and refusing to retreat.

'I guess Alice joined me during my trip... when she w-w-was with me in the flat... she got inside of my trip. She joined me.'

'Synergetic,' she announced, arching that eyebrow again and sitting back in her chair as though having proved a point.

'But she told me that she didn't have to be there at the same time in order to experience the altered state with me. She said she could have taken the same trip months before me... at least I think I remember her saying that.'

'Probably didn't want to give too much away. Didn't want to confuse you. The Phylogenic Memory is quite a concept to get your head around, especially when you're...'

'A bit thick and uneducated,' I said, immediately regretting the sourness in my voice.

'Oh. Nobody thinks your thick sweetie. We couldn't afford for you to be here if you were.'

'Who is the *we* Titania?'

She was about to reply, but the sound of the front door closing cut her short and we both looked at the door adjoining the entrance hall. It was Ober. He came in and sat on the end of the couch, looking from Titania to me and back again with a wary glimmer.

'How are you feeling?' he said, a peculiar stiffness framing the question. He shot a glance to Titania.

'A bit confused actually,' I replied, truthfully. I wanted to take the opportunity to pin down Ober on the weirdness that was engulfing me, but Titania headed me off.

'We're having some memory problems', she said, laying her hand on my arm as if protecting my interests. 'The usual thing -- patient can't remember us administering the 2C-E at all. I told him that the phenethylamines can affect the Hippocampus.' She turned back to me. 'Your perception of the event may have bypassed the Hippocampus and gone straight into another part of the temporal lobe... all unconsolidated. That will be most interesting when it surfaces again.'

I tensed up and my hands began to shake. This woman was taking the piss out of me. I was being treated like a bit of an imbecile under observation. Ober seemed to notice my discomfort and motioned Titania to follow him out of the room. As they both got up he placed a guiding hand on her back, from which she shied away slightly. Instinctively I averted my eyes, gripped by the anxiety of witnessing an embarrassing situation in an enclosed space. But just as they were leaving the room I looked back and saw them exchange a fleeting glance. I rarely trusted my own interpretations of other's actions when they were not meant to be witnessed by me, and in my current state I could not be sure of what I was witnessing anyway. But I swore that I saw humour dancing between their eyes. Just a glimpse. Just a momentary flicker of private amusement at my expense. It drew a cold shiver through me. I suddenly felt very alone, almost discarded. The trust that I had built up with Ober over the months was instantly diluted. I had no family, no friends and all of my emotional life had been vested in the only person who wanted to hear what I had to say. He had offered me a lifeline from my condition and I had grabbed onto it. But now he had shaken the rope. The moment of communion that I saw between them alerted me to the potentially precarious position I found myself in. I had been separated from my home. Ok so it was a dystopian hole of a home, but I still belonged to it in a way that I would never belong to the rural sumptuousness of Ober's house, and their shared knowingness confirmed my position as an outsider brought in to... well, I didn't know why. Why was I there? Who was paying for my regal convalescence and what parts were Ober and Titania playing?

I felt nauseous again. I tried deep breathing to clear the tension from my body, but the paranoia was hijacking my racing thoughts and I found myself tautening up again as I attempted to recount every moment from waking up in the car to the present. I wanted to find some answers to their mutual understanding of my condition and their reasons for arranging the situation as they had. But how could I do that now? My confidant was no longer to be trusted without question. He was in league with someone who, in our short acquaintance, I had been given little reason to like very much. And I couldn't even remember the sequence of events during the previous twenty-four hours, so how would I be able to piece together any meaning behind those events.

I got up, wrapping the throw around me, and tottered over to the bay window overlooking the garden. I pulled down the sash window and leant against the frame, looking out over the lazy, comfortable scene. I closed my eyes as the scent of Rosemary drifted up to me. The smell instantly conjured up the image of a Rosemary bush. How did I know this? I was fairly confident that I'd never seen or smelt Rosemary in the city. But something about that decadent, voluptuous, almost decaying aroma was able to open up the image of the plant in my mind. So where did it come from? Was it simply something that had been stored in my memory from seeing and smelling a Rosemary bush at some distant point in my past? Or was I receiving the recognition by way of Ober's Phylogenic Memory – a collective unconscious. And if that were the case, did I always have access to it, or was it only reached into during particular states of consciousness?

I opened my eyes, saw the Rosemary bush under the window and closed them again. What was the image in my mind? A sensory memory involving sight and smell. But how did the image form? Where was Mind? Was my cerebral cortex just processing neural information and displaying the results in a non-visual way? Or was Mind actually part of *everything*, a collective that drew on all knowledge and experience from all life, but which only had limited means at its disposal when attempting to formulate and display its recognition of things in the brain. Perhaps when a psychedelic flooded my neural circuitry Mind was enabled, in part, to escape the confines of the physical brain and become part of the collective unconscious. That was why it was always so difficult to explain the experience in words. How do you explain what Mind *sees*? It doesn't see it visually. It creates amorphous imagery based on visual and other sensory input but it *remembers* and *sees* everything in a way that simply cannot be explained. It can only be experienced. And the psychedelic experience is a direct participation in Mind. Perhaps it is one of the few ways to access what you really are without dying.

I opened my eyes and watched the clouds within the pale blue sky. They seemed, at that moment, to offer a partial explanation for my memory gaps. Their ever-changing appearance was simply an illusion. They were not the shapes and forms I saw with my eyes, but were intimately connected to and a part of the physical environment of the sky. They could not be detached from the sky and in fact had no real existence of their own at all. The clouds' constituent parts made up the whole, and each part, each atom, was unaffected by the passage of time; took no part in temporal movement at all. The existence of the clouds' atoms was outside time. They were, in effect, eternal. And if something is eternal then what need does it have for time?

I closed my eyes and tried to focus on an image of eternity, something without beginning or end. If Mind is eternal then there are bound to be times when it loosens the shackles of Time that it finds itself chained to whilst using the brain as a vehicle. Maybe I would remember what I thought had not happened when the time was right. Perhaps Mind was disturbed, or reminded of what It really is, by the psychedelics that allowed glimpses of freedom and reacted by taking the memories from the Hippocampus region of my brain and burying them in deeper cerebral recesses. Or maybe I'm just starting to imagine things after taking very large doses of extremely potent psychedelics. I'd have said both were possibilities.

I left the garden view, the Rosemary bush and clouds, and went up to my bedroom to get dressed. It was about time I got back into the real world, whatever that was.

X

It took me most of the afternoon to convince myself that I was able to go outside of the house and even maybe venture down to the village. The thought of having to interact with people there made me want to slip under the covers of my bed and hide myself away. As much as I had hated going outside my flat in the blocks, at least I knew what to expect there. I could limit the damage by attempting to appear invisible, something that I was, for the most part, successful at pulling off. But here it was different. I had the notion that the whole village probably knew what the house was used for, and that they would not be particularly amenable to its *inmates*. I knew that Titania lived in the village, but beyond that, and the glimpse I had had of it coming through in the car, it was a completely unknown quantity. It scared me as if it were a living threat, nestling in the English countryside like a sentient being just waiting for me to fall into its clutches.

And yet there was an internal voice urging me to get out of the house and put myself into an alternative social situation as soon as possible. I knew that if I didn't my agoraphobia would take hold of me and never let me venture outside the confines of the house. I would be trapped there, just as I had been in the flat in the blocks.

After several hours of procrastination, and several cannabis-heavy joints, I finally put on some jeans, a T-shirt and trainers and went out into the garden, which would, I decided, act to break me in to the alien environment. The garden was larger than it looked from the house. The trees that curved with the stream at the bottom of the sloping garden continued on the other side for about the same distance again, giving way to another grassy area enclosed by a wooden fence. I crossed a small, rustic footbridge over the stream and walked up a tenuously defined path to a stile in the fence. The spot overlooked the countryside down to the village and I traced the sinuous course of the stream through woodland and fields before it was canalised beside the road through the village.

A sentient being. From this distance the village did look kind of organic. It blended into the lush green and gold countryside, the mellow stone, tile and thatch somehow as much a part of the landscape as the trees and fields. It looked inviting. It looked like a representation of the perfect imagined England, all harmonious, settled and at one with itself. It made me feel nostalgia for something I had never known; something buried deep inside me that was awaiting the appropriate signal for activation. I couldn't quite grasp the meaning behind it but it was speaking to me from somewhere beyond me and yet still a part of me.

I leant on the stile and watched a couple of luminous dragonflies skitting backwards and forward a small distance in front of me. Perhaps they had a hypnotic effect on me, because after a couple of minutes I began to zone out and found myself fantasising about the landscape being a huge curvaceous woman gyrating and heaving with each heartbeat and breath. The vision of her geologically defined breasts and immense pregnant belly made me smile. I felt the urge to touch the earth, to touch her body. Slowly I sat down, placed the palms of my hands on the ground and massaged the soil under the rough grass. I closed my eyes and conjured up an image – an inarticulate image, impossible to describe because it was made up of an ulterior sense that does not allow its own representation. It was similar to being on a trip, but without abandoning all control.

I stayed there for ages. Then I climbed the stile.

And now I find myself on a wooded footpath beside the stream leading down to the road into the village. Something's going to happen. The weight of expectancy loads the atmosphere and I have tears in my eyes. Alice is with me somehow. It actually feels like she's wrapped around me, weightless but all over me. The excitement is tangible in all of my senses: I can taste the exploding pollen in the air; smell the transitory waft of thyme; touch the thickened summer air surrounding me as I move; hear the edgy birdsong reverberating around the woods; and see the sumptuous, energised vegetation expanding and contracting in green, brown and black. My heart pumps away. I haven't moved this fast for a long time. I'm tripping over brambles and roots and breaking into a run. The wood swallows me and then spits me out onto the road just in front of the first (or maybe the last) cottage in the village. Breathlessly I walk between the road and the stream, into the village.

Immediately I realised something wasn't quite right. I'd been thinking that Ober might not have wanted me to leave the house and there was a lingering sense that I may have been 'in trouble.' The acidic fear of the potential to meet people in enclosed social spaces was also eating away at my insides. But there was something else layered on top of the anxiety; a disquieting sense of abnormality that worked on a level just below my sensory radar. It had taken hold of me the moment I had stepped into the wood. I wanted to get rid of it as soon as possible.

Still short of breath I stopped with the intention of turning back, but just as I was about to a car came rumbling around the turn into the village from the direction I'd just come. I tried to look innocuous and casual by carrying on walking into the village but the driver had evidently seen me turn round and the car slowed as it passed me so he could get a look at me. It was an old sort of car, some type of Rover I thought, and the driver was equally antiquated with thick-rimmed glasses and slicked back hair. He shot me a quizzical glance as he passed, then clanked the car into a lower gear and carried on, pulling up some fifty metres ahead. I watched him get out, look back at me for a few seconds then go into one of the cottages along the street.

It was only after he'd disappeared into the cottage that I noticed how few cars there were parked in the street. The few villages I'd ever been in were brutalised by traffic and choked with parked cars. This street had no more than four or five cars parked up, all old models. It gave the place a stillness that was at once both quaint and discomfiting. And where were the speed bumps that had woken me up on the journey through the village to the house with Ober? My stomach muscles began to tense up and sweat broke out on my back. Again I turned to go back, but the recondite atmosphere of the place held me there. A spark of my old energy struck up and began to stave off the anxiety. I wanted to be there.

I took a few deep breaths and continued on into the village. The stillness was unsettling but I carried on, heading for... well, I didn't know what. And with every step the languidness of the air became more pronounced -- it surrounded me and fed the impressionistic aura of the place. The blurry rooflines of the houses, the washed-out colour of the sky and the ambiguous perspective further along the street – they combined with the stillness to impose an abstraction on my perceptions.

By the time I reached the pub half way along the street I was beginning to see movements in my peripheral vision. The movements filtered through the thickened summer air accompanied by sounds that seemed amplified – echoing sounds of life and death; insect larvae breaking out of their skins; small animals eating one another; dead organic matter mouldering and squelching. I stopped and closed my eyes, wanting to know what I would see. The images of the honey-coloured stone cottages stayed with me for a moment but were then replaced with strong, irresistible figures melding into the buildings and becoming one with me both at the same time. They were like androgynous humanoids expanding and contracting at will. I couldn't tell whether they belonged to this place or in my tired, reactive mind. Maybe both.

The figures turned black and disappeared into shadows. Their disappearance coincided with a sudden overwhelming urge to sleep. My head seemed too heavy to be carried on my body and I wanted to lie down and rest it immediately, anywhere. I tried to open my eyes but my lids flickered and refused to open. My head lurched forward and downwards. My mind followed suit and clunked down between whatever levels it existed in. It was like falling from a height but feeling nothing except the lurch in your stomach. Without thinking what I was doing I allowed my drained body to drop gently to

71

the ground and curled up into a foetal position on the tarmac of the pavement. It was blissful to allow my head to be supported. All of my tiredness swelled through me, completely taking me over. It was like being a small child again, sanctioned to behave in a socially abnormal way. In fact, at that moment I was pretty sure I was a child.

Stealthily the androgens emerged from the shadows again and came to stand over me, swaying and rocking like trees in the wind. They supported me, not physically but as a parent might, soothing and nurturing when the world has become too frightening and complex for an immature mind. I longed for them to hold me, but they did not seem able to actually touch me. There was some division between us that could not be brooked. It was a division of Time rather than space but I couldn't quite grasp the concept – I just needed a few more moments to understand, a few more moments and they would divulge their secret to me and I would be able to join them, become one with them.

I'm in the pub now, sitting in a corner of the gloomy interior looking out a small leaded window to a shady garden with plastic tables and chairs in the back. I have a newspaper on the table in front of me, which I have been pretending to read in order to make my solitude less conspicuous. It's an old newspaper, out of date, practically an archive piece. My mind is buzzing. I am trying desperately to remember something that has happened to me recently but which remains hovering just beyond the boundaries of my recollection. I can see it, like a distant feature in the landscape, but I can't quite make out the details. It's important as well. If I can remember what it is it will be a fundamental step towards me discovering my mental problems and getting rid of them. What is it? Tip of my brain. I feel myself physically urging the memory towards me with the beckoning motions of my arms. But it is stubborn and doesn't come. I slump back in the chair and sip from my cloudy beer. It doesn't taste too good. First time I've drunk beer in years. Years. That's part of the answer but I'm not sure what the question is.

I stare through the thick, dirty window glass again, wondering why I am here. There's no one in the garden but there is movement in the shadows amongst the bushes at the far end. I strain my eyes to see and then jolt suddenly at what I think I see.

'Mind if I join you son?'

I jerked my head round, then quickly back again to glance out of the window. There was nothing there, only a couple sitting down at one of the rusty old tables. I looked back to the man, my vision swimming. The last thing in the world I wanted to do was talk to a stranger – I had thought reading a paper on your own in a pub clearly signified that.

'Of course not... please.' I said, gesturing to the chair opposite.

'Eugene Quince,' he announced, sitting down.

'Hello.'

My sight had steadied but my stomach muscles were tightening again. I wanted to think about how I'd come into the pub. I wanted to concentrate on the sequence of events leading to that glimpsed weirdness in the bushes. When had I come through the front door? Who had I ordered the drink from? Hadn't I just been asleep? But Eugene Quince's presence subjugated any introspection. I was going to have to interact with a person for an indefinite time period, and there was no escape from the social environment I had somehow put myself in.

'You holidaying down here?'

'Um, yes, k-kind of.'

'Good good. Down from the city for some fresh country air eh?'

'Yes it's b-b-b--' I couldn't get it out. I knew my face was turning red and my hands were beginning to tremble a little. 'Sorry, I have a...' I gestured to my mouth, knowing he'd understand what I meant.

'Don't worry son,' he said, narrowing his eyes a little. 'What causes it?'

I hadn't quite expected that, but in a way it was far preferable to vacuous small talk.

'I have agoraphobia... and s-some other anxiety disorders. It sometimes makes talking to people... strangers, quite d-d-difficult.'

'Oh, so you're staying at the manor house?' He asked, gesturing vaguely towards the door.

I nodded. He'd worked that out pretty quickly. Maybe all the loons Ober brought down to the house pitched up in the village at some point. Mr Quince probably made it a habit to become acquainted with them. But despite his sharpness I couldn't help warming to him. He had an avuncular gait with his tweeds and brylcreamed hair. As if on cue he even brought out a pipe from his jacket pocket, quickly filled it with tobacco and lit it up whilst sitting back in the chair.

'We don't have much to do with the house here in the village,' he said, after filling his lungs with smoke and then steaming it out his nose. 'I think the villagers are a little apprehensive about it you see.'

'Why?' I asked, attempting to look as innocent as possible.

'Oh, it's not because of the poor broken people who come to stay. It's more... more the goings on there sometimes.'

He evidently had no compunction about labelling me a psychiatric case, but I kind of liked that. I appreciated the openness.

'Goings on?'

'Well, I don't want to say anything myself. It's just that this place hasn't changed much since the war and the villagers are... well, they're a conservative bunch you see. Good people. But they find it difficult to accept certain *new ideas*. Professor Liddell and his... compatriots... well, the locals just think they're a bit... a bit hippyish.'

I couldn't contain a smile. *Hippyish*. But the smile fell off my face an instant later. *Professor Liddell*. Shit.

'I know this will probably make me sound like a silly old fool who's been listening to too much village gossip,' he continued, apparently not noticing my widened eyes. 'But there are a lot of odd stories about the place since the... *group* took it on about five years ago.'

'What sort of stories?' I asked, realising that my piqued interest had relegated my anxieties and stutter and replaced them with the nervous energy of someone hanging on words.

'Oh, I don't want to make too much of it,' he said,

unconvincingly. 'It's just that they tend to keep themselves to themselves. And when they have their gatherings up there, they never involve anyone from the village.'

'What about Titania?'

Quince looked slightly put out. He took another inhalation and considered. 'Yes, Titania lives in the end cottage. She took up with them as soon as they bought the house. I think she may have known Professor Liddell from before. But I don't want to cast any insinuations. They have certainly saved the house from ruin – it was in an awful state before.'

He was evidently keen to move on from Titania, and politeness obliged me not to pursue the subject despite wanting to know all about her. I took another sip of the beer, even though it was starting to make me feel a bit nauseous.

'Drugs,' he announced, clandestinely looking about him. I tensed up. ' I think what the village is concerned about is that there may be illegal substances being used there.'

'What makes you s-say that?'

'Oh, I don't know. There is just some odd behaviour up there sometimes.'

'How do you know?'

He narrowed his eyes at me again. 'Well, the villagers like to keep an eye out... for their own peace of mind you understand.'

He relit his pipe and took a few puffs, clearly paving the way for an anecdote.

'About a year ago, one night, well early in the morning, in summer, about four am just as the sun was coming up, Professor Liddell and some of his group were found at the edge of the grounds, close to the woodland.' He stopped and smiled, but his eyes never left mine. 'Naked. The lot of them. Sleeping naked around the embers of a camp fire.'

I shrugged as if to say 'so what', but Quince held up his hand to indicate the punchline was about to come.

'The odd thing was that in the middle, next to the fire, there was one chap with... with deer antlers on his head and a hide wrapped round his shoulders.' He paused for dramatic effect. 'He was the only one who seemed to be awake. Staring into the middle distance in a trance.'

'Right.'

I wasn't sure if I was supposed to find this funny or profoundly disturbing, but what interested me most of all was…

'… Who found them'?

'They were just found.'

That was an odd answer. I had to suppress the urge to laugh out loud. But in a moment the suppression turned back on itself. Quince reloaded his pipe and carried on talking about the grounds of the house or something. But at the liminal edge of my audition I could hear a voice. It was at first indistinct, but then, as though the volume had been turned up suddenly, clear and whispering in my right ear:

Imagine if you were able to see every person in the world that happened to be defecating at a given moment, altogether at the same time.

I swung my head round. Two old geezers, gossiping over their pints of mild, looked at me.

In the other ear, so close that I swore I felt the breath against my cheek:

You would look up at a huge cavernous canopy of assholes excreting into a void above you.

I twisted round again in my seat and then stood up, knocking over my chair with a clatter.

'Are you all right son?' said Quince, reaching out his hand hesitatingly.

I stared at him. What must I have looked like?

'Yes… yes, I'm ok. B-b-but I think I should be g-getting back now.'

'Are you sure, you look very pale.'

'Yes, I need to get b-back.'

All eyes in the pub were on me, and I wasn't imagining it from the depths of an anxiety induced paranoia; they were really looking at me. I felt sick and slightly giddy from the beer and the stress was beginning to pull my stomach up into my mouth. I waved my hand at Quince without looking at him and hurried to the door. I opened it and was almost outside, but for some reason I glanced back to the bar before I closed the door behind me. The barmaid was looking at someone, it might have been Quince, pointing to her head and spinning her forefinger round.

I stumbled outside. The sunshine was brighter than before and I squinted and shaded my eyes before moving down onto the pavement, keen to remove myself from the vicinity of the pub. There seemed more cars parked up now – I had to squeeze between two to cross the street. I stopped in the middle of the road... on a speed bump, thirty centimetres high, painted with fluorescent yellow. I looked at it with big eyes and a swelling in my chest.

I had to get back to the house. I needed to extract myself from this situation as soon as possible and bunker down in a safe space in the house. I marched across to the pavement just before two cars whipped past me, two new sports cars, with assholes at the wheels and excrement coming out the speakers. They took the speed bumps without slowing down and quickly disappeared around the bend out of the village. The selfish extravagance of the drivers matched the new, angry atmosphere. Other cars moved up and down the street in an almost constant stream of never ending traffic. A strained tenseness was tangible. Noise and petrol fumes everywhere, infecting the air, causing the place to be diseased, informing its character and dictating the febrile mood.

I put my head down and started walking. There were quite a few people about and I had to avoid eye contact for the length of the high street. I couldn't allow anyone to see into me. I would have killed for a joint. I couldn't think of anything else that would mitigate the appalling pulses of adrenaline and God knows what else that were careering through my brain. Why were there so many fucking people about? And why were they all looking at me like I'd just landed from another planet? I gritted my teeth, fucking and cunting under my breath for no better reason than I couldn't stand to be there, ensnared in a village that had been overrun with a frayed tension. My anxiety was inarticulate. Words and concepts escaped me. All that I had were bubbling images of half-seen people, cars and stone cottages. Dirty cottages too.

Fume-blackened and sad looking, as if they were slowly dying beneath a layer of grime, palling away into the past.

I strode on, bumping into a couple of people who tutted me and ratcheted up the tension even more. By the time I reached the last cottage I was almost running. But I stopped when I passed it. I looked beyond at the red brick houses clustered around a newly constructed cul-de-sac. The last cottage was enveloped in the gloom of their shadow. Iciness ran through me, followed closely by a wave of tiredness. Hadn't I just been asleep? An indistinct and partial memory of the androgens slithered through my head. My eyeballs rolled in their sockets, flickering with irresistible fatigue. The new houses that were now the end of the village faded into the mauve blackness of imminent unconsciousness.

I needed to talk with Ober.

XI

I woke up in my bedroom as the shafts of a late afternoon sun cast their special light into the room. The longcase clock in the hallway below struck five and a lazy breeze filtered in through a half open window. I closed my eyes and tried to relax into the soft, subdued peace of the place. But my turbulent thoughts were awoken with me and my muscles started to tauten up, marking out a renewed agitation.

After a few minutes I got up and stretched at the window. I was lethargic and grumpy and so disinclined to think clearly, but I attempted to churn up the events of the past couple of days. There was no linear narrative. I just couldn't place one event before or after another. I groaned at each jumbled memory. They were like snapshots randomly mixed together, offering no sense of temporal movement. I didn't know what to make of my own memory. I was disorientated and subdued, trying to come to terms with being totally out of control of my own life.

Before I descended into a trance at the window I decided to hunt down Ober to talk with him. I needed someone else to get me straight, and whatever my inhibitions Ober was the only choice I had. I intuitively headed for the library. Sure enough, Ober was there inspecting a vinyl before putting it onto the turntable of a big 1970s-looking deck, all burnished silver, dimly lit dials and big knobs. I immediately suppressed the thought that I hadn't noticed this last time that I was in the library. I didn't need any more confusion.

'Good evening,' he said, glancing up at me for just a second. I couldn't work out whether his tone was friendly or critical.

'Ober, We need to talk.'

He let go of a smile that had started to form on his lips, and lowered the needle on to the edge of the record, spinning round on top of the speed-aligned chequered sides of the turntable. I didn't know what else to say. I needed him to give me some explanations but I wasn't sure how to elicit those explanations. The unquestioning trust I had always conferred on him had been bruised and damaged. I realised I was shaking slightly and that my mouth had become dry. I hadn't been nervous with Ober like this since I first met him in the hospital.

'I need you to give me—'

I was interrupted by Syd Barrett. The immediately recognisable strains of *Terrapin* came out of the speakers that were hidden somewhere amongst the bookshelves. Ober turned the volume down a tad and gestured for me to join him. I sat down in one of the armchairs but Ober remained standing, holding the record cover and glancing between it and me.

'What do you need me to give you?' he asked, tonelessly.

A tingle ran down my neck and dissipated over my chest. I was suddenly being interviewed.

'I'm getting a b-b-bit confused about things. I think there must be something affecting my short-term memory... the drugs... Titania did talk ab-b-bout them affecting the hippo...'

'... Hippocampus.'

'Yes. Is that true?'

'Mmm, to a degree.'

He didn't elaborate. I was starting to sweat and feel a bit sick.

'Of course most people think Syd Barrett just took too much acid and fried his brain,' he said, holding the record cover up with Syd crouching on his stripy floorboards. 'But I would suggest that perhaps he was told the meaning of life during one of his trips and was never able to fully integrate that information into his everyday existence. Never able to explain what he knew to other people. That would be enough to drive anyone insane.'

I tried to smile but I think it must have come out as more of a grimace. I didn't know whether this was leading to an explanation or not, but the marginally unhinged voice of Syd Barrett as a backdrop was distracting me to the point of not remembering why I was there. Perhaps this was the next stage in my treatment: associating myself with famous madmen.

Cos we're the fishes and all we do,
Move about is all we do,
Well oh baby my hair's on end about you.

'Well, I don't think I've been told the meaning of life yet,' I said, trying to untangle my thoughts from the lyrics. 'B-b-but I'm pretty sure that I'm losing control of my memory somehow. And I keep seeing things... strange things. Actually I'm not even sure if I see them – I don't know whether I see them with my eyes or whether they're in my mind. I think I'm beginning to lose track... you know, what I imagine and what I actually experience. I keep losing chunks of time and then they seem to come back as memories... but I don't know where they are supposed to fit. It's like time's messed up and I keep popping in and out.'

I realised I was not making a very cogent point. I couldn't concentrate properly with the music filling the air. But Ober was listening intently – he had that narrow-eyed look he got when what I was saying interested him. I shut up to see if I'd made any impression on him. He sat down opposite me and folded his hands together on the record sleeve.

'Did you have a bad experience in the village today?'

'Kind of, yes.'

He gestured for me to continue.

'Should I have told you I was going?'

'It doesn't matter. Just tell me what happened.'

I breathed in, deeply, and primed myself to provide a useful overview. But I realised that I just didn't have things straight in my own head. How could I describe sequential events to Ober when they were so tangled in my memory?

'I'm sorry Ober, I'm not quite sure where to start.'

'At the beginning. I saw you at the far end of the garden, up by the stile into the woods. Did you go down to the village along the footpath through the woods?'

' Yes. Yes, that's right... the footpath. But I think the drugs are acting residually... leaving a trace behind and popping to the surface like a flashback. But it's not like a real flashback because you just can't tell where it starts and reality stops. I know I was on the footpath but I can only recall it as a single moment. A single moment of leaves and sunlight and tree bark.'

'But isn't that how we always recall the past?' he said, looking genuinely engaged. 'It's never like watching a film. Our memories distil the progression of events into series of moments... sight, sound, smell, taste, touch... all into one multi-sensory instant.'

I frowned. How was he always able to correlate and articulate what I was experiencing so effortlessly?

'Mmm. I guess so. But when I got down into the village it was... it was odd. There was something about the air – it was cleaner somehow, and yet there was a muddy languidness about the place, like a dream – not like a trip -- but so crystal clear, so... *real*. There were hardly any cars and those that were about were all old models. And it was so quiet. It was as if it were the sixties or something.'

I had been talking without looking at Ober, but now I looked back at him and saw how he was hanging on my words. As soon as our eyes met he melded back into his usual impassivity.

'Did you meet anyone?'

'Well, I ended up in the pub, The Green Man I think it's called. But the thing is I don't remember going in. I only realised I had ordered a drink and sat down when I was sitting at a table looking out the window.'

I shifted in my seat. I didn't know quite how to talk about this.

'And before I'd gone in I kind of... well, I f-f-fell asleep.'

'Did you experience anything when you were falling asleep.'

He didn't seem phased that I'd been falling asleep on the village High Street in broad daylight. I tried to collect myself. I could sense Ober trying to extract as much information out of me as possible, slightly impatiently.

'I thought I saw... like... people. Androgynous people, flitting around in the corner of my eye. And then when I looked out the pub window—'

'Hold on. What about these androgens? What were they doing?'

He seemed to have accepted their existence remarkably quickly. I had been thinking of them as... 'Hypnagogic fairies.' I spoke the words but I wasn't quite sure where they came from.

Ober sat back in his chair. 'Did they touch you?'

'No.'

'Did they talk?'

I shook my head.

'Do you think they were *really* there?'

'You tell me, you're the psychiatrist.'

He smiled. 'And what did you see when you looked out the pub window?'

'A green man, covered in ivy.'

'Anything else?'

'Hooves, horns... I only glimpsed it for a fraction of a second.'

'And why wouldn't that just be a flashback?'

'Jesus Ober, I d-d-don't know.'

I sprang up from the chair and walked over to the hi-fi, gritting my teeth. But Syd was just getting into the jaunty routine of *Here I go*. I couldn't help smiling. He managed to dissipate some of my anxiety in just a few seconds.

This is a song 'bout a girl that I knew,
She didn't like my songs and that made me feel blue,
She said a big band is far better than you...

'I told you – it didn't feel like a flashback.' I said, as calm

as I could. 'None of it did. And then I met some bloke...
Eugene Quince.'

Instinctively I looked at Ober. He'd tightened up a bit.

'Do you know him?' I asked, feeling like I'd suddenly
regained some control over the conversation.

'Yes, we know him. He's a policeman.'

'He didn't tell me that.'

'I bet. But I'm sure he was trying to elicit as much
information about the house as possible, wasn't he?'

'I suppose.'

'You must understand that we need to control your
contact with the likes of Quince for the time being. He could
set you back a long way.'

'Christ Ober, I think talking with some middle-aged bloke
in a pub is pretty f-f-fucking lightweight compared to what's
happened to me recently, even if he is a c-c-copper. You
don't raise an eyebrow when I tell you I've been seeing
skinny fairies on the high street and a green man in a pub
garden, but talking to Quince is beyond the pale for a person
in my *condition*.'

'Ok, ok. Calm down and sit back down.'

I took a few deep breaths and slumped into the chair. But
my agitation was still bubbling. I decided I should probably
carry on talking.

'So yes, I guess Quince was q-q-questioning me, but...
I... well, I heard some voices and so I was probably a bit
rude. I had to just leave.'

'Voices?'

'In my head... well, I think they were in my head. That
trip I had back in the flat, the sea of sphincters... they were
talking about that.'

'Talking about it?'

'Describing it... as if they were reading out a description
of what I saw.'

Ober nodded but his eyes had taken on a thousand-yard
stare. I couldn't tell whether what I had just said disturbed him
profoundly or if he was just getting bored. I also considered
the possibility that he might be experiencing both feelings at
the same time.

'Anything else?' he asked, tonelessly.

'Well, I rushed out the pub and everything had changed.'

He didn't move a muscle but I sensed Ober's attention snap back into a groove.

'Changed?'

'It was busy, lots of people about, cars everywhere. It was so utterly changed from when I had gone into the pub. It had become... angry, tense. And, I know this sounds stupid, but there were houses at the end of the village... I saw the last cottage on the way in but on the way out there was a new cul-de-sac there as well.'

I shifted uneasily in the chair. If I'd been someone listening to me I'd be thinking I was talking bollocks. I decided I had said enough. Ober was stock still, his eyes not quite meeting mine. Abruptly there was a tension in the air, a quality of importance being flagged up by some abstruse force that inhabited the library with us. My heart pumped in anticipation and I instinctively gripped onto the side arms of the chair. As if in collusion with the atmosphere even Syd had stopped singing and the needle-arm returned to its rest. Ober brought himself up in the chair so as to lean slightly forward, now looking me straight in the eye, and evidently aware of the pressured ambience. He allowed it to linger. I think I knew what was coming but the blood was pumping in my ears so hard that it was difficult to keep a thought in my head. The only image I could conjure up was Alice Liddell's cartoon face just before she disappeared over the parapet outside my flat. But where did that image exist? I was the only person to have seen her face, from that perspective at that particular moment in time, but where was the image stored? How could I be sure it was any more real than an amorphous dream?

'There never was a real Alice.'

A wave of dizziness filled my head.

'We just put her into the trip to help you. Went a bit wrong, but nothing too bad. Nothing too long-lasting. You see...' Ober paused and looked at me with his piercing multi-coloured eyes. 'You see, the drugs allow us to manipulate time.'

The dizziness took over. I wanted to shout out loud, wanted to cover my ears and shout NO, NO, NO. But I knew I couldn't make a sound. I knew I was under the influence of something that I couldn't resist but I had no idea when it was being administered to me and no idea what it was. I closed my eyes and opened them again. The gloaming library was still there and Ober had got up to replace the record at the deck, apparently oblivious to my distress.

'I think you'd have got on quite well with Syd Barrett,' he said, swivelling the vinyl between his forefingers before putting it back on the turntable.

I just stared, open-mouthed, my head still swimming with whatever was controlling it.

'And that's definitely a *good* thing.'

Trip to, heave and ho, up down, to and fro,
You have no word,
Trip, trip to a dream dragon
Hide your wings in a ghost tower…

Shit.

XII

I rushed into my bedroom and shut the door behind me. I could still hear, faintly, Syd's music, as though it were infiltrating the wooden beams and floorboards and dissipating through the entire house. My stomach was tight and sick and my head was beginning to throb. I sat on the bed and tried to still myself, tried to centre and control all of my racing thoughts. I lit up a joint I'd prepared earlier and attempted to focus on Alice Liddell. I wanted to recapture the moments we were together *before* we took the drug. That wasn't part of a trip. She had been a person interacting with me in the normal course of my shabby existence. I closed my eyes and tried to picture her but, as before, I couldn't quite bring her face into relief. There was just the cartoon image borrowed from the *Wonderland* illustrations.

After a couple of minutes without being able to conjure her up I started to drift into thinking about my Alice. How I wished she were here. I would have done anything to hold her one more time, to have her tell me it would all be alright, that there was nothing that could stop a brother and sister if they set their heart and mind to it and worked together.

A knock at the door pulled me back. I really did not want to talk to Ober. He was scaring the shit out of me and I simply was not ready for any more.

'Yes,' I said, in a tone meant to inform him that I wasn't receiving. The door opened and Titania came in, shut the door and approached the bed.

'May I?' she asked gesturing to the bed.

What did she want? Was she privy the conversation between Ober and me? She was not someone I wanted in my personal space at that moment.

'You're going to have to know some things before too long,' she said, sitting down on the bed without my leave. 'I realise this is hard for you, and that there are things you do not understand... but you're part of something very large... very large indeed. One thing that you will have to learn to accept is that whatever sufferings you may have to undergo, you will be doing it for the benefit of the greater good.'

I did not want to hear this. 'If you don't mind Titania, I would really like to be alone right now. I'm g-g-getting scared and I am beginning to doubt everything I see or remember, and with all due respect I don't think there is anything you can say at the present moment that is going to make me feel b-b-better.'

She nodded slowly as if acknowledging my summary of how I felt, but at the same time knowing better. She sidled her position on the bed and I noticed the slight contour of a suspender belt under her skirt. I felt an involuntary rush of blood to my face and looked away to the window on the far side of the room.

'Has Ober told you about Alice... Alice Liddell?'

Despite myself I couldn't help engaging. 'Kind of, I guess... if she ever existed of course.'

'She did exist, still does exist. At least as far as you're concerned. And has he told you about what happens to you when you are medicated?'

'Medicated?'

'Your medication.'

'Tripping you mean.'

She pursed her lips and nodded her head again as though just made aware of something. She put her hand onto my arm and my chest started to contract. I wished she weren't quite so good-looking. And that she wasn't emanating quite so much empathy at the moment. It had been easier to dislike her.

'What you've been taking is a new mixture of drugs.'

'Phenethylamines?'

'Partly.'

'Hold on, what do you mean, *partly*? Ober explained these drugs to me. I've seen dozens of experience reports on websites. They either are or aren't. And you told me before that I'd taken 2C-E.'

She flashed her eyes and smiled a little – involuntarily I thought. I began to feel a bit thick, unable to decode all the nuanced behaviour going on around me.

'I'm not the person to explain the way these drugs works,' she said, unconvincingly. 'But I do know what we can achieve by using them. They are potentially the golden key.'

I waited for her to continue but her attention seemed to have drifted. Her eyes had hazed over a little, her pupils dilated.

'The golden key?' I asked, sensing the thickening atmosphere in the room.

'Imagine a world,' she said, her eyes re-focussing on me, flashing again as the subdued early-evening light from the window caught them. 'Imagine a world where the fear of death has been overcome. Where everyone on the planet knows that death means no more than the falling of another drop of rain into the ocean. Imagine knowing with absolute certainty that your existence is an application of the universe and that it is eternal.'

Her tone was perhaps mocking, perhaps not. But she was building up to something. She was setting me in place like a mother manipulates a recalcitrant child.

'It sounds a bit sinister to be honest,' I said, immediately feeling unnecessarily facetious. She ignored me though, and leant a little closer.

'No time, no death, nothing... the Void... and you are the Void.'

I started to feel the first breakers of a panic attack lapping against the shoreline of my brain. I'd have been happy to have this conversation with her if I were stoned and we were talking drug-induced theory. But there was heaviness in her tone and demeanour. She meant it. And it scared me. It scared me more than Ober had. The sickening waves of anxiousness began rolling over me and I started to glug back air as if it were in short supply. Titania put her hand on my arm then moved up on the bed behind me. I was too tense to react, too excruciatingly trapped to move a muscle. She gently manoeuvred me down on my side and pulled my legs up so that I was lying down in a foetal position. She shifted herself behind me and pushed her body against me with her arms wrapped around me. The tenseness in my muscles began to relax and I allowed myself to engage with her warm body, her nurturing touch. My breathing slowed to match hers and I closed my eyes.

'It's coming isn't it?' she whispered, her long fingernails digging into my arms slightly.

'What is?'

'It's about to tell it's tale, about to loosen another chain from around you. Just relax. Just wait for it to come and take you there. Don't worry, you'll be back. It won't be final.'

The rush of the drug was shockingly intense. It came from nowhere and infringed upon me as if my entire body was being replaced, atom by atom, with another made of silken air. I wanted to cry but I was too taken over, too different to be permitted such extravagance.

A minor chord, repeated indefinitely, filled my head. Or was it everywhere, filling everybody's head? I couldn't tell the difference anymore. I didn't want to tell the difference.

XIII

'... Four, five, six. You're there.'

I am here. Titania and my mother are one. They are the same. They are one with all women, with a goddess so inexpressibly huge that it fills multiverses. And I am inside them. I am drifting in this stone-lined chamber, encased within the Earth, and feeding on the womb. The dimly defined edges of smooth boulders surround me and the musky scent of millennia fills my head. I've fallen here from somewhere unremembered but now I am suspended, curled up as a foetus in thickened liquid. The thumping beat of a heart reverberates around me, shaking the stone core of the barrow and providing me with sustenance. The vibration reaches me as neither sound nor touch, but as a throbbing sensation derived from nothingness; a vacuum, the Void that has long ago swallowed all birth and death and now controls all from a place that is infinite.

I spread myself out. My senses begin to incorporate the stone boulders and my liquid surround. I no longer know where they begin and I end. The disarticulated bones of a dozen generations buried in the barrow meld into my barely formed skeletal frame and become one with me.

And there are voices. I don't hear them, but they are infiltrating me without respite. They are sonorous and low, and they tremble through stone, liquid and bone. They are telling me something in a language of wind, warning me with fire, protecting me with earth and soothing me with water. But it is not a language of words. It is a language only heard, seen and felt at birth and death, at the two moments when humanity experiences the Truth of beginnings and endings. It is the language of oneness, of a mother and a child inside her, of the rocks communicating with the stars and the air congealing into the earth.

I spin, slowly revolving in my dense liquid, becoming stone and earth and bone and then flesh. I know that I need to remember this. This cannot be allowed to drift into a forgotten time. Time. I'm not quite sure what I mean by Time. Everything that has happened? Or everything that will happen? But it seems so obvious that they are one and the same that I just cannot get on top of the concept of Time moving. Our lives are just one single happening that we experience as a linear movement. Outside of us is nothing and everything – all Space and all Time, collected together as the Void. And the Void is all that matters, because ultimately that is all there is – an infinity of stillness.

Now there is a sound, a definite *heard* sound. It is like the deep cry of a creative life force, of a mother bringing a child into the world. The sounds drift out of range and become incoherent, become... synthesised. A synthesised pulsing bleep.

'Five minutes in. 45mg. You'll be fine.'

The rush is extraordinary. I'm coming apart from the stones to the accompaniment of the unnatural synthesised pulses. I'm suddenly compressed through a narrow aisle in the barrow, glancing, with difficulty, at the collections of bones in the side chambers, some of which form into human skeletons, waving and grinning at me. They seem to think this is quite funny. But I don't. I'm being ripped away from something that is everlasting and all encompassing and being thrust alone through aisles, tubes and canals filled with blood and slime and all manner of organic perinatal matter. The pressure makes me think that I'm about to implode. And I do.

It is night and I'm prone on the ground looking over an obsidian landscape lit by ritual bonfires and shooting stars. In the distance a vast forest stretches into an endless valley filling it with foliated blackness. I shift to a sitting position with my back to one of the barrow stones. With eyes closed I feel myself starting to melt back into the stone, becoming one with it again. But it is soon displaced by her body. I try to sink into her, but I can't. She must have something to say. Communication prevents oneness.

'I'm pleased you've made it this far,' she says. 'We were starting to have our doubts.'

The shooting stars are taking over the sky and I know that I could join them, somehow. But I can't remember how.

'Oh, there it is again. Can you see it?'

I close my eyes and see it clearly. The hammerhead machines are lying at the side of the road, broken up and in pieces. The road looks as if it is made of some living vegetation, but that can't be because as I visualise it I am able to range close up to it and see that there is a car driving along it. I can see the car from many different angles but I can't see who is inside. Or can I?

I just turn back time a bit. It is night. The car's in front of a concrete garage, waiting for someone, some people. And here they come.

Oh no.

XIV

I woke up not knowing where I was. Or should that be not knowing where I am... or will be. I knew that I could no longer trust myself to know whether things were in the past, present or future. I was adrift. It was terrifying and yet somehow liberating. I was half-sure that I didn't even need to get out of bed and things would just happen. My trips seemed to be taking me out of myself and into a place that was not concerned with the practicalities of everyday life.

But after touching my face, the bedpost and the sheets I pulled myself up in bed and looked out the window opposite. It framed a translucent white sky and the swaying tops of trees, divided up by the diamond lead quarries. The view looked and felt real. It seemed to be as it should. It was flat and pointless and naggingly depressing. Some voice deep inside me was attempting to remind me that I no longer had to put up with such constraint, such an imposed perception of the world and all that was in it. And yet there it was, the lumpen reality of another day that would come and go and then live in the memory. It would become "the past". Even such a worthless and nondescript memory as those treetops set within their hazy white sky had already lodged itself in my brain somewhere and was perhaps even now informing a great collective subconscious that sucked everything -- past, present and future – into it in order to inform... inform what?

I pulled away from the thought. I could sense a surging wave of depression about to overcome me and take me away on its black tidal current, and I didn't want to give it any more power. Such desperation. Such nihilistic wretchedness. I had thought I'd always been prone to depression before Alice and my mother died, but it was only afterwards that I found out what real depression was. The knowledge that everything you are is nothing, and that you are trapped in the corner into which life has manipulated you. All of your perceptions, thoughts and dreams, through your whole life, mean no more than those of the first human three million years ago. They are as nothing. Sometimes I found that if I concentrated on the pointlessness of existence for long enough, for hour after hour, the depression would atrophy and I would reach a point where there really seemed to be nothing: a Void. The Void would come at me like a formless abyss and swallow me into it, swallow up all the tears, self-loathing, hatred and despondency and replace it with nothingness. It replaced reality with something so utterly different that it is impossible to describe.

My body tensed up slightly in bed. The memory clicked into my head of my panic attack in the shop, all those months ago, the one that got me sectioned. I hadn't made the connection before but there was an instant, just a split-second, immediately before I passed out when there was nothing... absolute nothingness. The people in the shop, the old woman who I'd smacked, and the ground I was standing on – gone, swallowed up by the Void. And its formlessness was so radically different than normal reality that my memory had probably just let it go, allowed it to pass straight into my subconscious without any consolidation. Perhaps these extremes of emotional behaviour, these depressions and psychotic episodes, actually allowed momentary access to a universal reality; a reality made up of the formless Void where nothingness is everything. And maybe that's the same place the drugs were taking me. Psychosis or drug-induced altered states – both were showing me an inluminous *other*, which was currently way beyond my ability to understand it.

I got up, rolled and lit a joint, then moved over to the window, feeling as if I'd touched on something important. The mere fact that I thought anything could be *important* suggested that I had waylaid the depression that had been lapping at my door and so I was able to look out over the garden with a renewed acceptance. Perhaps the stillness and peaceful ambience of this place were starting to act as shields or barriers against the depression that had, in the blocks, found it easy to take a grip and hold me down. Whatever else was happening to me here I was at least being given some protection against the assertions of my affective disorders.

The sunless morning sky cast a shadowless pall over the view. The trees bending with the stream seemed caught in a midsummer slough of decadence, limbs and leaves hanging in the air waiting for the sun to return. I closed my eyes and tried to regulate my breathing: four counts breathing in, hold for two, four counts breathing out. I had to ensure the shields stayed up.

Those androgens are looking more like proper puckish fairies now, like those alien-fairy madmen in the illustrations of Brian Froud. They are outside of time and they know it. They can simply come and go into the world and you won't know whether they're a memory or a premonition.

I opened my eyes slowly and looked around me. Inside my head – the whispers were just inside my head. I tried to deflate my tense body. The whispers were just a slippage. I didn't want to think too hard about it. Instead I concentrated on the real world. I closed my eyes again. The sounds of the garden filtered up to me: small animals rustling in the bushes, birdsong emanating from the trees and somewhere far away the glistening sound of church bells brought in and out of audible range by the vagaries of the gentle wind. The more I concentrated on the sounds the more well defined they became. Soon I was able to make distinctions between the rustlings and the birdsong, picking out each shuffle of a restless mouse and each thin, sharp call of countless birds. But the church bells always remained as a backdrop. They drifted away and then back again, but always stayed as a presence, underpinning the audio landscape and announcing the existence of a world beyond the immediate environment. I strained to hear the range of the bells, the modulated keys in alto, tenor and bass. I allowed the notes to conjure up an image of the church with its parapeted tower and the bellringers in the bell-chamber on the first storey. Of course, the images were made up in my mind, but they constituted a form of reality created by nothing more than the vaguely heard carillon of ringing bells. It was a reality over which I had control, a reality created by me despite its reliance on the amorphous sound of distant bells. I could change it at will. As long as I stuck to the basic rules outlined by the bells I could impose any form and structure onto my composition. The church could be deep in a forest, its newly built limestone tower glaring in the sunlight of a fifteenth-century summer. It could be nestled within a village unsoured by noisome modern brutality, with the bellringers garbed and gaited like characters from a Breugel painting. Or it could be the ruined shell belonging to a long forgotten religion, where only the tower with its peal of bells remained, ringing out a warning against an invader; an invader so different from us that we might not even know what it was when it attacked us.

The bells stopped. I opened my eyes slowly and let the visuals of the everyday take the place of my mind's-eye imagery. The residual of my created reality drained away and I was left with a day that was still flat and oppressive, the sky a single colour of blanched whiteness. Whether it was the dreary numbness brought on by the monotone day or just a leftover emptiness from what had been happening to me I couldn't tell, but for almost the first time since I'd woken up in hospital after the stabbing I felt locked into normality. Of course, I wasn't at all sure what normality was, but it seemed well represented by what I could see and hear. I decided that it might be time to take advantage of such dismal predictability and go downstairs to do some reading.

The library seemed grey and characterless in the subdued morning light. The colourless day had leant torpor to the place. I made a half-hearted effort to take down a few books and read the blurb on the covers, but I was too distracted to open any. I kept getting momentary glimpses of hidden memories, which welled up to the surface of my consciousness before disappearing into nothingness the instant I attempted to extract anything from them. The fragments meant nothing. They had no context: a car, an earthen mound, my knife wound, Alice Liddell, my mother and sister. I simply could not remember whether I had been dreaming, tripping or if what happened in my everyday existence had become so blurred that all I was left with were degraded moments in time, confused snapshots all out of order.

I went over to the shelves holding the vinyls and pulled

out a batch. More or less the sixties and seventies collection I had expected: Pink Floyd, Led Zeppelin, Genesis, King Crimson, Van der Graaf Generator. But there was also some more obscure stuff from the late sixties/early seventies: Stone Angel, San Ul Lim, 3 Hurel, Dando Shaft... never heard of them. I took out some more, folky stuff: Fairport Convention, Pentangle, Nick Drake. There was nothing past about 1975. I went along the entire three shelves of records, there must have been near on a thousand vinyls, but I didn't find anything later than the mid-seventies. It shouldn't have disturbed me, but it did. Evidently Ober had a retro musical taste (I simply presumed the collection was his) but there seemed a significance about the homogeneity of the records that was edging around the boundaries of my mind and threatening to crossover to tell me something I was not going to like. But it was just another vague, unrooted notion – what was I supposed to do with it?

I made sure all the records went back where they came from – they seemed to be arranged thematically: folk, blues, prog, electronic -- then pulled out Tangerine Dream's *Phaedra* and put it onto the turntable. Doomy, early electronica -- it wasn't exactly what the doctor ordered for someone with an affective disorder, but it seemed to capture the moment, seemed in correlation with the greyness of the morning. It was trippy too. Ever since I'd first taken LSD I had recognised that so much of the music of that late sixties/early seventies era was the product of psychedelic inducements. *Phaedra* was certainly there – the repetitive, swirling, synthesised sound that swims round the head during the early stages of a trip were mimicked and reproduced, if not matched. The airy, echoing austerity of the music was nothing more than a paean to the psychedelic world.

I sat down in the gentleman's chair where I half remembered uncovering my knife wound... how long ago? Was it days or weeks? And what did I see? I trawled through my memory attempting to pin it down. But I couldn't. I could not concentrate on my own memories. There was a blockage, self-imposed or put there by the drugs I didn't know.

Outside some crows were cawing. The sound mingled with the music, lending it a hypnotic effect. The caws seemed modulated with the dulled pulses of synthesiser and sound effects, layered into the air as though designed to fit together. The music and cawing became perfectly balanced and in harmony, invoking the atmosphere of the shapeless day. I shuffled in the chair.

'It is a mysterious semblance at the stand of nightmares.'

The voice was low, nasal, jokey... in my head. I closed my eyes but saw the library as though they were still open. I tried to open my eyes but could not.

'I was *long gone* by the time this came out. 1974 if my memory serves me right.'

I 'looked' to the other side of the hi-fi stack where an armchair identical to the one I was sitting on had been taken by a young man with a shock of unruly, dark, curly hair. His purple paisley shirt was half unbuttoned and his Cuban heeled boots were resting lightly on the occasional table to the side of the chair.

My head seemed to shuffle, seemed to fan open and then shut like a pack of cards. I knew I still had my eyes closed but there was glimmering light from somewhere, allowing me to see the library and the man in peculiar, iridescent detail. My depressed emotional reaction to the dull day remained as before, but he was outside of it, lifted into my space by something... well, just something.

'Crazy this light huh?' he said.

'Yeah, is it always like this?'

'For me? Guess so. It needs to be though. It needs to be consistently abnormal otherwise it just wouldn't work. But then, consistent abnormality actually becomes normal after a while... if you believe in after a whiles.'

I stared into his deep, hazel eyes, aware of the impossibility of the situation but also aware that at that moment he was the most tangible reality I had. He was like an embodied memory, a recollection, or more accurately, a series of recollections made into a material presence.

'The thing is Syd, if we're really sitting here together, either you're a ghost, I'm seeing things, or it's 1967 and I'm a time traveller. Because I hate to say this, but I know that you died. You've left us.'

He looked at me with those diamond eyes and sat up

slightly in the chair as though excited by what I had said. He chuckled and winked.

'Died, yeah, kind of. But what really died? Some tired old man that had nothing to do with *me*. You see, once you find your way to the... to the, er, astral plane you just realise that you can imprint yourself on it and it lasts forever, ready to be tapped into by anybody on the same... the same, oh what's the word... wavelength. The same wavelength.'

'The astral plane?'

'Yeah. Bad term really. Ye know, much maligned. Basically it's a recognisable aspect of the Void. A place where you can travel to without all the inconvenience of taking your body there, but which is familiar enough for you to interact with, with your, erm... mind.'

'So do you exist?'

He laughed and smiled pixie-like, then lit the cigarette he had been twirling about between his fingers.

'Obviously. You're talking to me aren't you?'

'But I talk to people in my dreams and they don't exist.'

'Ooh, big mistake,' he said, drawing hard on the ciggy and sinking back into the chair. 'Just because you don't have your body with you doesn't mean you're not experiencing a reality. Do I not exist when you listen to one of my records put down in 1970? I'm there. Audiologically, I'm as real as when I recorded it. Sounds, memories, smells, wishes... they all get... get... what is it I'm trying to say... *burned*. They get burned into the astral plane, the great collective consciousness, and there they stay for infinity. And of course, you know that infinity is the Void.'

My eyeballs were cold and dry with being open so wide. Of course, my eyes were still closed, but I was just starting to forget where they were closed and who was closing them. The affinity I felt for Syd had started to make me a part of him. I was beginning to sink into my armchair as he was in his, and I even found a cigarette in my hand burning some unconventional tobacco.

'So what is this reality I've been experiencing?' I asked, thinking that whatever I said or asked would be intuitively understood by Syd. 'There are things happening to me that I don't understand. I don't seem to have any control over what happens. For Christ's sake, I'm sitting here with my eyes closed talking to Syd Barrett as you were in 1967... and this is just after thinking today was a normal, boring, slightly depressing day. Do you have any answers?'

He shrugged and smiled, ran a hand through his hair and took a couple of drags on the cigarette. 'Well, ye know, there's probably nothing I can tell you that you don't know already. You're ill, probably much more ill than you think you are. But then so is everybody. The whole western world is suffering from diathetic illnesses on a very large scale... very large scale indeed. I mean, sometimes it's just a case of coming to terms with the illness... even allowing it to give you access to other altered states. Schizophrenics do that all the time – they can dance away from their ego and be somewhere else. Of course, they don't have any control over the dancing but they *know* that existence is much more than... well, more than this.'

Syd gestured around him vaguely and narrowed his eyes a little.

'But I'm not schizophrenic, I'm depressed, I have anxiety disorders. I shouldn't be seeing fairies and losing all sense of time and happening. I'm totally disorientated. The weird thing is that what I think of as my illnesses actually seem to be getting better – this house seems to... to repress them. Maybe that's just because I've been pulled out of my world and then kept in a state of almost constant confusion. No time to ponder what's wrong with me.'

I realised I was starting to talk to myself, work things out in my own head. But Syd looked interested, looked as if he wanted to encourage me to continue.

'I can't even remember how many times Ober has given me the phenethylamines since I came here. In fact, I'm not quite sure what I'm being given.'

Syd half raised an eyebrow. 'That's interesting.'

'What is?'

'You not being sure what's causing your altered states. You probably think that I was a permanent acidhead after '67.'

'Sorry Syd, that's usually the general consensus. Isn't it true?' I asked, before suddenly remembering Ober's comment about Syd finding the meaning of life and being unable to integrate that knowledge back into everyday life.

'Depends from whose perspective. I actually discovered a lot of things when everyone else thought I was just fried, especially after I moved into Cromwell Road in '68. That was a time of revelation for me. And you'll probably be soon finding out that the acid was perhaps not quite what it appeared to be...'

I was hanging on Syd's words. I knew this conversation wasn't going to last long and I felt as if some mighty revelation might be about to pass his lips. I attempted to choose my words carefully.

'Do you think Ober... and Titania, aren't telling me why I'm really here? After all, it's a bit of an expensive way to carry out psychiatric treatment.'

'But you're on a programme of research aren't you?'

'Yes. Yes, I am, but I'm not quite sure what they're researching... or actually who is *they*.'

'Well, ye know, you'd better find out... although...'

'Although?'

'Well, maybe they know best. I mean, they're educated people. They probably know what they're doing. Maybe they've got a plan to cure the Western World or something. And after all why do you need to be in control of things anyway. Perhaps they're keeping you out of control for good reasons.'

I pondered that. Maybe my illnesses *were* much more serious than I thought and the treatment was overwhelming me because that was the only thing that was going to work. I'd been brought to a controlled environment where I could be given massive doses of drugs that would flood me and wash me out, carry away all the disorders that were crippling me.

Syd raised a brow and nodded, as though he'd heard what I just thought.

'What about time though?' I asked, 'I just can't remember the order of things here. Ever since I came round in the hospital my memory keeps getting things muddled up.'

Syd began moving his head to and fro. 'Muddled up. Good name for a song that... muddled up, cuddled up, forgotten my name to the turtle's shame.'

I laughed, and for a moment I started to rationalise what was happening: I was giving material to Syd Barrett who was then constructing rhyming verses from it and singing to me as the person he had been in about 1967. But the process of rationalisation broke down almost immediately and was replaced with simple acceptance. Why not? Talking with Syd in a country house library was hardly as far out and leftfield as being reborn from a burial mound... a Neolithic long barrow--

I started from the recall. I remembered it. Not as you would remember a dream, but as you would remember from real life, something everyday. I could feel the liquid compression on my body, smell the musty ancientness of the boulder stones, and visualise the darkness of both the barrow interior and the black landscape, where the vague shapes of forests and fields were accentuated sable and inky beneath the star-filled sky. I knew I had to hold on to this, it was important. What was next? Something about a road... a car... some people--.

'I guess time only really exists on the physical plane... ye know.'

I knew Syd had interrupted my thoughts on purpose. The imagery disappeared and the next part of the memory vanished like sand through the funnel of an egg timer.

'You're only really constrained by it because you're in a body. As soon as you're out it's all over the place.'

'Out?'

'Well, what do you think the drugs do? If you take enough of the right drug often enough then you'll be putting yourself in all sorts of periods and settings that for whatever reason have helped contribute to your subconscious understanding of things. Like, for example, you are probably too young to have been around in the sixties, but there are all sorts of influences on you from that time that make it real... in a sense, ye know, real but not history. You can go there whenever you like, but you have to leave your bod behind.'

'So I am a time traveller.'

'Well, yeah, kind of. But you need to understand that there are lots of different types of time. And they can be changed to suit a perspective.'

'Changed?'

'You'll find that some histories... *degrade*. You'll wake up one morning and find that what you once thought of as the past was only a delusion or a half-remembered dream. And in its place is a whole new history, a new reality. After all, everything you think of as the time you grew up in is only cobbled together from memories from your own hazy perspective. It's not the Truth or anything. True reality can only be formed by the collective consciousness – a trillion, zillion perceptions rolled into one. We've got to just hope that there's someone around to make sense of it all. Make a final *true reality*.'

I was getting a bit tense. My memory was heaving. If I allowed it to have free rein it might completely engulf me. But I could allow bits through – I pictured the Green Man pub in the village. Did I fall asleep there? I reached down deeper. Did I really see the androgens and the Pan in the garden? Or was I just having a drink with Mr Quince? Both?

'I did like Alice Liddell,' said Syd, lighting up a second cigarette. 'She was kind of cute.'

The pub disappeared in my head and was replaced by the cartoon Alice. 'Did she die?'

'Well, I'm not really sure. But suppose; right... just suppose that you've been on these drugs for much longer than you think. Say, since you were first in hospital, say since you first met Ober. They've been, let's say, administered to you in slightly increasing doses until you reached a threshold, a threshold that required a new type of drug... a drug that could take you to a place that lets you kill a part of yourself. The drug could have enabled you to make this person up, say as a representation of your sister, and you killed her. You killed all the guilt and sorrow you feel for *your* Alice.'

Syd's voice had changed a little. It had lost its offbeat, nasal tone and become more precise and well enunciated.

'But I didn't take the phenethylamines till after I'd met Alice Liddell. I took 2C-C for the first time when I met her.'

'Oh, she was probably a real person, and probably turned up that night to take the drug with you, but everything else was a new reality created by you.'

I tried to release the knot that was forming in my

stomach. I attempted to picture Alice, naked, on top of me. But I got my sister's face and body instead.

'What about the knife wound?' I said, indicating the spot on my abdomen. 'Is that real or not?'

'Well, your belly has a wound. Your physical belly that is. Don't know who did it though.'

'What do you mean?'

You don't really think Alice's brother did it do you?'

I was going to say yes, I did believe it, but my words were halted by a whirring, clicking noise in my head that sounded like a metal spring cascading down wooden steps. I held my temples and attempted to push the noise from my head, but it continued: whirr, click and thump... whirr, click and thump...

'There's always something isn't there?' said Syd, evidently aware of the sound but apparently unaffected by it. 'It probably means that I have to leave.'

'I wish you wouldn't,' I said, still holding my head and gritting my teeth at the noise. 'You seem to know a lot... I've got more questions... why am I really here Syd? What's really being done to me? Where are my mum and sis? Syd. Am I going mad... is this what happened to you? Syd. Syd'

But Syd was fading away, fading away to somewhere I couldn't follow, fading away into the past where he would become what he once was again. He'd come out especially for me and now he had to go back. But I'd connected with him and forged a link. He was a part of me.

I began to feel my eyes folding shut with an irresistible tiredness. And as they did so I also felt them opening, opening to bring me back to the library. Slowly the room gained substance and I found myself gripping on to the sides of the chair, my heart thudding. The needle was stuck half way through the record on the turntable: whirr, click and thump... whirr, click and thump. I kicked the stack and it righted itself, continuing on its journey and picking up the grooves of the record to fill the library with its austere, synthesised 1974 sound.

I pulled myself up in the chair and looked around. The same grey, featureless light crept into the library filling it with tiredness and monotony. And I was filled with tiredness and monotony as well. What was I doing there? What was I allowing to happen to me? The depression that had been threatening to get hold of me since I woke up that morning was now somehow highlighted and solidified by my conversation with Syd. I had no idea if I'd been tripping, dreaming or both, but the luxurious resonance of seeming to be in the past talking with a legend who appeared to be tuned into my wavelength was gone, and there was only a dull emptiness to replace it. The *real world* was shit. I didn't want to be there. I wanted to escape back to a world of compassion and meaning. I wanted the specialness and understanding of an altered state. I wanted to belong to that world and to be freed from my own lumpen, disparaging reality. I wanted to talk with Syd some more.

There was only one thing for it.

I needed some more drugs.

XV

I wasn't sure if Ober kept any drugs in the house but I was going to find out. And seeing that I was in the library I thought I'd start there. Systematically I went through the drawers of the bureau and a dozen or so box files with spines to make them look like leather-bound folio books. Nothing. I thought about checking behind the books but after a dilatory effort at a single row I realised that it would have taken all day to go through every book and so I moved into the drawing room next door. I opened and checked every closed space, even checked for wonky floorboards. Nothing. The search was only about fifteen minutes old but already my natural inclination towards abandonment and resignation whenever things got too difficult or complicated was starting to suppress my initial enthusiasm.

I slumped down in the window seat, closed my eyes and thought of my Syd experience. It suddenly seemed to have happened years ago, like a half-forgotten dream. I wanted to go back and speak some more with him but the deadening weight of reality was pressing down on me and I began rationalising the experience to fit into the banal normality of the flat, lifeless day. I had always done this. No matter what sensory landscape I was taken to by psychedelics I always had to make it fit into the normal everyday afterwards. Even now, after spending most of my time during the last two months in a mental whirlpool, instead of questioning the nature of reality my first instinct was to explain what had happened to me using logical rationale. As far as my Syd experience was concerned, it must have just been a flashback or a half-dream. The stifling, grey tendrils of depression ensured that my imagination enquired no further. I had gone from excitedly seeking out drugs to renew the experience to settling for the mundane in less than a minute. It was as if I were on the brink of crossing a border but couldn't gain the inertia to move forward. I had to stay where I was even though it was a barren, empty land.

After half an hour of staring into space I got up and moved mechanically to my bedroom. I just couldn't think of anything I wanted to do more than go back to sleep – to escape the brutal, desolate meaninglessness of the day.

Half way up the main staircase I noticed, for the first time, a small cupboard with doors affixed to the boarded balcony wall. I tried the handles but it was locked. My enthusiasm was sparked, not by much, but by enough to make me look for the key. There was a big bunch of keys in the kitchen, which I brought back up to the cupboard and began trying each key in the lock, no matter how unlikely the fit. Of course, none of them did fit. But as I tried each key in turn I noticed that the lock was quite flimsy, it was probably just a small strip of metal holding the doors shut. I ran back down to the kitchen and through to the... the scullery I think Ober had called it, where there was a box of tools. Large screwdriver in hand I returned to the cupboard ready to jimmy it open. I looked around and stopped still, holding my breath for a few seconds to make sure there was no movement in the house.

Was this a very sensible thing to be doing? However carefully I broke the lock it would be noticed eventually. I could claim diminished responsibility due to my conditions but that might backfire if Ober thought I was going to start causing damage and hassle. He might decide to send me home, and no matter how often depression threatened to get hold of me in the house, I knew that going back to the blocks would send me over the edge. A fleeting, chilled image of the concrete view out of my flat window made me shiver physically. But he'd invested too much time in me to simply send me packing for breaking a lock. And anyway, I could claim I was using my initiative -- I was in need of an entheogenic experience and I sensed that this cupboard was the secret store. No harm done. I slotted the head of screwdriver into the slot between the doors and made ready to angle it against the lock.

'I have the key if that would make it easier.'

I jumped hard and had to hold on to the banister for support. An electric pulse surged through me ending up slithering out through my fingers. I dropped the screwdriver. Titania stood at the bottom of the stairs holding a key in front of her.

'Although there's nothing in there. Not last time I looked anyway.'

Despite the shock my initial response was to wonder how she had known what I'd been up to in order to get the key. Was she now bluffing about the contents of the cupboard? If she had the key on her surely there *was* something there. Her expression was of amusement.

'Why is it locked then? I said, defensively. I was shaking.

'Why not?'

There was no response to that. She waited a moment and then came up to me on the stairs, unlocked the cupboard and opened the doors.

'See, nothing in there. Are you disappointed?'

'I... I-I-I...'

'Mmm, that's too bad. We thought we were getting rid of the stutter. Always bound to come back in moments of crisis though... or at least moments of *perceived* crisis.'

'I th-thought there might be drugs in there,' I said, deciding candidness was probably my only option.

'Why, are we not giving you enough?' she replied, turning one corner of her mouth into a smirk.

I was grateful for her good humour but still didn't know what to say. Why was I always so tongue-tied? She locked the cupboard back up and took hold of my hand.

'Come on, let's go outside and sit in the garden. It's a nice day.'

'No it isn't,' I said, picturing the blank white sky I'd been seeing out of windows all morning. 'It's dull and depressing.'

She just shrugged and led me down the stairs and through the house to the French doors in the drawing room. It was a bit awkward being led through the house by her, but by the time we reached the doors I seemed to pick up on her cultivated calmness. It reinforced the shields that kept at bay the depression that had been nipping at me all day. It had to slip away back into whatever form it resided when not inhabiting me.

She let go of my hand and opened the doors. The sun was warm, shining through a patchwork blue and white sky.

'Seems to have cleared up,' she said. 'No more dull and depressing. Mr Blue Sky's come out to play.'

We sat down on two loungers and she reclined hers further back so that her face was almost horizontal. I kept mine upright.

'I'm sorry about the cupboard,' I said, unable to think of anything else to say. 'I'm not sure what came over me.'

'Doesn't matter,' she replied, closing her eyes and stretching her arms out beside her. 'It's only to be expected.'

What did that mean? I could feel the tightness in my stomach returning. Her coolness was putting me back on edge. But at least with her eyes closed I could give her a quick scan over. She was a damned fine looking woman – one of those women who come to a natural fruition in their forties without the abdominal ravages of childbirth. She was wearing some body-hugging black outfit that made it relatively easy to imagine what she'd look like out of it, and her dark hair seemed to glitter in the sunshine... just like my mother's hair used to glitter. I closed my eyes and pictured her standing on the walkway outside the flat, taking in the twenty minutes of sunshine during a summer afternoon. I reveried the image until the usual churning guilt and grief began to make itself felt.

'What do you think of the house?' she said, still with her eyes closed.

'The house? I replied, dumbly.

'The big fifteenth-century building you've been living in for a week. It's right here.' She wafted a finger in the direction behind us and then squinted at me under the shade of her hand. She also opened her legs slightly and shimmied around a little. I gulped.

'Yes, s-s-sorry. It's great... yeah, great.' This was in danger of turning into a very awkward conversation, for me at least, and so I decided it was time to jump in with something useful. 'How do you know Ober?'

She pondered for a moment before answering. 'I've always known him. We've been friends and colleagues since the beginning.'

'The beginning of what?'

'Just the beginning.'

I wished I wasn't there. Her refined crypticness was not something I knew how to deal with, and I was beginning to stare at the well-defined shape of her vulva through her pants.

'But are you a psychiatrist too?' I asked, trying to patch up the gaps in the conversation that were starting to ratchet up my anxiety.

'I'm a psychoanalyst,' she said, smiling out the corner of her mouth. 'And I have some other useful skills that Ober can use with patients. I guess I'm what you'd call a facilitator.'

She seemed slightly derisory of the term, but I couldn't be sure if that wasn't just me overinterpreting her languidness. 'Are you like Alice then?'

'Alice Liddell? Yes, sort of.'

Why was she always so luxuriously evasive? And why was my heart beginning to hammer away again? She must have brought me outside for a reason.

'But I'd like to ask you a question or two if you don't mind. Your assessment probably needs to be kept a bit tighter than at present. Do you mind?'

'No.' My palms were sweating and the drumming heartbeat was making me shake. 'Not-t-t at all.'

She sat up a little, which made me feel a bit safer, but then she began slowly rolling a thumb around her nipples, one after the other, bringing both to hardness underneath that tight top. I tried desperately not to look, but the arousal was already at work. I had a sudden mental image of me sucking at her breasts. My cock attained full hardness.

'Do I remind you of your mother?'

I gasped involuntarily. 'My mother? Yes... I guess you do a little.'

'Like Alice reminded you of your sister?'

'Yes.' I looked away.

'Then we need to have a full session – an anaclitic therapy session – for you to get across to her. We'll organise it when Ober gets back.'

'Anaclitic therapy with you?'

'Problem?'

'No... no.'

I tried to prise open my dulled memory. Had I not already had a session with Titania? No, that wasn't right. But I had come down from a session with her sitting with me. Or had I?

'Good, because we need to start sorting out your traumas: mother, sister, guilt, grief – they need the clear light of a heavy-duty entheogenic episode to get them all untangled and manageable. At present you're using too many weak archetypes and symbols and things you're probably just picking up by accident from the collective. We can only do so much with rebirth from Neolithic long barrows.'

My eyes were wide at this. Her words dredged up something deeply buried, but essential. For an instant the smell of damp stones, the inky darkness and the sensation of being suspended in thick liquid filled me. But it was fleeting. Two seconds later it became nothing more than a vague, foggy resonance lost in my jumbled memory.

'No, a nice clearly illuminated session is what's needed. I think we should have worked out your dosages by now.'

I came round at that. 'Yes, my dosages... Titania, I need to know what I'm taking. Sometimes it feels like I'm almost constantly on something... you know, like all the time I'm tripping, and sometimes it's quiet and at other times there's a surge.'

Her body language changed, almost imperceptibly, but there was a stiffening of her upper body. Her eyes creased slightly. I wanted to take advantage of this.

'I need to know if there's a residue always in my system

after I've taken the phenethylamines... because... well, I'm feeling out of control and I think I can feel my depression trying to come back. That's why I was trying to get some drugs from the cupboard, I was desperate to get out of my normal life... to escape back into the psychedelic world, especially after I met... after I, er, m-m-met Syd... Syd Barrett.'

The smile returned to her face.

'And what did he have to say?'

'He said that I killed Alice Liddell in my own imagination in order to kill the guilt and grief of my own sister's death.'

'Sensible interpretation. Did you ask him about his own disorders?'

'Not really.'

I hung my head a little realising that I had been given an opportunity to talk to Syd Barrett and I had just talked about myself.

'Shame, might have helped. Next time eh?'

'Yeah, next time,' I said, unsure whether she was telling me there would be a next time or if she was teasing me. 'But what about the dosages? I need to know what I'm taking... after all, it's not everyday you get an audience with a dead rock star. It could only have been the drugs. Couldn't it?'

She pouted her lips and reclined back into the lounger.

'Well, you must understand that the drugs are only facilitating experiences and events that are an intrinsic part of you. They don't create the experience; they simply allow you to overcome the obstacles created by your ego and to tap into what you *really* are. A bit like when you make love with someone, you will only be able to orgasm if you have sufficiently let go of your inhibitions and have become willing to let the other person see your uninhibited self.'

She looked at me and moved a hand down over her pronounced vulvic bulge. My cock, which had been on the wilt, immediately stiffened up again. I tried to adjust myself accordingly, but Titania curled her lips in recognition of my discomfort.

'You have to be able to let go of your ego,' she continued, 'to recover from the suffering that life will throw up. All your negative emotions: grief, guilt, selfishness,

109

loneliness, depression, anxiety – they're all propagated by your ego. You'll only get them all under control when you are able to bring to your life experiences that have been developed without the ego, experiences that are outside of *you*. These drugs allow that.'

She spoke with a laconic drawl, slowly but purposefully. She kept her hand over her bulge, moving the middle finger rhythmically back and forth. I took my eyes away and pretended to find interest in the blackbird singing on the roof of the house. I needed to calm myself otherwise I'd be stuttering away like an idiot when I tried to speak.

'Whatever you experience, it really happens to you. Don't make the mistake of thinking that everything that happens outside of normal everyday consciousness is not real. Once you accept that it is real you can extend yourself... find the golden key that will lead to Samadhi.'

'Samadhi?'

Titania didn't answer. She just let out a single low gasp and jerked her ass up a little. She drew her hand away from its vulvic duties and put it to her mouth, licking gently on the middle finger for a few seconds. I couldn't help but stare.

'Yes, Samadhi,' she said, absent-mindedly, apparently not noticing my staring. 'Lots of words for it -- choose your own.'

She closed her eyes again for a moment and then sat up with purpose. Her drawl turned sharp. 'Do you remember me telling you about the golden key?'

I drew my gaze away from her and tried to remember. My memory chugged. 'No... well, maybe...'

'We are helping you to find the golden key, and you are helping us to learn the best routes to it.'

'Routes?'

'You wanted to know about the dosages, what you are taking.'

'Yes.'

'You are on something all the time. Your medication is constant.'

I gripped the handles on the lounger. 'What do you mean?'

'We're applying the medication regularly, tinker-winkering

110

with the doses. Then DMT is administered at appropriate moments. Letting time slip and slide... slide and slip. You just never know where you'll end up or who you'll meet. Tickety tickety click. Clickety clickety tick.'

'What?'

'Tickety to, tickety to. Clickety tock, tick tock.'

My tight grip loosened and my hands began to shake. Desperately I tried to focus on Titania and stop the weirdness. But the shaking snaked up my arms and then devolved to different parts of my body where it took over all motor control. Worst of all were my eyes – the eyeballs rolled, uncontrollably, up and down and from side to side, blurring the world into a confused mess of fast-moving colours.

'Clickety tick. Tickety click. Tick tock.'

They are somehow connected to the plant life in the garden. They are elementals tending every individual flower, herb, vegetable and tree. But when they realise that you can see them they morph into androgynous fairies and pay you attention. It's not all good either. Some of them are angry. They are communicating grievances but you can't understand what they say yet. But you do understand that their concept of Time is radically different than yours and that they want to make this perfectly clear to you. One of them is now going to touch your arm--

I bolted in my seat, eyes bulging and heart careering.

'Tickety click?'

'What?'

'Are you all right now?'

Titania was kneeling beside me on the lounger with her hand on my arm. Instinctively, I snatched it away. At least I thought I snatched it away. But when I looked down it was still there. In fact, I was looking at myself lying on the lounger to one side of Titania. It didn't seem that odd, but the sound of whispering voices made me on edge, because I knew they must have been whispering about me.

Corpus callosum, dentate gyrus, septem pellucidum,

consolidation, neocortex, reconsolidation, zif268, receptors blocked.

'You're having a catatonic episode. Just relax and you'll be back with us soon. This drug formation activates anisomycin... it'll affect your ability to reconsolidate the memories of what happens to you during the times when you are clear of medication. But it will also help you to understand what an illusion time is. Just relax. That's good... you'll be ok.'

'Tickety click?'
   'What?'
   'Are you all right now?'
Titania was kneeling beside me on the lounger with her hand on my arm. Instinctively, I snatched it away.
   'What's happening to me Titania? Is it normal now... or not?'
   I looked around, wide-eyed, for the androgens and whoever had been whispering. Titania let me expend some nervous energy then put her hand back on my arm.
   'You had a catatonic episode. Don't worry about it; it's bound to happen with someone who has such major anxiety disorders as you do. The medication is activating certain inhibitors in your brain... well; you don't really need to know the details. You just need to relax.'
   She rubbed my arm, then ran her fingers through my hair and leant over to kiss my forehead. I was still frozen to the spot, but she lingered over me for a second before running her lips over my cheek and withdrawing back to her original kneeling position.
   'Just relax.'
   Slowly, I sunk back into the lounger, my hands still shaking and my head starting to throb with the beginnings of a migraine. I closed my eyes and attempted to regulate my breathing. The tiredness was immediate.
   Titania. Did you say that I'm constantly medicated?' No answer. 'Just now, did you... did you... um... medication...and what... what is DMT? What is it... ?'
   My eyelids were weighed down but I managed to half

open my left eye. Everything was blurred: light and sound merging into one and then dissipating into something unrecognisable. Through my flickering lashes I could make out Titania, still kneeling at my side. She found the vein in my arm and inserted the needle.

'Just relax.'

XVI

Psychedelic trips are not like dreams. Well, they are kind of like dreams, in that they have the ability to create bizarre situations that seem somehow *deeply* real, as though you've abandoned all the social and cultural restraints that hold you down in everyday life and are suddenly given leave to feel and understand everything at a profoundly emotional and meaningful level. But there is no mistaking the fundamental differences between the two experiences. A trip tends to have a story curve. That is, things seem to move from one stage to the next, not so much in terms of time but in terms of ideas. Wherever you are when you are tripping there is the impression that it is everything. Your ego has been devolved into something else and there ceases to be any memory of who you are or your usual physical and mental attributes. All is dependent on the new reality, which can be *so* different that it cannot be translated into words or images. A dream, however, uses the everyday to construct the content. That content may be extraordinary, even deranged, but it's still taking things that are generally understood at a cognitive level and allowing them to be touched by collective human imagery and symbolism. Ober says that dreams are just scraping the surface of the Phylogenic Memory whereas a trip can take you through and out the other side of it.

Or did he say that? Why is it that I seem to be systematically losing parts of my memory? And where am I when I'm thinking this? What if I were to be tripping whilst asleep and dreaming? Is that possible?

This is a dream. I am intensely aware of the fact that I am dreaming. The action and emotional content skip around in no particular order but at the beginning and end of each scene I am able to stand back and analyse my perceptions, knowing full well that what has been happening has happened in a dream. But this is also a trip. Those perceptions are not my own. They are generated from an emptiness where there is no memory and no individuality. They are coming from something that is, at the same time, so immense and so minuscule that the shock of its proximity is totally overwhelming. It contains everything and nothing: every thought of every human and non-human and also the nothingness of infinity that exists without time. It is the vast unfathomable Void, but it's allowing my dream to act out some kind of performance that might be better understood by my dreaming self.

First off are some crazy images of a gigantic Mr Gloop wanking into a huge plastic bag made of see-through bison skins. When his penis ejaculates his groans resonate throughout the world and form a kind of matrix around the globe. The matrix is the Internet, which covers the world like a thick, sticky web that gradually congeals into a mass of effluent, bubbling and rasping from within. This goes on for ages. I keep seeing Gloop, wild eyed and flashing teeth, bringing himself off again and again until his semen has filled up the universe. There's no meaning in this – the dream is just being adapted for use by the trip. It's like a sound check. But after Gloop disappears amidst a universal ocean of his own spermatozoa there is a clearing of sound and vision. We can begin.

27 January 1967. We are here. There is a dull white light shining into the orange night at the end of the stairs as we walk up together. The warm, tobacco-scented air from the smoky underground begins to give way to the freezing cold winter air and I rub my hands together, as much in excited anticipation as to dispel the cold. We mill about on the Tottenham Court Road outside the club for a while, watching the straights come up the road from the Dominion Theatre and chatting aimlessly to some of the freaks in the queue inspecting the luminescent red and yellow metallic-ink posters on the wall. The skippy feel of expectation is making me light headed and I breathe deeply, looking around me to soak up the atmosphere.

'It doesn't look much,' I say, nodding towards the half open door with flaking green paint and a dirty old Guinness clock above it. 'Looks like it's still a down at heel Irish club to me.'

'Well,' says Ober, taking a last drag of his spliff before dispatching it under foot, 'it is most of the time, but outward appearances can be deceptive. It's turned over to the UFO at the weekend. It's been going for less than a month. Come inside – it's a different world.' He stops me for a moment at the threshold, holds my arm and stares at me intently. 'And remember, this moment is important. Everything else in the future depends on it. This is where the particle meets itself.'

He doesn't give me the opportunity to question him. I don't have any idea what he's talking about. He gives the freak on the inner door two pound notes and takes two blotters off him. As we walk down the dingy stairs into the darkness Ober presses one into my hand and I pop it into my mouth.

'It's always top notch stuff here,' he says. 'It'll keep you involved till dawn and take us where we need to go.' He gives me a meaningful smile and breaks into a trot when we reach a corridor.

The darkened corridor leads into the low-ceiling basement hall. It's a narrow space with a tiny stage area; all lit by a crawling, multi-coloured light show of globular images produced by some clunky slide projectors on a small scaffold rig. It's packed with people, mostly freaks with crazy clothes, probably supplied from the *Granny takes a Trip* stall in the corner. Frilly shirts, old hussar uniforms, kaftans, leather tricorns – the place has managed to draw in the alternatives and they have made it their home. The air is thick with incense and dope and up on the stage there is some wild improvisation being played by five guys with saxophones, cellos and guitars.

'Who are they?' I ask.

'AMM Music,' says Ober, as he accepts a generous hug from a topless girl with a huge garland of flowers wrapped round her head and shoulders.

Ober moves away with some preppy looking guy in a Panama hat (he looks out of place but seems to be in charge somehow) and I shift closer to the stage. I'm still not too comfortable here – I haven't been able to dilute my everyday uptightness and adapt myself to the loved-up, drug-induced freak out. I'm trying to remember how I got here in the first place, and why everything seems so... so *authentic*. Authentic compared to what? I sit down with some freaks next to the stage and watch the guy who had been playing the cello pick up a glass jar with an applied microphone and start rubbing it up and down to produce a weird industrial sound, like a crane swivelling on its axis.

After this the acid starts to kick in. I come up very quickly. This is lovely stuff. I'm not uptight now. In fact I'm playing with a beautiful flower child, placing our palms together and moving them along with the oily bubbles of the crawling light show. Laughing. I'm so in love with her and everyone here.

Then time squeezes itself through a vaporous tube full of swirling lights and we are further into the night. My body is buzzing. I'm still sitting down close to the stage and the light show is casting grainy gold and electric blue globules over The Floyd. It makes them seem to be moving in a staccato slow motion, shadows drifting half unseen around the stage. They're only just into the set. Syd Barrett's in the middle with his painted Fender Esquire and the whole world seems filled with the whirligig, tripped-out, slightly sinister sound of *Interstellar Overdrive*. It starts to take over all the senses. The puncturing bassline is touching me, bouncing on my skin with its rounded, blunt edges, and I can taste that spangly guitar note, repeated again and again and again. I'm being washed over by the soundscape and the light show, inside and outside. I am pervaded by it. The music, the lights, the sensuousness of being able to experience it all as a multi-sensory episode – this is a place of magic, a place where we realise that all consciousness is a universal One and that the recognition of this will change everything once the secret is out.

I close my eyes and allow the improvised sounds to carry me along on their back. The oily light show penetrates my eyelids and I slither over each globule until I fall from one and drift into a further darkness. There's a voice in my ear, whispering. It's telling me that something is about change...

no, *everything* is about to change. This is it, the moment in time when we breach the barriers of consciousness that civilisation has forgotten.

There is an expansion.

'That's good my little baby. That's so good it's amazing.'

Titania's lips were tight to my left ear and she was moving her body over me, grinding, rubbing, and caressing. 'I shouldn't be doing this yet, but we've got to take it as far as it will go.'

The watery sun appeared as a remnant of the light show through my squint. The needle pricked the vein in my arm.

'Oops a daisy. 100mg. Bit much. Never mind, you'll be all right.'

'I'm going to keep this as simple as possible.'

I feel horrendously sick and the veins in my temples seem ready to explode. With my eyes closed I can't stop the sensation that I'm falling from a great height. But every time I open my eyes I'm in a garden with fluorescent green vegetation and a circle of dark yew trees with a turquoise coloured pool in the middle. I close my eyes again and I'm falling, propelled through the air at an unimaginable velocity. I open my eyes. Ober is standing next to the pool beckoning for me to come and look into it. He's wearing an outfit made of sound, shimmying and reverberating over his body.

'Simple. There are seven phases.'

I nod my head. When the nod reaches its lowest point and my head is momentarily at rest above the pool it instantaneously expands to encompass infinity. The moment becomes all I need to see what Ober is showing me – my consciousness takes in everything from the beginning to the end and then round the back of it. There are no senses – sight, sound, smell, touch or taste – just pure consciousness. It can't be explained in language. But it translates like this:

'Phase one,' says Ober, enunciating his words as though talking to an idiot, 'is this.' He shows me a forest glade with a hominid picking some red and white mushrooms and stuffing them into his mouth. 'This is the source of humanity, when

117

consciousness was first recognised for what it is. It actually happened to the Troodon dinosaurs first, in the late Cretaceous, but the meteor wiped them out before they got a grip on it. Anyway, *Homo Habilis* here is the source, about three million years ago, and this is the moment of realisation, induced by an entheogenic episode after eating about seventy-five grams of *Amanita Muscaria* -- the fly agaric mushroom.'

The scene shifts. I watch again as a group of the *Habilises* gather round a dead companion. They cover her body with branches before setting fire to her. They then proceed to munch down handfuls of fly agaric and one by one fall into slumbering sitting positions. I range close up to the face of one and he opens his eyes. They are black but they show a depth of realisation and a great wonder at the mysteries of life and death. For an instant I am that hominid: fearful, confused, grief-ridden, but at the same time accepting and deeply content. There is no difference between our consciousness. We are both everything and nothing at the same time.

'Phase two,' says Ober, abruptly severing my link with the *Habilises*, 'is a hunter-gatherer society with an embryonic shamanic priesthood. Possessions are a bad idea because they'll just encumber you as you live a peripatetic existence, constantly on the move with each season. No land ownership either – everything communal within each extended family group. And the groups of any given region meet once or twice a year to engage in ceremonies led by shamans to whom the responsibilities of consciousness expansion have been divested.'

I look into the pool and see a gathering of peoples on a hill with a large oval plateau. It seems to be midwinter and they're all wrapped up in hides and furs. All except the shaman who stands on a circle of burning embers, naked apart from the skeletal remains of a deer skull and antlers tied to his head. He's out there – far out. He's actually achieved his altered state of consciousness not with any type of drug but with a ritual of fasting, drumming and exposure to the icy cold for weeks. I join him as he first flies above the landscape and then delves into the near future to see what might be best for each of the gathered social groups.

'In many ways this is the apex of human civilisation,' says Ober. 'It is the time when everyone has to be a fully functioning part of a group and where any type of selfishness or egotistical behaviour is detrimental both to the group and to the individual. Their shamans are powerful repositories of all knowledge. They can plug into the Phylogenic Memory whenever they need to, purely for the health of the collective groups. There is a deep understanding of the nature of reality by all. Life and death are but different attributes of the eternal.'

I'm lying down on the hilltop with my cheek to the cold, hard ground. I *am* part of this Mesolithic gathering. I could stay here if I wanted to. Part of me does. I join with one of the women. Her consciousness seems linked to the others in an explicit way, as if they're actually in direct communication. There's quite a lot of pain, but the inclusiveness of it is... not human... they are fundamentally different from us in the way they think and act. They have a collective ego. And they are hearing things... voices...

'That's correct,' says Ober, reading my mind and pulling me back to the edge of the pool. 'Now, phase three is something you have already plugged into. That's almost certainly because it appeared to be the most useful phase to your mind in its entheogenic state – the mother goddess symbol is strong here, and you needed a mother... and rebirth.'

I look into the pool and find myself looking through the eyes of someone – male I think – winding along an avenue made up of two parallel rows of huge standing stones, sticking out of the ground at regular intervals. Jeez, he is really stoned. He can hardly put one foot in front of the other. And he's hearing voices. There's a constant stream of whispering voices travelling from one side of his brain to the other. He seems perfectly happy with this; it is evidently normal. But I don't understand the voices. I'm not really a part of his bicameral existence – I can't share his consciousness.

'That's because they're becoming individuals. Collectivity has been broken down by ownership: land, resources, people. The introduction of agriculture and the subsequent need to own land and possessions has started to erode the metaphysical bonds between people. They are still able to rely on a shamanic priesthood of course, but the shamans have to take larger and larger amounts of entheogenic drugs – the type of drug depends on the environment – just to maintain contact with the Phylogenic Memory. Still, they do have a great line in Goddess worship – obsessed with pregnancy and birth. I mean look at that.'

My stoned human vehicle obeys a voice in his head that tells him to look beyond the stone avenue to an enormous artificial mound towering over him. He sees it become the swollen belly of a gigantic earth woman made up of the landscape, and then with the sparkling water of a spring flowing at its base a crack dilates and...

'And this is the most depressing phase,' says Ober, taking hold of my head and directing my eyes to a murky corner of the pond covered in scum and debris. 'Phase four is dogmatic religions and materialism. Every person for themselves and hollow belief systems that have forgotten what consciousness is. Humanity is living under an astounding delusion that is fed and propped up by the ego – strongest it's ever been... or ever will be again.'

I see murder, war, rape and greed on a prodigious scale. But I can't get inside the heads of any of these people. I just have to watch the mayhem from a distance. It goes on and on and on and on. But it ends with a suburban scene, early 22nd-century Amerika: tree-lined street with big neutron guns at either end. The street is covered with heli-cars and big houses... then I'm inside one. All the attributes of wealth are there: virtual TV walls, sauna pods, robot maids, silver-dream sleep chambers etc. etc. A family sits around a 3-D screen planning a virtual holiday with all emotional responses included. They eventually plump for a tour of the African desert Wastelands followed by a short stay amidst the flooded delta cities of south Asia and returning via the decimated cityscapes of their own country's east coast.

'Can we go to Europea too,' whines little Jimmy, his fat body jerking with indignant excitement. 'I've been told they do cannibalism in the new cities. I so want to see that. Can we? Can we?'

'You know very well that the Church doesn't allow virtual trips there,' says mom. 'The people there are... are evil. They are evil drug taking unbelievers.'

'But I want to, I want to, I want to, I want.'

'The last days of the old Western civilisation in Amerika,' says Ober, as the scene fades. 'The high watermark of the ego, when selfishness and dogma have complete control over human consciousness.'

'So how is it rescued?' I ask. 'Or is the fifth phase even worst?'

'You've already witnessed the genesis of phase five,' he says, as the pool briefly relives my 1960s UFO club trip. 'Its furtherance just requires a quorum of people in positions of social and political authority who have realised that the only way to overcome the inherent selfishness born of materialism and power is to change fundamentally the nature of the ego. They achieve this realisation through the controlled use of entheogenic substances, which give access to the collective consciousness – the Phylogenic Memory. They achieve Samadhi. They touch infinity... the Void.'

'And what about everyone else?'

'Within three generations, and after the environmental crisis has had its demographic effect, eighty per cent of the world's reduced population outside Amerika have background levels of entheogens inside their brains at all times, and high levels at prescribed moments. Extra DMT can be administered to those most in need, or those who are resistant to the entheogens. Everyone is in touch with the Collective and no one *wants* anything. The entheogens banish misery, suffering, greed and ownership forever. No one does anything unless it is beneficial to the group – the Collective. And it allows everyone to see beyond death, to see themselves as part of the infinite, ever-living Void. The fear of death is overcome. The golden key has unlocked the door.'

'And what about individuality?' I ask. 'Do people not have choices anymore?'

Ober doesn't answer. He just lifts up the surface of the water in the pool and shows me phase six.

The world is beautiful. Canopies of rain forest and temperate woodland stretch over vast swathes of land, reaching the edges of uplands and mountains, which are dotted with crystalline lakes and tarns. There is no sign of humanity anywhere. The ancient cities, villages, freeways and installations are long since collapsed into archaeological stratigraphy and exist now only in the dreams of those who are left. And who are they? I lower myself beneath the upper reaches of an oak, birch and lime woodland and descend to a clearing. Spaced around it there are seven mounds made of clay – each one is somewhere between a ziggurat and an anthill, reaching up to the lower branches of the surrounding trees. It is tranquil and balmy. There is the slight scent of incense in the air and the lazy calls of midsummer birds echo round the stillness of the woods. My attention is drawn to a movement on one of the mounds. Someone is coming out of a circular hole near the base. She moves strangely, her arms compensating for some kind of disability in her legs... or maybe they're not legs. And she's wearing some type of armour. I float closer as she turns her back to me and starts to stoke what looks like a fire contained within a circle of stones. I move closer and closer, but I'm getting the impression that she knows I'm here, that she can actually recognise me as a real entity in her world. I stand stock-still and try to regulate my breathing but there is something about her gait that implies she is just biding her time and trying to work out how to interact with me. She's probably frightened. Yes, that's it – it can't be everyday she gets a visit from a disembodied consciousness. She's sensed me but is too afraid to turn round and look me in the eyes. I wish I could let her know that I'm not in any way a threat.

I wait a while then decide to ease up closer and inch between two of the stones. Shall I announce my presence? Ah, no need, she's turning. But as she does so she moves quicker than I would believe and races up to me no more than a hand-span from my face. I'm unable to feel such a human emotion as shock but it's close. How can I say this... she's part human part cockroach.

Her shiny brown exoskeleton covers her upper body and her legs are not damaged, they are just thin and wiry with external joints. Her pointed facial features retain their humanity and the antennae are nothing more than stubs that seem to pull the corners of her enormous almond-shaped eyes to the top of her head.

'Beautiful huh?' says Ober, who has stagnated time in order to whisper in my ear. 'This is as good as it gets for us in phase six. *Homo-Cryptocercus*: the result of genetic modifications made possible after the genesis of the twenty-fourth chromosome. There are still some twenty-three chromo-humans knocking about, mostly in Amerika, but not many, and their days are numbered – they're disease riddled and, worst of all, incapable of thinking as a collective.'

Time comes back online and now I'm with her, inside her. But to be with her is also to be with the group... no, wait, not just the group, but *everybody* everywhere. We're networked, connected to a universal consciousness with our minds acting as one, for the common good. And oh, how good it is. The ego is obliterated and replaced with a common, collective identity. Individuality is banished. No greed, hate, loneliness, despair, envy or ownership. The ecstasy is almost too much to take, and they're like it all the time. How can they accommodate so much?

But I'm a bit of an anomaly. I have no body. They've recognised my presence but can't quite accept it. Some other people come out from within the mounds – they appear to float a little above the ground – and form a circle around the stones. They meditate together then the female who I saw first comes to me again.

'It's time for you to go traveller. We could be damaged by your continued presence. Our collective must find the likes of you of our own accord. Go with our love.'

I turn to look for Ober but he's not there. I turn back, but I'm in the garden again looking into a dusty crater where the pool had been. I'm feeling sleepy.

'What's phase seven?' I whisper, tiredness engulfing me. 'Samadhi? Do I get to see that? What happens to the cockroach people? They were wonderful.'

There is no answer. There is just the wind blowing through the trees. I'm coming down.

XVII

After polishing off a couple of morning joints I sat down beneath one of the oak trees lining the garden on its eastern side. The midday sun was oppressively hot and even within the shade of the tree the closeness of the day coupled with the cannabis encouraged inert sluggishness. I dozed for a while and then woke up clammy and restless. But I couldn't get myself moving. There was nothing to do anyway. Titania and Ober seemed to have disappeared and getting myself motivated of my own volition was only a slight possibility. And yet... and yet I felt all right. I felt light and almost contented. I thought back to the equivalent situation in the flat on the blocks. How many empty, wasted days had I stayed curled up on my bed, utterly unable to make myself do anything at all, depression coating every thought and memory with thickened despair. I realised now that I had, since their deaths, been completely at its mercy. Sometimes it would render me useless for days at a time. Then, when I was forced up and out of the flat for provisions, it would mutate into the anxieties that made me sweat, shake and stammer through a trip to the shops. And once safely back in the flat, relieved of my fear of people, the depression would start stalking me again. Sometimes it would lay low, at bay, and let me drift along, but it was always there, just awaiting the opportunity to consolidate its grip on me. It was a many-tentacled beast and it loved to wrap itself around me. Not here though. It had been trying to get me but it was finding it difficult to survive in such an environment.

I slid my back down the trunk and sidled about until I was comfortably prone. The sunlight sheaved through the leaves, touching my face and bare arms with slivers of heat. It still seemed a luxury to have the privilege of lazing around outside in complete privacy. In the blocks we had no outside space at all apart from the walkway, and the public parks in the district did not encourage solitary wanderers. There was an unwritten social rule of who or what had rights of presence in the parks. In the daytime: kids playing, dogwalkers, semi-organised games of football and winos. At night: ominous gangs of teenagers, thrashed out sex and... winos. There was no place for a male on his own unless he was quite clearly off his head, in which case he was safely ignored or beaten up. If you were not inebriated and walking around the parks on your own during the day, you were most probably a paedo. Walk around at night and you invited target practice and/or robbery/assault. And since my anxiety disorders had taken control of me the social stigma or danger of wandering around public places on my own had become personal anathema.

But, of course, at the house this was all changed. I had a private space, a delightful private space where I could simply hang out and not have to worry about other people. It would never be a place to which I belonged but it was starting to do things to me. It was isolating my depression and anxiety disorders and making them seem somehow less real.

Real. The word kept coming to me, bobbing to the surface and reminding me of... but no, I was trying to banish my intermittent memories of those different realities. For now anyway. Moments would come flashing back to me, but I knew I wasn't ready for them. It had been three days – I think... maybe four -- since I'd been with Titania on the lounger and not an hour went by without some imagery from the trip seeping back into my thoughts from hidden places. I closed my eyes and saw the big almond eyes of the cockroach girl. The image was shockingly vivid, and I opened my eyes with a start, sensing the residual memory slinking away into the garden, ulterior to my mind and existing of its own accord. For an instant it formed into an androgen and then became dim and unseen in the shadows of the herb garden.

Always with us they are, most of the time scornful and distrustful, but sometimes so compassionate that they weep for our grief and disappointments as though they are us. As though their minds and ours are as one.

I quickly turned my eyes from the herb garden and shook my head violently, attempting to get rid of the whispering voices. I knew what I was seeing and hearing but I didn't want to deal with it. I didn't want to overwhelm myself with making adjudications on reality. I needed to know first how much I was being 'aided' in my adjudications by drugs. I had spent most of my waking hours dredging my splintered memory for a coherent story, a plan, a sitemap for what was happening to me. But every time I thought I'd gripped onto something it either shattered into unrecognisable fragments or dwindled into nothing. I was pretty sure that I was being given a drug on a daily basis. Hadn't Titania told me so? Maybe. But how this was being done I had no idea. And the injections – I had holes in my arms and bruising. DMT... what was that? Why couldn't I ever fucking remember anything? If the place had a computer with web access I could search for some solutions, but as it was I just had to live with it and try to work things out for myself.

Was this how Ober was scheming things out for me? And was it for *me*? There must have been easier ways to treat an anxiety-riddled depressive without going to such lengths. What was in it for him... and Titania... and the *we* that I'd still got no closer to finding out about? One thing was clear to me; they were doing everything they could to ensure they didn't have to answer any of my questions. Every time I got them alone they would manipulate the situation so that--.

'Hello young man.'

I started violently and scrambled up from underneath the tree. Squinting into the sun I saw Mr Quince standing somewhat uncertainly a few paces from me.

'Sorry, I didn't mean to startle you. I had just come up to see Professor Liddell about a few matters... parish business.'

I swayed a little, light-headed and dizzy from getting up too quickly. For a moment Quince's features were dark and silhouetted with the sun behind him and a barrage of red and orange spangles danced around him as my head rush completed its cycle.

'We're closing in on them.'

The spangles fizzed out and I started to make out Quince's face.

'Pardon.'

'I said, we're closing the village shop. Just for a couple of weeks whilst it's renovated. Very old fashioned, needs a bit more than a lick of paint see. We want to bring in some cold storage as well. You know, a refrigerator, maybe even a frozen food cabinet.'

'A freezer?'

Quince looked a bit bemused. 'Yes. Yes, I suppose that's what it would be.'

I took a deep breath and relaxed my shoulders a little. Quince had his pipe with him, and took advantage of the momentary lull to relight it and take a few puffs. The aroma of tobacco wisped past me and mixed in with the garden smells. It evoked some memory – too deep to come to the surface without further bidding but able to make me want to pursue it. Something sad, something long ago.

'They've underestimated us.'

'What?' The memory shrank away.

'I said I hope they'll understand. I know it will be inconvenient but the parish thought it was about time we brought the shop up to speed. A village needs its general store and the parish council has agreed to help out with the costs of renovation you see. It will be a kind of loan. Lowest possible interest rate of course. I was here to ask Professor Liddell if he might be able to contribute something. It would be a gesture of goodwill.'

'A gesture of goodwill,' I repeated, squinting at Quince and trying to work out if there was some coded meaning to the words. But he just hummed in the affirmative and sucked on his pipe, looking round at the house.

'Does your parish always do this kind of thing?'

He took his pipe out of his mouth and fixed me with slightly narrowed eyes.

'Mr Snout, the shopkeeper, like many of us, is a war veteran. He has found it difficult to keep the shop going on his own in such a small community, and the parish feels duty-bound to offer him some assistance.'

'A war veteran?'

'Yes.' He turned to the house again, making it clear that he would rather be getting on with his objective than standing in the garden talking to me. 'Is he about?'

'No. It's only me today. But I'll give him the message if you like.'

'No, don't worry about it. There's no desperate rush. But perhaps I could borrow the lavatory… if you don't mind.'

I gestured agreement. 'There's one on the ground floor, underneath the staircase.'

Quince set off. He seemed in a hurry. I remembered Ober's disquiet when I had told him I'd been talking to Quince before, and realised that he would have probably not wanted him in the house unchaperoned. Too late. Did it matter? I shuffled about nervously, wondering if I should go into the house and speed Quince on his way. I waited five minutes then walked up to the house. But Quince was gone. I called for him, but there was no response. He'd evidently just made his own way out.

He'd put me on edge. I didn't quite know why. He was just an old fashioned sort of bloke; the usual type of middle aged soft reactionary that I imagined to inhabit all English villages. But there was something reverberating about and around him, as if he were a character in a movie – pretending. Yes, that was it, it was like he was acting a part and what I saw was just a glossary of the real person. Turning up in the garden when it was only me there, getting himself into the house unsupervised, and then disappearing without notice. It was like someone taking part in a pre-ordained story plot, with me as an unwitting device. And what he'd been saying had already begun to mix itself up in my head. I got a fleeting image in my head of him talking indecipherable code. Was that right? Had I been meant to understand something from what he had said?

I sat down on the stairs and attempted to regulate my breathing. My heart was pounding away for no particular reason and my hands shook slightly when I held them out before me. Perhaps I'd had a bit too much sun. I got up and started to make my way to my bedroom for a lay down, but stopped halfway at the little cupboard in the balcony wall. My heart was now thumping in my mouth – my face was flushing hot. Without really thinking about what I was doing I tried the handles on the cupboard. It was unlocked. I hesitated for a moment, holding the doors ajar but not opening them. Then, with one quick jerk I opened them.

Inside was a human brain, glistening wet and grey. I

ran my fingers over its smooth, contoured surface then lifted it up to look at the underside. The two bulbous hippocampi glowed red in the medial temporal lobe. I touched them and closed my eyes. Instantly I was flooded with memories. They flew at me, and they were all in the right order. Mum and Alice; the news of their deaths; my six-month descent into a welter of psychiatric disorder; my sectioning; Ober and my therapy; Alice Liddell; the house and the jumbled series of drug-induced events. Everything blew through me like a mental hurricane. I knew it only took a few seconds, but I had remembered everything, in startling detail. And Titania injecting me with DMT. I could see myself on the couch with the chemical compound flashing up in front of me as if I were on TV: *N, N-dimethyltryptamine*. I watched the needle sink into my vein and felt myself coming up immediately--.

'Not again. Poor love.'

I opened my eyes and saw Titania on the stairs. There was nothing inside the cupboard. I wasn't coming up. She led me into the living room took me in her arms and hugged me hard. Her body sent electric through me – not sexual, but rather... motherly. I pressed every part of my body against her and held on like my life depended on it. Maybe it did.

'I think I'm remembering things Titania. It feels a bit like the lid's popped off something and all the memories are coming back.'

'Good.'

'I touched the brain... and it feels like something has touched my brain.'

I smiled wildly, tears blurring my vision.

'I think maybe you need to tell me about it,' she whispered, her lips brushing against my ear.

'Yes. I think I do.'

XVIII

There was an iciness travelling up through my chest. It's not very nice having memories come back at you as if they were entirely new thought experiences – especially when they are so fucking nasty. But then that's probably why the subconscious goes to the trouble of repressing them. It knows what the conscious mind can and cannot handle.

Titania sat me down on a hard-backed chez lounge in the darkest part of the living room, away from all the windows. She was scrutinising me as she moved about in front of me. She looked as if she were stalking something.

'Don't rush anything,' she said, her voice low and toneless. 'Recall can be a painful business.'

I followed her eyes. I was glad she was there; I needed someone to whom I could spill out everything that was rushing back from wherever it had been until now. But the feeling left by her embrace had quickly dissipated and her cat-like migration from one end of the chair to the other was starting to make me feel vulnerable and agitated. It even occurred to me that perhaps she didn't want some of my memories coming back.

'What do you want me to tell you?' I asked. It must have sounded cagey as Titania stopped still and squinted at me. It was a look of unmitigated suspicion.

'Whatever you want to,' she said, before resuming her movement with arms folded. 'Is the recall prior to your sectioning?'

'Yes. No... well, mostly.'

'Tell me then.'

'Well, it may not sound much... but I've just remembered hearing about their deaths. There was a copper... and a social worker. I'd completely forgotten about them. They came to the flat on the day it happened to tell me... oh Jesus.'

The mental image of the policeman and social worker folded into the centre like a closing book. Taking its place was a room lit with a cold blue light. In the middle of the room were two bodies laid on two tables covered with white shrouds. An attendant drew back the sheets and asked me something. Alice's face was barely recognisable with a massive fleshy gash running from what was once her mouth up to a dismembered eye socket. I mechanically looked from her to my mother. Her face was more intact, but the top of her skull seemed to be deflated. Or perhaps there wasn't anything there at all. I closed my eyes. The image remained.

Was I there, or was I in the house with Titania? I heard the sound of the attendant nervously shuffling about and sensed the emetic effect of what I had seen beginning to force bile up into my mouth. I was trembling violently. I wasn't just remembering this; I was there again. The fucking drugs – they'd put me back in that room, that morgue, that charnel house. I was being forced to experience it over again -- to experience the soul-sucking nightmare for a second time. And at the moment it felt as if it would last forever. I couldn't open my eyes. I couldn't risk opening them and seeing the carnage that I'd caused. I did not want to be there again. I shook my head furiously, shutting my eyes tighter and tighter until it hurt. They had found out how to manipulate time all right – and here I was suffering the consequences. I reached out for my mother, blindly wanting to touch her corpse.

'It's ok, it's ok.'

I jerked and recoiled from the touch on my arm, instinctively opening my eyes. Titania's face was close to mine. I could smell the faint scent of her moisturiser. Of course it was the same as my mother's. She also had two different coloured eyes. Or maybe they were turquoise. It was difficult to tell.

'It's not surprising you should bury and repress something like this sweetie. Your conscious mind has to be good and ready to carry around this sort of thing.'

Did she know where I'd been? Had I been talking? What was she talking about? I closed my eyes again. The image of the shrouded corpses remained, but it was a clearly marked out memory, delineated as such in my mind. I wasn't there again.

'You should be starting to realise how your medication works by now,' said Titania, apparently in reply to my unspoken questions. 'It would be no good us just pumping you up with every entheogen under the sun and letting you get on with it. We're all plugged into the same network. As long as you're on the correct medication all of your thoughts are ours as well.'

'What?'

'And morgues are never nice places to be are they. Especially when you have to see what you have seen.'

She stroked my hair back out of my eyes and delivered a feathery kiss to my forehead. I quivered at her touch at first but then reached out to hug her. She held me and let me rest my head against her shoulder for a minute before gently releasing me and sitting down on the end of the chez lounge.

'What else?' she said, folding her fingers together. 'I know there's more, but you've got to allow it to come back from your subconscious before we can help you.'

I held eye contact with her, not something that was ever easy for me, and tried to calm myself. I was still trembling at the image of the brutalised bodies of my mother and Alice, but there was more to come – a swelling of things past, being heaved to the surface of my consciousness by something outside of me, something external. It was the drugs I supposed, but somehow it didn't seem so. I wasn't experiencing any of the usual rush and visuals that symptomised a trip. Although maybe I was just being fooled. Maybe the drugs were more intelligent than me and were able to make me believe that their reality was my reality. If they allowed other people access to my imagination then they must be able to do almost anything. I breathed out a shaky breath and closed my eyes.

'You need to tell me how this works Titania. How do I know these memories are real? How do I know whether what's coming back to me hasn't just been put there by the drugs? How do I know they aren't all just psychedelic flashbacks?'

'Well, I guess you'll just have to trust us sweet thing. Why would we be implanting false memories in you? And HPDDs hardly ever take the form of *remembering*.'

I listened to her whilst the swell of another 'memory' came up from the depths. 'What's an HPDD?'

'Hallucinogen Persisting Perception Disorder... a flashback.'

The words triggered the memory. I visualised myself in the flat with Ober. I was lying on the couch and he was kneeling by my side with his hands clamped to my head. I opened my eyes in the middle of a mind-bending trip and saw him through his spread fingers. Except it wasn't him. It was Alice... Alice Liddell. No... it was my Alice.

I opened my eyes, the trembling had got worst. 'I don't think I can trust my memory,' I said. 'It's telling me things that just can't be true.'

Titania smiled. 'Is it indeed.'

'Yes.'

'Do you not think you were brought in to identify your sister and mother?'

'I-I guess, but why would I forget it?'

'You know why... it's called dissociative amnesia. Something your subconscious thinks is too painful for everyday consumption.'

'And so why should I remember it now?'

'Because you're being cured.'

'Of what?'

'Everything.'

I heaved a sigh and realised how taut my body had become. 'But I remember a trip with Ober, in the flat, one where he'd mentioned HPDDs before for some reason. You saying it brought the memory back. And now I remember opening my eyes and seeing not Ober but... but Alice.'

'Your sister?'

'Erm, yes.'

'Not Alice Liddell?'

'Maybe her as well.'

Titania raised one of her sharp eyebrows and parted her lips with her tongue. She allowed me a few seconds to dwell on what I had said before moving a bit closer to me on the chez lounge.

'Have you considered the possibility that almost all of your memories are just manipulated images. They are manipulated by you, me, Ober, society, the passage of time... but none of them are *true*.'

'Bullshit.'

'Ok, what if I were to suggest to you that you are part of an experiment whereby everything you've experienced since you first kissed your sister, or when you first *thought* you kissed your sister, has not really happened. In fact, let's just say that it goes even farther back and that your whole existence since you were a little boy in the mid-seventies, from when your sister Alice was born, has been manipulated by us. Your entire perception of reality is based on the constructs of the entheogenic medication that you've been given in varying doses until it was finally made explicit after your breakdown in the shop.'

'Woah – stop right there Titania. I'm as real as you and this house. Look.' I thumped the cushions and pinched my cheeks. 'I don't want to hear any more fucked-up theories of reality and my place in it because I know what I've experienced – ok, so I might have forgotten some of it, but that doesn't make it any less *real*. It's just the drugs. It's just the fucking drugs mixing up my sense of time and making me forget things... and making up other things.'

'Are you sure that it isn't the drugs that are making you *remember* things? Perhaps they are even allowing you to know things that would otherwise be beyond your memory.'

I made a dismissive gesture and tried to get up but she pushed me back down. Her countenance suddenly took on a febrile shimmer and she used her surprisingly balanced agility to pin me down with one hand.

'You're just a little pawn in a very large game,' she said in a lowered voice. 'But you've had access to what things are really about. The recall of your own suppressed memories is just a side effect. I'm all for your psychiatric treatment here, but I don't think you should be as sheltered as you are from the bigger picture.'

'So why don't you just tell me what the bigger picture is?'

Titania grabbed me by the hair and forced me further back into the chair with shocking strength. She pushed her breasts against me and brought her face to within a few centimetres of mine.

'Haven't you realised yet,' she whispered with bite, 'you aren't told, you experience. Our language isn't capable of dealing with it. You have to go there and be part of it. Everybody does. And everybody will.'

She thrust me back again and stood up. I was thinking that I should have been scared, but I wasn't, I was turned on. My breath came in short, sharp expulsions and the air thickened around me. And, of course, my straining cock was on full alert. Titania retrieved a small bag from somewhere in the room and took out a plastic cylinder. For a fleeting, outrageous second I thought she was taking out a strap-on dildo, and my lungs contracted. But it wasn't a dildo. It was a tube containing a hypodermic needle and vials of liquid. Expertly she fitted a vial into the needle casing, straddled me and tightened a strap around my forearm. And with the cephalic vein standing proud she poised the needle.

'You're going to see exactly what happened to your sister and mother,' she said, her eyes flashing. 'You already know. But you have to be reminded. Reminded by medication. 75mg of N, N-dimethyltryptamine to be precise. It's going to take you on another phylogenic journey my little sweetness.'

She took my face in her right hand and squeezed my lips apart. I was frozen to the spot, unable to move. She ground around on my cock for a few seconds then, with a pouty smile on her face she expertly inserted the needle into the purple vein.

The DMT took seconds to reach my brain and relieve it of its usual take on reality. My head lurched from Titania's hand and thumped against the back cushions of the chez lounge. But that was the last I knew of me. I was pursued by Titania's voice, but I was leaving it behind to go somewhere else.

'Enjoy.'

XIX

It is night. The car's in front of a concrete garage, waiting for someone, some people. And here they come.

Oh no.

Mum is pulling hard at Alice's arm, dragging her towards the car. Alice cannot remember ever having seen mum like this. Withdrawn, tearful, cold – yes. But never angry. Not this angry. It scares Alice like nothing else she can think of. Mum opens the passenger door and throws Alice into the seat, knocking her head against the frame. But Alice doesn't feel a thing. The adrenaline coursing through her acts as an anaesthetic, at least a physical anaesthetic. Her mental world is swirling around and pressing in on all sides. Pressing in on what? Pressing in on everything she knows and has known.

'Don't even think about moving,' spits mum, slamming the door behind Alice.

Alice couldn't have moved even if she had wanted. Her breath is coming in fits and starts, her hands are quivering and she tries desperately to gather her thoughts together and work out what is going on. At the baseline she knows, but the turmoil inside her head is preventing her from making any assessment. It affects every part of her. She even has to remember to breathe, as though all her automatic critical faculties are closing down and she's having to exist on manual.

Mum thrusts herself into the driving seat and slams the door behind her. Alice can't look at her but she feels mum's eyes boring into her with... what is it? Hate, disgust, fury – probably all three, but there is something more. There is disappointment as well. Alice senses the deep reservoir of disappointment surfaced with all the more visceral emotions blowing around on top. And then something even deeper: black, fathomless, unoxygenated regret. Regret. The thing is, it seems almost as if she is regretting something in the future. She thinks mum has been given access to what will happen by giving herself over so completely to this weltering storm. And what she feels most of all is regret. Alice feels her entire frame tremble at the realisation.

'Look at me,' snaps mum. But Alice can't. 'Look at me!' she shouts, grabbing Alice's chin and forcing her head round. With her free hand she slaps Alice's face hard. Alice doesn't feel a thing, but both eyes start watering.

'How could you do this? To us. To me.'

Mum lets go of her face and fumbles with the keys. She starts the engine and pulls away from the garage forecourt with a reckless abandon that makes Alice grip the door handle. Away from the blocks and onto the main thoroughfare she drives, clanking the gears as though she has forgotten what a clutch is and jerking away from stops as if daring the cross traffic to hit them. She only remembers to turn on the lights after the second horn-blast from another car. Ten nerve-racking minutes like this, then they come to a queue of traffic creeping forward towards a distant junction. At first Alice thinks they are going to career headlong into the back rearmost car, but mum slams on the brakes at the last minute and they screech to a halt amidst the pungent smell of smoking rubber.

Alice looks out the corner of her eye at mum. Her face is streaked with running eyeliner and she's gripping the steering wheel so hard that her fingers are turning red. Alice runs her tongue around her bone-dry mouth and tries to form some thought that she would be able to turn into words. But she can't. All she can think of amidst the chaotic internal psychobabble is that mum's fury is being mutated by the regret. Maybe she knows this just because she knows mum so well. Or maybe the blood connection of mother and daughter holds some implicit emotional link, dormant for most of the time but active at times like these: times of crisis, when the usual personal and social barriers necessary for everyday life have been dismantled.

'I want you to tell me when it started, why it started and what you are going to do about it.'

Mum enunciates every word like she's talking to a foreigner, except that every syllable is laced with a slithering vehemence that makes Alice think someone else inhabits her body and mind. Someone she doesn't know. And does mum know everything? How does she know? Of course, she'd have to find out eventually—'

'WHEN!'

Mum's scream makes Alice jolt from the seat. A ripple of nausea waves up from her stomach and seems to find a staging post in her gullet. She opens her mouth to speak but her lips are thick and swollen and they quiver with a chaotic energy.

'When your dad died,' continues mum, suddenly and freakily softly spoken. It's her usual voice, but as if spoken by an insane person mimicking her. 'I made a promise to you that I wouldn't involve myself in any relationship until you'd left home. That was when you were two and your brother was six. And I stuck to it. Twenty-one fucking years. I'm fifty seven years of age and I've devoted the best part of my life to raising you two at the expense of myself, and this is how you reward me.'

A stream of responses whipped through Alice's head.

She plucked one at random and regretted it immediately. 'We never asked you to do that.'

'WE! You sound like you're one fucking person issuing a statement.'

'I didn't mean that—'

'Well what do you mean? You've had every penny I earned. Every penny so that one day your education would get us out of the shithole we live in. I've loved you, worked sixty hour weeks packing boxes and stuffing chickens' asses, done everything I can for you, just waiting for the day when you'd pay me back and say "hey mum, we don't have to live in the blocks anymore, because your son and daughter want to say thank you for all your sacrifices. Let's move out. We can go anywhere with my job and money."'

'But I don't earn that much—'

'Well you earn a fuck site more than me and your brother put together. God, I was too lenient on him. He's never done a proper day's work in his life. He's spent his adult life *improving himself*, reading books, listening to music and fucking about on his computer like some independently wealthy toff... and all subsidised by me... and you probably. Oh God, I see it now. The two of you together, laying plans for the future, dividing up the spoils.'

Mum stops and breathes deeply. She probably realises that she's starting to sound unhinged. She's moving the car along in awkward jerks, sometimes getting horned by the cars behind as gaps are left in the crawling queue.

'I love him mum.'

Alice immediately realises that is an honest response, but quite a foolish one.

'He's your fucking brother, of course you love him. It doesn't mean you have to let him screw you, like... like a pair of fucking chimpanzees.'

Alice attempts to retreat further into the seat. She's hardly ever had a crossed word with mum. All through her teenage years when her girlfriends were poisoning their maternal relationships with poorly comprehended angst, mum and Alice just drifted on as they always had: a gentle breeze of a mother-daughter relationship. She can't even remember hearing her swear before. It's like sitting next to a stranger. It adds to Alice's internal chaos. She has grown used to the Secret. Grown used to all the little things that need to be done to maintain it. But she has also grown used to it being kept. And now it's out of the bag, out in the open. She thinks she could just about deal with mum knowing. They could integrate it into their lives somehow. But now there is more to the Secret, and in a moment of stomach-lurching realisation Alice sees that her mother only has half the picture.

'I've been asking myself how it could happen,' continues mum, her watery eyes staring straight ahead but turning occasionally to cast a withering look towards Alice. 'When he came back from staying with those friends of his – he was only round the corner but we'd hardly seen him for the best part of a year – you might have seen him as someone else... not your brother. Is that right?'

Alice couldn't find an answer. 'Maybe... I—'

'Or was it going on before – is that why he went away in the first place?'

'No. I don't know. Mum, please—'

'Don't fucking *please* me. You know, one of the worst things is that it was going on under my nose. I guess you had plenty of time to get it on whilst I was working nightshifts. God, I was always so proud of how the three of us stuck together, how we managed to cope with all the bullshit that made other families – often two-parent families – go under. I thought we were a team, the three of us united against the world. A single mother and her courageous son and daughter overcoming the odds of living in a crime-riddled, concrete hell-hole without falling into the crap that's all around us. That's what I thought. But I was wrong wasn't I. 'Cos all the while you two had your own little secret, your own disgusting little secret.'

'Mum, it wasn't like that.'

'No? What was it like then? Please do tell me because I'm having a little difficulty under-fucking-standing it.'

Alice tries to control her breathing, which is beginning to turn into jittering sobs. 'You know how he is mum,' she says, still unable to look her in the eye. 'He listens; he understands and tries to help. Just think about some of the losers I've been out with in the past. They were all just out for

themselves. Most people are. But... but he isn't like that.'
Alice clenches her fists, using one to wipe away the tears.
'You know this. You know what he's like. He's devoted
himself to you and me. I guess I realised there would never
be anyone else like that. And when he went away and we
didn't see him for so long... I... I came to see how much I
loved him—'

'Love is not sex.'

'But we—'

'Brothers do not have sex with their sisters. It is
disgusting.'

Mum's anger seems suddenly focussed and controlled.
Alice thinks that she would find it easier to deal with outright
unfocussed rage.

'When he came back,' continues Alice, attempting to
formulate her justification, 'and you started working nights,
we... we comforted each other. We were both so lonely.
Neither of us seemed to have any friends. You know what I'm
like. And even his old flatmates went away somewhere else.
We were just two human beings needing... needing
compassion.' Alice knows she's making a pig's ear of this but
her brain isn't firing on all cylinders and she can only put
together her reasoning in formulaic clichés.

'Compassion? Compassion is not sex.'

Alice looks sideways at mum. She is trembling and
blinking her eyes like she's in a sandstorm. Alice decides that
she needs to undercut the conversation. 'Do you regret
having us?'

'Do I regret having you?' Her words are pitilessly laced
with affirmation. 'I regret everything. I regret giving away
everything to you two, I regret marrying someone who
estranged me from my family to live in the blocks and then
left me alone, I regret... I regret ever having lived...'

Alice holds her breath as mum pauses without finishing.
A prescient notion seems to pass between them. The notion
is one of emptiness, of a void. It is as if she has been made
suddenly aware of an emotion that was previously unknown.
It is like turning a corner and seeing the sky a colour that
does not exist. A wave of nausea sweeps through her again.

'... Ever... ever.' Mum's voice is lost amidst the engine

140

noise as she pulls away from the lights and onto a stretch of dual carriageway where the traffic is free moving.

It starts to rain drizzle. Alice hugs herself, holds her belly and looks through her tears at the blur of lights swirling around in the night. They drive for another twenty minutes or so in silence before mum pulls off the main drag and through a residential area that leads to an unlit road on the way out of the city. There's not much traffic here and the headlights illuminate small animals scampering off the road into fields that form black silhouettes against the backdrop of orange light pollution from the city.

'Where are we going mum?'

No answer.

'You probably shouldn't be driving when you're like this.'

Mum looks at Alice. She can't interpret the look, but shadowed by the night it seems bereft of humanity. Her personality seems to have drained out of her like a... like an insane person. Alice's heart pushes out a massive beat.

'Mum, you're scaring me. We should turn round and go home.'

'No we shouldn't.'

'Mum!'

The car's near side flirts with the unseen ditch at the side of the road and mum's instinctive response is to brake and pull the steering wheel in the opposite direction. The car swivels on the greasy surface, rights itself and then realigns to the middle of the road. Mum takes her foot off the brake and onto the accelerator.

'Mum, please slow down. Mum!'

She does slow down a touch but the car still feels as if it's not quite under her control. Alice digs her nails into the palms of her hands. If a vehicle comes round a blind corner they're going to hit it.

'Where are we going?' asks Alice, unable to stop the wobble in her voice.

'Where are we going? Mum repeats. 'The road to recovery. The road to nowhere. A dead-end road. The long and winding road. You tell me.'

Frozen tendrils reach down Alice's lungs. Some creature made of ice is hooking itself on to the inside of her chest. It is difficult to speak but she manages to mumble out the words: 'What does that mean?'

Mum flicks her head round to look at Alice. Her glacial eyes fix her own and within them lives... nothing Alice can understand.

'It means that I'm taking you on a journey. I'm taking you on a journey into nothing.'

Alice tries to say something but she's become dumb. She is frozen into dumbness. This isn't her mother.

'You know he's watching us don't you?'

Alice starts trembling all over.

'I can feel him here. Can't you? And you know what; I think he's watching us from the future. Long after we're dead. He's found a pathway back to us from some far off future when you and I are nothing. He's come back because he has to come back and confront what he has done to me and to you. Can't you feel him Ally? He's here... inside of us.'

Mum takes both hands off the wheel and cups them around Alice's face.

'MUM!'

The shout jolts mum out of her freakiness and she clasps the wheel again, pulling the car back onto the left side of the road. Alice unbuckles herself from the seatbelt. The next chance she gets she is going to open the door and dive out.

'I have been on the edge for so long,' says mum, her voice angry and vitriol-fuelled again. 'I have been on the receiving end for so, so long. I have held it together over the past few years because of you two. You haven't even noticed. And now I find out what you've been doing... you haven't noticed me because of what you've been doing. I gave birth to you. I brought you into the world. Then I was left alone to cope. And this is my reward. My fucking reward.'

The rain is now lashing against the windscreen but mum hasn't increased the wiper speed. The water on the screen turns the road ahead into a melange of disassociated lights and dark shapes.

'Everything always seemed so calm,' she continues, the unhinged lilt returning to her voice. 'So many people on the blocks lead such chaotic lives, always pumped up with some emotion or another, and usually on drugs. But we, we happy three, we were always mellow and calm, and aware of each other. No arguments, no feelings hurt, no... no despising. But now I know that that was probably because you two realised your secret would be best kept by an environment without hysterics.'

Mum's shoulders slump as if she were spent. Nothing left to say. Alice takes her left hand from the door handle.

'You don't really think he's watching us do you?' Alice doesn't know why that matters quite so much, but it does. She feels that perhaps mum's psychotic behaviour allows her access to certain realisations that are usually kept under wraps. She had always suspected that mad people had a better grasp on reality than everyone else... even temporarily mad people.

Mum slumps again. She takes her eyes from the road and then butts her forehead against the top of the steering wheel. Alice's hand automatically darts for the door handle again. But she knows she won't jump. It's not that she is afraid of hurting herself, rather it is because it is now clear to her that she needs to stay with mum, to see this through, wherever it is going. Funny, she had always thought that the reason the three of them stuck together so well and for so long was due to not needing anyone else. They were always a self-contained unit. But the Secret has now caught up with her, with them.

Mum continues to drive with her head unnaturally stooped and lowered. The rain is getting heavier, but still she isn't turning up the wiper speed.

'Have you ever taken a psychedelic drug Ally?'

The words are slurred and for the first time Alice wonders whether mum has been drinking. 'Ecstasy,' she replies, tensing up at where this might be going.

'This feels like I'm on a trip,' says mum, ignoring Alice. 'It isn't real is it? At least it isn't a consensus reality.'

Alice's eyes grow big. *Consensus reality.* Mum must have been reading another self-help book. The thought momentarily makes Alice smile, but it is no more than a moment.

'Do you know what I think?'

Alice bites her lip. 'No.'

'I think that what we think of as everyday, normal life isn't real. It's only when we take a drug, go mad or have some enormous emotional upset that we can find out what reality is really like.'

'You sound like—'

'Your brother. Yes I know. And do you know what else I think? I think he's taking some very special drugs in the future and coming back to us... watching us, feeling everything we do – all as part of the real reality.'

Alice suddenly realises that the shock of discovering the Secret has tipped mum over the edge. All the anger, hatred and regret are just the automatic reactions of a person who has flipped their lid. They're not real. They are just the outward appearances of madness covering itself – giving itself time by fooling other people that the host is reacting in a normal way when in actual fact insanity is taking over every region of consciousness.

'I don't think so mum,' says Alice as gently as she can.

'I can feel him here. I feel him like I used to feel him in my womb. It's as if we are one.'

Mum closes her eyes and the car drifts back towards the side of the road. When the near side wheels bobble against the verge she opens her eyes with a start and pulls the car up straight again. She looks at Alice. Alice can't decide what the look means, but there is a hint of questioning in it. Her mouth speaks words without her thinking.

'Mum, I'm pregnant.'

They don't exist in the way existence is usually understood. They slink around at the borders of perception, inhabiting a folkloric reality that you will only occasionally touch, if you're lucky... or unlucky. They'll be there when you die though. And you're gonna need 'em.

Can things happen without any time passing at all? As the car speeds up and starts to slide sidewards towards some kind of big machinery parked up in a lay-by Alice is as sure as she can be that the passage of time has stopped. She glimpses the branches of trees through the side window, their wet leaves not moving. She stares at the water on the windscreen static and globular, reflecting shafts of atrophied light in its stillness. And there is no sound. There is an audible resonance but it is not produced by anything external to Alice. It's inside, deep inside. In fact, it's so deep that she begins to think that it's not actually a part of her but part of something bigger, much bigger... infinitely bigger.

Her eyes focus to the glistening road ahead. There is still no movement beyond the car but there are people in the road. There are little people dancing in a ring around an overgrown toadstool in the road. Alice knows they are not part of any world of tarmac and machines but she can't quite grasp how they seem to be moving when everything else has stopped. The car is spinning and turning over, she knows this but she can't feel it. All she comprehends is the little people dancing in a circle and the deep audio breaking against her consciousness like the non-existent underwater waves in the Sea of Tranquillity.

At the moment of impact they come up close to the little people. Alice smiles a final smile as she sees in detail their grizzled, grumpy little faces and their black, shining eyes. One of them breaks the circle and is immediately close to Alice. For an instant she knows what it is like to share an emotion with an alien being. It/he/she looks her in the eye and imparts an empathy that she didn't realise existed. In that instant she is released from fear and released from life. It helps to prepare her for what she's about to go through.

The vehicle hit the hammerhead cranes in the lay-by at a speed of between eighty and ninety kilometres per hour. The vehicle had probably already turned over several times after the driver lost control on the wet road surface and little remained intact of the chassis above the floor. The two females in the front seats of the vehicle would have been killed instantly upon impact, as it seems that the windscreen was the first point of impact. At that speed the chances of survival for the driver and front-seat passenger were nil. Neither female had been wearing a seatbelt, but it is unlikely that this contributed to the fatal injuries as the upper chassis was largely destroyed by the said impact. Both females received fatal injuries to the head. There is no evidence that any other person or persons were involved in the accident. The two females were announced dead at the scene of the accident and taken to the district hospital mortuary to await the pending identification by a relative.

The faery stoops over Alice's torn-apart body and sadly shakes its head. It turns its almond-shaped black eyes to me and they are filled with tears, one of which falls onto her blood soaked black hair that covers her smashed up head.

'We'll look afters,' it tells me telepathically. 'Violent deaths always most difficults.' It scrunches up its snubbed nose and scratches its shock of red hair underneath its tricorn hat. 'But you's been heres longs enough. Needs go backs. Oh, tells Oberon et Titania -- need tryptamine compound carrying second N-methyl group.' It winks. 'But only clue I'm geevings.'

Jesus H-pole-vaulting-fucking Christ.

XX

The hazy ambience of the late afternoon seemed to embrace all my senses. The heat haze hovering over the grass of the combe felt lurid against my skin and I smelt the sumptuous vegetative growth of everything around me in the heavy, honeyed air. In the background the lazy trilling of summer birds was layered over the hush of trees, whose gradual movement in the windless air was at the edge of audible perception.

Sweat coated my back, causing my T-shirt to stick to the skin and my eyes were tired from squinting into the bright day all afternoon. I'd forgotten to bring either sunglasses or a hat and so the sun was taking it out on me, making me a part of the unprotected environment. I wiped the sweat from my forehead and flapped my T-shirt to create some cool flow of air over my body. I wanted to take it off, but the combination of the bandage on my stomach and the thought that I might bump into someone prevented me. I was not ready for any interaction, but if I did have to speak to someone I didn't want to look like an escaped detainee.

I had found an old Ordnance Survey map of the area in the library and had followed a footpath that led from the house in the opposite direction from the village. I wanted to get into the countryside, away from the house, away from roads, and definitely away from people. I thought that the little red-dotted footpath on the map led up the side of a ridge, but my map-reading skills were evidently not what they should be as I found myself heading down into a riverless valley that ended in a steep-sided combe. I stood under the shade of a big oak tree and surveyed the map for a route that didn't involve climbing the combe-side, but unless I went back the way I had come there was no choice. Slowly, with a determination that was mimicking self-flagellation, I started the slog up the combe, following the slight footpath to the top.

It was worth it. As I reached the crest a view of summer pulchritude spanned out before me. It took in the easily defined patchwork of brown and yellow fields within a mile of my view, the indefinite green wooded hills in the middle distance, and on the far horizon the glimmering, nebulous line of the sea. I sat down and squinted at it. My heart pumped hard from the climb and I was feeling a little dizzy. This was the most exertion I had had for a long time and the hot sun sapped me further, so after taking in the view I laid back and closed my eyes. My heart was still working hard and its thumping superseded the sounds of nature around me. Somehow the throbbing seemed divorced from my environment. It was subterranean; existing in spite of the vast array of the landscape that I presumed still existed beyond my closed eyes. I was an implant there, a transitory visitor amongst a world that worked on a circular, seasonal basis of time that continued unaffected by my linear intrusion. My pulsing heart signified the difference.

After a while of internal chatter, structured around the vibratory resound of my heart, my mind started to turn back to the trip. I had suppressed the recall all day but now it was pushing aside all other thoughts and forcing me to confront it. What startled me most was the clarity of it. All I had to do was call to mind Alice's face and she would be there. I had every detail: her reddened eyes, the tear droplet running between her breasts, the nervous shaking of her hands. But most agitating were her thoughts. I had them all as though the neural activity were my own. Everything was there, the whole gamut of quivering, fear-filled emotions blurring the distinction between her and me. But most of all it was the sorrow. I had never touched anything quite like it. Alice clung to it like a life raft. Amidst the storm of mum's disbelieving rage Alice had this to keep her afloat. And somehow it was an *old* sorrow. It was that of an old person whose life-long partner has died – not the immediate grief, but rather the all-encompassing, sickening sorrow that settles in afterwards and never leaves. Alice had this and embraced it. She used it to stave off the madness. It comforted her. And I would never have understood it before I was given access to her internal world.

I shifted my position uneasily and opened my eyes. I breathed deeply and closed them again. She was there once more. But what did I mean by *there*? This problem was still travelling with me, still lodging amongst the everyday. How is a memory trapped in consciousness? I'd heard the explanations from Ober but the descriptions always fell short. I could understand the mechanics of it: hippocampi accept new input from external source, input becomes consolidated in the temporal lobe, and memory exists. But how is this *experienced*? What is the experience of that existence?

Since I had started to take psychedelics with Ober I had begun to realise that in an altered state of consciousness there is an awareness of the experience. The nearest I had ever got to pinning it down was that it was like a consciousness observing itself. The existence of a memory is observed and therefore it exists. When you have been taken over by a psychedelic you become a third party to whatever depths of your subconscious you happen to be observing. But it's more than just ego breakdown and disassociation; the memory is getting burnt into something bigger... Ober's Phylogenic Memory. I got the impression that there was a subtle difference in meaning between this and the collective subconscious -- something about the level of control an individual could exert on them -- but to be honest I was quite certain that I simply did not have the intellectual ability to grasp it. It would, like so many things, always be beyond my mental grasp.

But what I did know was that the imagery in my head was clearer than I could ever remember. A residual of the super-reality of the trip was lingering and making my thoughts sharp and pristine. The memory of it was not the foggy sense of half-formed images that usually represented people, things, places, spaces, smells and stimuli for me. Instead, with my eyes closed, I could experience the car journey trip as though it were happening again. I could open my eyes and escape, but as soon as I shut them again the shocking realism of Alice's and mum's emotive existences made me shudder and gasp for air. It was a reality that eschewed the five senses and relied instead on a sense that collected its information from an unknown space, a space where time didn't exist, a space of infinite capacity. A space called God—

I jolted alert and instinctively pressed my palms to the ground to assure myself I wasn't falling. Why had that trip happened? Why had my mind been carried there to witness... to witness what exactly?

I rolled over onto my side and looked through the blurry grass stalks into the distance. I didn't want to believe what I had seen – more than seen: felt, experienced, lived. My stomach lurched as the crystalline images flooded back to me. As much as I wanted it to go away I still couldn't stop myself closing my eyes again and allowing it back. It came in waves. It washed over me like a liquid presence. Alice's sweet, sweet face and her every whispered thought that had synchronised with my own. We had always felt the connection: the knowing looks and touches with which we sometimes communicated, especially after we made love. But this had been different. I was the same person as her; we shared the same mind. And however much I attempted to rationalise it I could not believe anything else, because the trip had had the substance of concrete reality.

Concrete. My internalisation turned back to the blocks. It seemed a long time ago since I lived there. The year of existence in the flat after they died was cloudy and insubstantial. The only memories that stood out like beacons were the LSD trips. The recollection of them actually seemed to be getting stronger with time rather than diminishing. I thought back to the ceiling of assholes. It seemed a definite place at a fixed time. And it was a place and time that was linked to all the other trips; all the other altered states of consciousness.

I stood up with the thought. My heart began to race. It was as if there were a door opening. I closed my eyes and there it was -- the abrupt unfolding of a silken door. The memory of my trips on the phenethylamines started to slot into place. Ever since my trip with Alice Liddell I had been visiting the same place. It was not somewhere that could be pinned down or be made to fit neatly into our consensus reality. It didn't share the same physical laws and it didn't share the same time. In fact there was no time there. It was a place where everything that has ever happened, anywhere anytime, exists as a single entity, which can be accessed under special circumstances. But it's more than just a recording of life or history past and future. It has every thought, feeling and emotion ever experienced by every species that has ever existed... on this world and on other worlds.

I opened my eyes and started to pace around. I was on the verge of some sublime understanding. I was sure that I just needed to tip this over a touch and all would be revealed.

I closed my eyes. I swayed. If only I could just apply some logic to this I could begin to answer questions. The imagery of my altered states was beginning to flow back to me. It was like a river... no, not a river, a flow of information, a surge of atoms that contained within their whole... everything. Why had my trips taken me to certain places? I scrunched my eyes as if this would help me concentrate on an answer. Was it for help? I thought of Syd Barrett, the rebirth from the prehistoric barrow, and the six phases shown me by Ober. They didn't happen sequentially with normal reality. They were death, dreaming and infinity, and I was able to touch them when the neurotransmitters in my brain that usually kept control of reality were morphed by the chemicals into something more... something more real.

But was it all just designed to help cure my depression and anxiety disorders? Who was controlling it? Did anything control it? I cursed my limited intellect. If the meaning of existence was going to be revealed to anyone why would it be me? I was just some underclass nothing whose inadequate attempts to educate himself had merely shown up the limitations of someone with restricted abilities. I knew I was on the edge of some realisation but I couldn't quite take that extra step. I was unable to take it.

I breathed deeply and sat back down on the grass, eyes closed. The sharp imagery of the UFO club implanted itself before me. I could see the creases in one of the freak's clothes, smell the cannabis and hear the distorted music as clearly as if it were happening in front of me. 1967, five years before I was born. Why had the trip so immersed me in it? Why there? Why those people, that place?

A squawking crow overhead brought me back to the hillside. Or maybe not. Once again, things weren't quite right, weren't quite as solid and trustworthy as they should have been. The ground under my feet was amorphous and insubstantial. It was as if I could sense the world turning on its axis.

I breathed deeply once again. With eyes closed my imagination switched to the village and my visit to the pub. Until that moment I'd remembered it as something that had got mixed up with the trips before and after. I had thought I'd been imposing psychedelic imagery onto a normal, if somewhat traumatic, memory of a sojourn to a slightly odd country village. But suddenly, for the first time, I realised that perhaps the things that had happened to me in the village were the result of me being only partially there. I was tripping when I went there and some of what I experienced was happening in the... whatever it's called... the Phylogenic World. The androgens, the green man, the falling asleep – they only seemed to happen because I was on something, and that meant that I might well be on something all the time. Titania had said as much, but until this moment I had got her words muddled up and confused with so many other things that it hadn't meant anything. And if I was on something then, why not now?

I started off along the ridgeway, marching along the footpath with my hands in my pockets. It was there again, like an ambient tune in the back of my head, creating a backdrop to everything I experienced. It was nothing more than a vague sense that I was about to be switched on to something over which I had no control but its presence was unmistakable. Where the fuck was it coming from? I was getting agitated. I stopped and rifled in my small backpack for the joint I'd pre-rolled before coming out. I lit it with a shaking hand and took the longest draw I could manage. I must have rolled it a bit strong because immediately it sent the shivers round my skull and down my spine. But it was good. The agitation slunk away and I resumed my walk easier, less worried.

After a while I came off the higher ground and followed the footpath on the map down into a wooded valley. I was heading for a little hamlet from where I could pick up a minor road that led back to the house – about five kilometres I reckoned. Once in the wood and on the clay path I started unconsciously to filter out the physical surroundings of leaf, bark and undergrowth and to allow the images of the car journey to reform.

Alice was looking at me, but not with her eyes. It was just pure contact between us, a brother and sister who had shared the same womb interacting at a level that I was beginning to understand could only be touched when a psychedelic enabled it. At least *I* could only touch it when a psychedelic enabled it. Her image was unreal and yet so astoundingly present that I knew some chemical was working on my brain. It wasn't the cannabis. It might be a residual from my last trip, seeping through in the form of a muted flashback. But flashbacks usually announced themselves more sharply, more completely than this. This was more like the ambient tune floating around my head, suggesting, intimating, and whispering ideas -- powerful, infinite ideas. I was expecting the world around me to alter, but it didn't. I just kept getting closer and closer to Alice. I had been with her in the car and she was with me now. She was nurturing me. Or was it mum nurturing me? I was beginning to get Alice and mum mixed up. Their characters were dissipating and becoming one. They were fading away like shadows into the night. They had become the night. It was folding its nocturnal arms around me and telling me everything was ok. The voices whispered.

There is no death, there is no individuality, there is only oneness. You're experiencing oneness with them. You touch them so that they become you. And it is at that point you realise you are being held and stroked by intercessors, because it is they who know the truth and will be able to guide you through when your own deluded view of reality has broken down.

I'd come to a halt, instantly tired. My chin had dropped into my chest. I slowly raised my heavy, ponderous head. The greens and browns of the wood blurred and then sharpened into definite, recognisable shapes but the underlying, whispering intelligence was still distorting things. The intelligence was both loving and menacing. I attempted to understand it but I couldn't. It contained mum and Alice but they and it weren't being experienced from any perspective. There couldn't be any perspective because everything was one.

I blinked hard several times, shook my head then walked quickly through the remainder of the wood. It all began to fall back into normality. The clay path became hard-standing, then, beyond a metal gate a tarmac lane. This came out into the hamlet. It was starting to get dark. Christ knew how long I'd been in the wood. I made my way past the few thatched cottages clustered around a crossroads and then onto the narrow sunken road that my map assured me would take me back to the house.

But my head was in an in-between place. The car crash was beginning to repeat itself over and over in my mind. It was like a neural stuck record. It was almost as if it were attempting to burn itself into my memory, attempting to ensure I got the message.

The tree-lined sunken road became darker in the gloaming twilight and I kept my eye on the mauve and orange patch of dusk sky in the distance where the holloway rose up to a level with the surrounding fields and became free of trees. Within the sable ambience I sensed the intelligence. It postured and filled the space. It followed me and surrounded me. It melded into the darkening silhouettes of trees and slithered along the banks of the road. It had a message but it wasn't sure I was ready to receive it. It spoke in the voice of insects and birds filling the air with its arcane evening sound.

I walked on and reached the spot where the road rose up from its sunken route. I stopped, slightly breathless, and went over to a wooden field gate breaking a barbed wire fence that ran along the side of the road separating it from the pasture fields beyond. The fields stretched upwards on a shallow rise. The twilight coloured them a deep satin green. I realised I'd never seen anything like it. I leant on the gate and looked back over my shoulder at the road. It had blackened. I couldn't decide if there was something there or not. I turned back to the fields and strained my eyes to the top of the rise.

The summer dusk took over everything. I was no longer certain whether I was tired or just being lulled into a warm twilight world where tiredness is simply a state of being. All was encompassed within the lazy, drowsy ambience of the place. There were no people, no buildings, and no sound except the background drone of unseen life. Two electric-blue butterflies skipped by the gate and swirled and zigzagged their intertwining way into the fields until they were subsumed by the deep shadows. I squinted to follow them but they had disappeared. I closed my eyes. I swayed. This place was so far removed from the violence of the car crash and yet it contained something of the same overwhelming sorrow that I had shared with Alice at that moment. Did this particular piece of landscape really contain feelings? Or was it simply me imposing the detritus of my past on it, triggered by the suppressed gloom? Perhaps it was both.

And then I heard children. They were laughing and screaming in the distance, only barely audible. I opened my eyes and looked again to the top of the rise now silhouetted against the cloudless crimson sky. At one end of my view I noticed for the first time the uneven rooflines of a cluster of buildings, probably a farmhouse or something. The laughing seemed to come from there. The sounds ebbed and flowed with the dictates of a light breeze but second by second they became louder until I could almost differentiate individuals amidst the clamour. I enjoyed it. Their unfettered childish joy seemed to match the summer dusk and the rolling, barely visible landscape. I pictured Alice as a child, screaming her head off in wild abandon on top of the slide in the fenced-off playground in the blocks. I was older and was slightly embarrassed by her wilfulness, but that didn't matter as much as the connection between us. We belonged to each other. It was just another moment from the past, but it had been activated by my present. Alice was there, existing in my mind as completely as if she had been standing in front of me.

But then I made the mistake of closing my eyes. The little girl became conflated with the grown woman. Both were my sister but the woman now came laced with the association of guilt. I had witnessed the crash because it was my fault. The drugs had found out what was hidden at the heart of me and exposed it in every last shuddering detail. My stomach lurched and I instantly slipped over the fine line that depression draws in weak, feeble minds like mine. It never took much and this was more than enough. I slumped against the gate.

In the distance the shouts and screams immediately lost their exuberance and became panicked and afraid. It was as if they were mimicking my own mood slippage. Oh... they were.

The sky is blood and the courtyard farmhouse is a knotty, medieval construction from a particularly nasty folktale. The children are screaming. Their fear thickens the air. It is unadulterated fear, fear that only shows itself in the innocent mind. No fucking wonder either. They're being herded out of the farmhouse and into the courtyard. Their clogs tap out a tuneless percussion on the cobbles. Who's doing the herding? I can't see them at first, but they're big. They loom over the cordon of children. I don't want to but I'm going to have to range up close. I have to know. I zoom in. They are, of course, aliens. They are huge, barrel-chested beasts with cloven hoofs and maniac faces. Jesus, that's horrible. Half a dozen of them push and kick the tied-up children to one side of the courtyard. Everything is red. The whole scene is cast in a relentless reddened sheen that seems to accentuate shadows over light.

And that's where they're going – to the gallows. There are three massive gallows constructed out of living trees in the corner of the courtyard. They are beech trees I think, moulded into shape especially for the kiddies. Mummy, mummy, mummy – that'll do you no good now little ones. These fuckers don't care about you beyond the fear they can extract. And up goes the first one – neck stretched, hands tied, legs flailing, eyes popping out. They're all made to watch. Their faces are wrenched by the beasts, made to look up at little John Paul. Woah, they are fucking wild. They know death is coming and that it's going to be particularly painful. Up goes number two and three. The beasts are having a fine old time. They're loving every minute of it. But three gallows is not enough. The leader of the beasts intones his unseen god and there are suddenly enough gallows for all. Up they go, beast-handled into the nooses, all of them. They're swinging in the red air. They are dead and dying, the latter in the greatest of pain. How the beasts laugh and guffaw at their suffering. The last to die has her feet tugged hard by the leader. She snaps. The leader turns to look at me--.

I opened my eyes. I vomited into the bush at the side of the gate. The vision of the noosed-up children flooded my brain. There was only one solution to my predicament. If it hadn't been for the headlights coming up the road and turning dusk into an artificial space, I would have been hanging on the back of an overdose before midnight.

I was kneeling on the ground. The car stopped in front of me, the engine and headlights were switched off and Ober got out.

XXI

The sudden loss of light made everything seem black. It must have taken me a minute or two to re-associate myself with the ground, the bush, the gate and Ober.

'I thought I might find you here,' he said, offering me his hand to pull me up. 'Are you alright?'

I looked up at him then got up to my feet without taking his hand. It was too quick though and my head rushed creating a spangled world of my own. I grabbed the gate for support. The children and the monsters were funnelling off into the nether regions of my brain but the experience left a grimy residual that made me want to crawl into the darkness and be alone.

'How did you know I'd be here?' I asked, attempting to sound in control.

'I just did. I've told you that you need round the clock monitoring.'

'Monitoring?'

Ober didn't reply. He offered me a small bottle of water. I took it and drank. It was good to wash away the acrid taste of vomit. I wished the images of strung up children could be dealt with as easily.

'Are you alright?'

'I guess, yeah.'

He allowed the silence to douse the moment. He evidently was not too concerned with what had just happened.

'Titania tells me you had a high-grade experience yesterday.'

'High-grade?' I was testy. I didn't want to discuss anything at that moment, and certainly not the car crash.

'A trip from which you remember all the details in high-grade detail.'

Ober leant against the gate looking over the darkened fields beyond. Behind him the last vestige of the summer sun smattered a lone cloud in the west with an underbelly of deep, unearthly red. I could just make out his unmoving features.

'Yes. I saw them killed in a car crash.'

'And did you think... do you still think you saw what really happened?'

I leant on the gate looking into the same blackness as Ober. 'I don't know. I seemed to be inside Alice's head, feeling everything she felt, experiencing all her emotions. It was like there was no difference between us, no separate identities. It was like... like I was touching her memory.'

'That's a nice way of putting it,' said Ober, sounding genuine. 'You know you can touch it at any time you want when you've taken an appropriate dose and the set and setting are right.'

I shuddered and my stomach started to feel queasy again. 'I don't want to experience that again thanks.' A crystal clear image of Alice's face being lacerated by a giant shard of broken glass swept through my brain. 'Once was enough.'

'I don't mean the crash. I mean your relationship with your sister... and your mother. You can access their memories any time. And you can access your memories of them at any time.'

I turned to Ober, but his features were hidden in the dark. I realised that I was never sure if he was simply engaging in conversation with me or if everything he said was part of a contrived psychological design, all planned out as a grand catechism. I moved my hands over the roughened wood of the gate. I was tensing up.

'How do you know this Ober? I hardly told Titania anything this morning. How do you know where I went on my trip?'

I sensed him smile in the darkness.

'You are recovering my friend,' he said. 'You've gradually been working towards an acceptance of what has happened in your life. You will, in time, be able to integrate all aspects of your past into your present and then allow them to form part of your future. The crash was just something you needed to know about. And you might be blaming yourself and be having thoughts of self-harm on the back of it...' he paused and looked at me. I caught a tiny glimmer of light in his eyes. It must have been reflected starlight -- Venus hanging low above the horizon. '...But, you need to see this as a pivotal moment in your development rather than a reason for any guilt-induced thinking or actions.'

Ober's words bypassed me. I had other things dumping their load on me.

'She was pregnant.'

'Alice?'

'Yes, Alice.' There was a quiver in my throat. 'And... and I knew it. I knew it before the trip. Some of the LSD sessions had shown me it, shown me the truth of it. She was pregnant with my child.'

The tears started to sting my eyes. The crash had made implicit knowledge explicit. How had my life come to this?

Was I just stumbling through a pre-ordained existence like an automaton without any free will at all? Did any of my choices matter? I hung my head.

'Is this what this is about?' said Ober, somehow making it quite clear what "this" meant.

'It was a... what do you call it... an HPDD. There were kids and monsters up on the hill. They were hanging them, killing them. Not nice.'

'Indeed.'

'I'm surprised you didn't know all about it.' The irony sunk quickly.

'Mmm.'

'Oh, you did know. So what does it mean – anything?'

'I don't think now is the moment to psychoanalyse it my friend. I think we should probably be heading back to the house. Titania's been cooking something special. One of her Vegan rarities I believe.'

'Are the kids our dead children, and the monsters our incest?'

'Incest?' he said.

'Yes – the gruesome beast.'

'First time you've used the word.'

'Is it?'

'Yes. Come on, let's go.'

We got into the car and drove off along the lane, moths and insects dying violent deaths amidst the momentary illumination of our headlights. I closed my eyes.

Titania was standing at the cooker range stirring the contents of some big copper pans as we came in the kitchen door at the back of the house. I was still shaky and a bit queasy. The flashback, or whatever it was, kept pinching me and imposing its greusomeness on me. But the kitchen's ambience was soft and distilled from the world outside and Titania's cooking smelt wonderful – exotic and heavily spiced. She looked pretty wonderful as well. She seemed to get younger and better looking every time I saw her. And her clingy purple dress was setting off all the right curves. The car crash and the kiddies on the gallows had made the physicality of humanity repulsive to me, but I seemed to be able to make an exception for Titania. I knew I was probably starting to idealise her – her kooky behaviour should have made me want to keep my distance but instead I found myself wanting to be close to her... closer and closer.

'You've found our wanderer then,' she said to Ober, turning for a second to arch an eyebrow.

'Yes... I think perhaps a rest before dinner would be good. How long?'

'Forty minutes.'

I spent most of them in the bath, attempting to cleanse the day out of me. By the time I came down Ober was spreading out some heavy clay dishes onto the kitchen table, each one containing some delicious looking beany or rice concoction. Titania brought a plate of fresh flat bread with a pitcher of water and we started to eat.

It was the first time since I'd come to the house that I'd spent any time with either of them talking about nothing in particular. Titania told us how she'd made the East African Vegan food and Ober talked about the difficulty of finding building contractors in this part of the country with the traditional building skills to work on the house. It was just normal small talk chatter but it felt good. It completely overturned what had happened earlier. And trust began to embed itself once again, squeezing out the juicy paranoia that I'd started to attach to the motives of them both. I still had the underlying suspicion that they were manipulating every second of my life but they were evidently making an effort to restore my confidence in them and I appreciated it. In fact it felt like a turning point, it felt like I was moving upwards.

I didn't stutter at all.

Afterwards we retired to the living room with some weird spiced-up coffee that Titania had made and a small tin of nice looking resin.

'I was at the local hospital today,' said Ober, firing up his zippo under a resin block. 'There's a large psychiatric ward there – I worked there for several years some while ago.'

He was sounding a bit stiff. It was fairly obvious that the narrative was a lead up to something involving me. Titania moved onto the couch next to me.

'Don't worry, we're not going to get you admitted,' she

said, smiling out the side of her eyes. 'Not unless you're a particularly bad boy that is.'

I laughed nervously.

'There is also a patient there who I've been working with over the past few months, continued Ober. 'He was diagnosed as schizophrenic about a year ago.'

'And he had a pretty hard time of it,' Titania cut in, 'too much Clozapine and not enough people listening to him... it's an antipsychotic drug used to treat positive type schizophrenia in its acute phase.'

I looked from Titania to Ober. 'You don't have him on LSD now do you?'

'No, he is on a programme of medication with 2C-B.'

'*Really?*'

'Really. It's one of the mildest Phenethylamines. It does just enough to help us... understand the meaning of the psychosis. Not that psychosis is the term we should be using. Schizophrenia is in many ways no different than your own anxiety disorders – there are several similar symptoms.'

'He's just a sensitive soul dealing with a difficult world,' added Titania. 'The 2C-B is helping him come to terms with it. Just as we try to help him understand the meaning of his inner voices, so he helps us from his own perspective.'

Ober had packed an old-fashioned looking pipe with the resin and tobacco and lit up. It came to me via Titania.

'I thought that schizophrenic inner voices were just hallucinations,' I said, feeling the smooth uplift from two or three tokes. I was trying to think of the voices that had been appearing in my own head.

'No more than your trips are just *hallucinations*,' replied Ober. 'The content of what the voices say is important. They are not simply meaningless neurological symptoms brought about by a mental disorder.'

I was well aware that although I'd told Ober about hearing voices in the pub, I had not told him about the running commentary that had sometimes infiltrated my head since I'd come to the house. I tried to remember what they said but couldn't.

'There is a theory,' said Titania, taking the pipe and inserting it carefully between her lips, 'that previous to ancient civilisations becoming reliant on the written word everybody's consciousness was bicameral and that humans based all their decisions on the voices of the gods and goddesses that were constantly in their brains. That is – *everyone* was schizophrenic.'

I suddenly recalled my stoned stone-ager, hearing voices telling him to observe the opening of the goddess womb in the landscape. 'And so where do the voices come from?'

Titania flashed her eyes. 'Maybe you should just wait to ask him what he thinks.'

'Huh?'

'Francis.'

'Sorry?'

'Francis the Flute is the name he likes best, and he'll be joining us here for a little while from tomorrow. We're anxious to take him out of the hospital environment, even though his condition is still... acute.'

I took the pipe from Titania, her fingers brushing against mine. She looked at me as though I should understand some implicit signal.

'Don't worry, we'll be able to limit your contact time with him,' said Ober. 'You'll be under no pressure to interact any more than you want to. But you do need to know that he's been hospitalised for as long as he has for good reasons.'

'Violent?'

'Only to himself. He was first sectioned when he attempted to cut the voices out of his head with a Stanley knife.'

'Ouch.'

'But he's an interesting character. There's no reason why you can't be good for each other.'

'Is that why you're bringing him here?'

'Not really. His treatment is just part of the design.'

'The design?'

'Yes.'

I took another inhalation from the pipe. It must have been a lens of concentrated resin because it hit me like a train. I sank back into the couch and allowed the cryptic imagery of the high to meld in and out of my vision. The flush ran up my throat and around my skull. The air in my lungs tingled and

162

then expelled itself, hot and filled with its own energy. When I opened my eyes again I realised I must have lost time as Ober was gone and Titania had shifted her position on the couch. She looked like she'd been there for a little while.

'Still with us?' she said, her words echoing slightly.

'Yes... sorry. Where is... where's Ober?'

'He's left for the night. So it's just you and me.'

'Oh, right.'

'And seeing we're feeling cosy and a bit stoned I think you should talk to me a bit more about Alice... your Alice.'

Even under the influence my stomach leapt at the instantaneous image of Alice. 'Is that a good idea?'

'For sure. How do you feel now that you know she is pregnant?'

'*Was* pregnant.'

Titania shrugged. 'How do you feel?'

I took a couple of deep breaths. 'Well, to be honest, I feel a bit disgusted. I've always had a bit of an aversion to pregnant women. There's something alien-like about a creature growing inside another creature... like a ... a parasite.'

'And you even feel like this about Alice... and *your* child?'

'A bit. I'm sorry, I know it sounds odd.'

Titania waved away the apology. 'What else?'

'What do you think – sorrow, grief, pity... guilt.'

'Do you think Alice and the child still exist?'

'Still exist? In my memory?'

'In the Phylogenic Memory.'

I rubbed my fingers over my temples. 'I suppose. But that doesn't help me in the here and now does it.'

'Not even if you know their deaths are no more than a transition from one state to another. And you do know it don't you. Where do you think your treatment has been taking you?'

I was going to start crying if I wasn't careful. The shadows of Alice and mum were like a presence at my side and the impressionistic image of the foetus of *our* child was beginning to form more clearly in some part of my brain. I breathed deeply again. 'Is this what this is all about Titania? Are you conditioning me with the drugs like a ... a guinea pig.

163

Is this what the *research* is about? To see if people get better when they're not so hung up on themselves all the time.'

'We're hoping you'll do a little more than *get better*. But tell me more about Alice. Why were you in love with her?'

'Why? I guess we found a little bit of ourselves in each other. Our blood connection just seemed to make us different to everyone else and we both realised it. We'd always been close as kids, always cuddling up and hanging out together despite the age difference. And looking after mum drew us further together. There was so much love between us, all three of us. You know?'

'Love... yes, I know.'

'I can't remember a serious argument in all those years, just affection and mutual co-operation. Around us on the blocks families seemed to be in constant meltdown, permanent crises fuelled by drugs, poverty and hopelessness. I guess it enhanced our feeling of specialness, made us recognise... made us value the love. But then Alice went through a few bad short relationships with guys from her work. It distanced her from us. Quite natural of course, but it didn't feel like it at the time. So I moved out with some fellow losers on the blocks, for about six months I think. I hardly saw mum and Alice during that time.'

'And when you came back?'

' Mmm. When I came back Alice and I fell for each other. What else can I say? I'd never known anything like it. It was as if all of that affection, understanding and love that had built up over the years just suddenly exploded and became something much more. We couldn't keep our hands off each other. Of course, we had to hide it from mum, but that wasn't so hard. I don't think either of us even felt guilty about it; it was simply what had to be done. I loved her and she loved me and we had to be together no matter what.'

I took a breath. The cannabis was enhancing the visual imagery of Alice. I closed my eyes for a moment to see her more clearly. When I opened them again Titania had moved close to me and was scanning me with her luminescent turquoise eyes.

'But the sex was only a part of it,' I said, sensing the need to apologise without really knowing why. I started to come out with some hackneyed explanation of our feelings for one another but Titania pressed her index finger to my lips and shook her head.

'No need for that,' she said. 'I know what you felt. I know about the love. I know.'

She moved off the couch onto her knees at my feet, her dress hitching up over her knees. She put her hands on my thighs and stared at me for a moment, her eyes turned dark and glistening. I closed my eyes and silently asked Alice for her approval. I couldn't be sure whether the internal chuckle was hers or mine.

'You need another session soon,' she whispered, 'very soon. But there's been something missing from your treatment. It's been missing since your mother and Alice died hasn't it?'

I gulped and writhed under her touch. What did she want me to say? She moved her fingers up to my groin.

'Yes, I thought so. In my professional opinion I'd say what you need before we go any further with the treatment is an exceptionally hard fuck.'

I agreed.

XXII

They'll always be on your side, even when you think their voices are your own madness and their appearances nothing more than the hallucinated maelstrom of a drug-induced delirium. They are real. They are more real than anything you will ever know in this world. They are you.

The voices faded and became the vague creaks and shifts of the house timbers warming up with the new day. I opened my bleary eyes and made out the dull lines of window blinds keeping out most of the morning light in an unknown bedroom. I sat up in the bed, alone. A few moments later I had recovered most of the details from the previous night. Jeez she'd been wild. I felt the scratches on my face and back and my cock was painfully sore. I was red-faced embarrassed, despite being alone. It had been so different with me and Alice, and that was all I'd known of sex for years.

Unless, that is, I counted Alice Liddell, but I was still unsure about her place... her reality. Titania, however, was very real – very real and very much a woman in control -- big time.

In fact, she was so in control of everything that I wondered why she'd bothered with me. I was just a zoned out fruitcake from the city who was wandering around his own life as if it were someone else's. She must have been able to take her pick from anyone she wanted, including Ober. She didn't have to resort to screwing me. The suspicion that last night was just part of an overarching plan about which I knew nothing became stronger the longer I dwelt on Titania's motives. Everything could be made to fit into a preconceived scheme: the relaxing dinner, the strong dope, Ober disappearing, the tight, tight dress. But I had no ideas as to why. Maybe it was time I simply asked. Although asking Ober or Titania about anything rarely resulted in any type of clarification.

And then there was the memory of Alice. It was almost as if I were cheating on her. Was everything that had happened between us just for nothing? Had I merely fucked up both our lives, caused her death along with mum's, and then spiralled into mental illness? Being so easily seduced by someone I didn't know very well suggested to me that perhaps the connection I thought I'd had with Alice hadn't been as special as I'd believed. And if that were true then I should really be feeling guilty about what I'd pulled off.

But no, some perspective was needed here. It had been a year since they were killed and I'd finally felt able to get physically close to another person. Alice would understand. She was the most understanding person I'd ever known. Sex with Titania didn't diminish what there had been between us... between sister and brother. Nothing could.

I allowed myself to dwell on thoughts of Alice for some minutes before they started to drift back to the remembered scenes from last night. Titania had the most amazing body I'd ever seen. I started hardening up just thinking about her lithe muscularity and feral sexuality. And then embarrassment again. How inadequate I must have seemed. I was far more suited to the soft intensity of the lovemaking with Alice. But then we didn't have to try – the familial link ensured the depth of every touch and penetration.

The sound of a car drawing up on the gravel outside brought me to. I remembered Francis the Flute – another nutcase turning up for convalescence and whatever else Ober had planned. I wondered if Titania would fuck him as well.

I made my way out of the strange bedroom and back to my own at the other end of the landing. Five minutes later I was in the library, standing by the hi-fi stack pretending to leaf through a book when Ober arrived with his new psychiatric protégé. My stomach tensed up a bit but I was alright. I was going to cope with this. Ober moved him into the library. He was carrying a little longhaired, brown cat.

'This is the chap I've been telling you about Francis,' said Ober, his tone flat.

Francis was wide-eyed but seemed relatively calm. I had been expecting him to be babbling away to himself, but that was probably just my own clichéd ignorance.

'Yes, I know,' said Francis, his voice nasal and playful. 'I am Francis, Francis the Flute to friends like you.'

I studied him. I didn't want it to be true, but it was. He looked like Syd – Syd Barrett – without the hair. His hair was short and dyed bright red.

'What's your cat called?' I asked, unable to think of anything else to say.

'Bottom.'

'Right.'

'I am to sit down in this chair now,' said Francis to Ober. 'I will be able to gain a good perspective on the library then.'

I glanced at Ober who avoided eye contact. Francis handed him the cat, sat down with what was evidently a ritualised set of movements – straighten up in front of the chair, look around, then slowly lower the posterior with hands clasping the arms – then breathed deeply and closed his eyes. Ober smiled at him and grinned at me.

'Here, you take Bottom. I'm off to the village to meet up with Titania. I'll leave you two to make each other's acquaintance.'

The compliant, purring Bottom was flopped into my arms and Ober was gone. I sat down with the cat and observed Francis. He still seemed to have his eyes closed but I got the distinct impression that he was actually watching me from beneath his lashes. If I'd been told beforehand that I was going to be put into this situation I would have resisted totally. I should really have been shaking, sweating and ready to stutter when prompted. But instead I was calm and quite mellowed. Perhaps the absurdity of my circumstance had overridden my anxieties.

'I am told not to make small talk,' said Francis, without opening his eyes. 'We know each other's situation so there is no profit in exchanging meaningless pleasantries.'

'Ok. Who's telling you?'

He flicked open his eyes. I couldn't quite make out the colour but I could make a pretty good guess. He stiffened his lips into a strange, plastic smile.

'You know very well who is telling me,' he said, bringing his fingers together. He beckoned to Bottom who jumped down from my lap and onto his. 'You know I have been diagnosed as a schizophrenic?'

'Yes I do.'

'But you also know that Oberon has recognised the consistency of the contact and messages that are given to me.'

'Well, he hasn't actually told me that much to be honest.'

Francis cocked his head and lost eye contact for a moment. He was beginning to make me feel more normal than I had for a long time.

'I am to tell you. All in a straightforward fashion so that there are no misunderstandings.' He leaned forward in the chair. 'I have been much better since Oberon took me under his wing and made me aware. I did not understand things until that time.'

'Good... that's good.'

He sat back stroking the cat and cocking his head again. I felt an obligation to speak but thought better of it and just waited. About a minute later he regained tentative eye contact and started speaking.

'They used to frighten me – the voices. They came out of nowhere one day, as I was waking up in the morning, yelling at me, screaming orders in my head. I was living in a squat see, and I was sure the others had implanted something in my head, some kind of transistor. I thought they were operating the voices themselves. They never liked me. Always trying to get rid of me.'

He stopped abruptly, closed his eyes and smiled. He was speaking at breakneck speed in a voice that was all accents and none. I was quite glad of the intermission.

'Yes, always,' he continued, eyes opening slowly. 'It went on for days. The voices got clearer and clearer. They never stopped until I went to sleep. I was crazy at the others. Eventually they got me and beat me up. And as they were beating me up the voices were laughing and telling me that it wasn't them who were doing the talking. There was no transistor – the voices were the voices of the gods.'

'The gods?'

'Sumerian gods. They had been made quiet by humanity for thousands of years and were angry and bitter. But some people could still be made to hear their pronouncements and orders. I was one of those people. They whisper and then... SHOUT!'

I started in my chair. I wanted to laugh but I wasn't sure how he'd react so I stifled it. He grinned and continued.

'After they beat me up I was told by the gods to build a ziggurat in the front room. So I brought in all the earth from the garden, made it wet and started to build it up as they told me to, right up to the ceiling. The gods were going to appear at the top when it was completed. They provided full instructions.'

'What did your housemates think of that?'

Francis pulled a worried looking face. 'Oh, they were angry. They were very angry. They threw me out on the street. The gods would not stop yelling at me when that happened. I could not shut them up. They just kept ordering me to do things, first of all saying that they would help me and then turning on me and castigating me for my stupidity. In the end I had to try cutting them out of my head. I had been sleeping at the dump for weeks. I found a sharp knife and tried to cut them out. They screamed, but their screams were in Sumerian so I did not understand.'

I attempted to keep my eyes from widening too much.

'And then I was in the madhouse. Strapped down at first. It was probably the nineteenth century when that happened.'

'Pardon.'

'Nineteenth century – you know. The gods came with me. Kept calling me a cunt, although I am not too sure of the Sumerian translation for that.'

'Slow down Francis, I'm not quite sure I'm with you here.'

'Well, it does not matter too much. The drugs did not work for me – probably because they were so Victorian and old-fashioned -- so they gave me one called Clozapine. That brought me up to date all right. And it shut the gods up. They had to go back to their mangy old tombs on the Euphrates. But the drugs gave me a fever and stabbing palpitations... I thought my heart was going to break out of my ribcage. And that is when Ober took over. Swept them aside he did. Started to talk to me. No one had done that before.'

'You were taken off the drugs?'

He nodded. 'That brought the voices back, but...' He moved his head from side to side for a few moments. '... But they were now different. Ober was helping me to understand them – translate them.'

'So they weren't Sumerian gods anymore?'

Francis gave me a pouty smile. 'You know they were not. You know where they come from.'

'Do I?'

He leaned forward as far as he could with Bottom on his lap and placed a conspirational hand to the side of his face.

'The Phylogenic Memory,' he whispered. 'It is imparting its wisdom to me.'

A tingle buzzed around my skull. His eyes were turquoise.

'The voices were never Sumerian gods. I simply misinterpreted them. They are admonitions and directives and help from the great universal consciousness of which we are all a part.'

'Did Ober tell you that?' I asked, trying to think on my feet and ensure I said the right things.

He looked perplexed. 'Ober did not need to tell me anything. He just pointed me in the correct direction. Schizophrenia can be harnessed. It can be used to impart wisdom. Divine wisdom.'

'And what happened when Ober started to medicate you with the 2C-B?'

He sat back in the chair, tickling the cat under its chin. 'Medication?'

'Ober told me he is medicating you with a phenethylamine called 2C-B.'

'I see. I do not think of it as medication. It is rather, a mysterious semblance at the stand of nightmares.'

I gripped the chair handle. The tingle in my skull returned as a stinging pain that ran down my spine and dissipated into my abdomen. The moment was melded with my conversation with Syd. For that instance I couldn't differentiate the two.

'Syd?'

'Afraid not,' replied Francis, apparently knowing exactly what I meant. 'Although I am able to tap into what he represented and what he still means.'

I relaxed my grip marginally and allowed the soft morning light in the library to bring me back from wherever I was about to go.

'Is that down to the drugs or the schizophrenia?' I asked, my voice wobbly.

'Both probably. When I take the drug I go to the place from which my voices emanate. But you know this – I have seen you there.'

'Seen me there?'

'Or I should say *experienced* you there. How do you think everyone is monitored when they enter the altered state?'

My heart hammered into my ribcage. Instinctively I turned my head to look out the window in an automated attempt to give myself an instant to think about that. But Francis broke in – he was becoming a bit excited.

'Have you not worked out what they are doing yet? They are taking the mentally ill like us, like you and me, and allowing us to wander about in the Phylogenic Memory. We access it easier than straight people do. We cure ourselves with the wisdom that is there and help them to see the future. But it is a future that can be used by them. Not changed, no never changed, but used. More and more of us finding out that death is not real and greed and selfishness are diseases. No more egos and no more individuals. Everyone part of a

Collective. One big collective intelligence here on earth. It will seep out see, knowledge and wisdom will seep out from the universal consciousness, the Phylogenic Memory, and then a tipping point will be reached where enough people think and act the same way. A new heaven and a new earth.'

I tried to gulp but my throat was too dry. Francis leaned forward again; Bottom nestled against his stomach.

'The first heaven and the first earth... will have passed away.'

His whispered voice reverberated around the library. I stared at him. His eyes were wide and his lower lip quivered. I steadied my breathing as much as I could.

'Francis, I think...'

But I had no idea what I thought. Had I just had some questions answered or was I simply face to face with a lunatic? And whatever the answer, why had Ober manoeuvred us into this forced session?

'You think what?' he said, sounding suddenly calm. It is no good thinking and not saying. Although I am told that you do not understand many things as yet.'

'Who's telling you Francis?' I said, slumping back into the cushions.

'No need for that exasperated tone. I know you hear them as well. They just do not talk directly to you as yet. Always describing themselves in the third persona.'

He smiled and closed his eyes. Bottom's purring seemed to mimic his contentment.

'Who *are they* Francis?'

But my new schizophrenic housemate had withdrawn into his own world, probably listening to his voices and rooting himself somewhere far away.

I got up quietly and left him in the library, Bottom observing my exit with an amused feline grin.

XXIII

Things were speeding up. Where was this impression coming from? I was just standing in the garden, watching the crows loop between the high treetops down by the stream in the early evening haze. But there was a ratcheted-up intensity gripping me that made it seem as though events were moving all around me without me knowing about them. It was probably simply the knowledge that there was another person in the house, another person who was evidently not used to dealing with the everyday. His presence was most likely putting me on edge. Or it could be the fact that I'd not watched television or listened to the radio since I'd arrived at the house. No Internet either. The isolation could be making me nervy, and nervy equalled a perception that things were speeding up, happening without me.

But that wasn't quite right. The calm summer balm of the garden was like an extension of me at the moment. The soft blurred waves of contentment were washing over me, leaving me still and pacific. The depression was dissipating, my anxiety was difficult to recall and for the first time since mum and Alice were killed I was able to visualise them both without the full emotional lurch propagated by guilt and grief. There was no nervous agitation. To prove it to myself I took a stock check of my breathing, muscle tenseness and shoulder tightness. Best I could remember them for a long time. They were in tune with the easy hushed ambience of the evening garden. So where was this vague awareness of speed coming from?

I hadn't seen Francis since we met in the morning but our conversation had been travelling around my head constantly all day. I was still conflating his facial features with Syd's, but the words were all his own. I'd never met a schizophrenic before. If I had met him before my own descent into anxiety disorders and depression I'd have just taken everything he did, thought and said as signs of insanity – markers of a mind damaged by a world that it could not understand or deal with. But now I was no longer able to take such an easy option. I knew that perhaps the lack of understanding was just as likely to be another appreciation of reality, seen from a very different perspective. He still seemed to be on a different planet but it was a location in space with which I had been made familiar, through both mental illness and the enormously high doses of psychedelic drugs that I'd been taking for over six months now.

I walked down the garden to the stream. As I sat on a

large flat stone on the bank Bottom appeared from nowhere and jumped up on my lap.

'Hello,' I said, automatically adopting the universal tone reserved for cute animals. 'You've made yourself at home pretty quickly.'

He looked at me and closed and opened his eyes contentedly before starting to clean himself half-heartedly, the warm evening rays of the sun dappling his fur and making it turn between brown and a rusty auburn.

'What's happening all around us eh?' I continued, stroking his ears and neck. 'Why does it seem that everything is starting to swirl? Is it just my anxiety? I don't feel anxious though, that's the thing. I feel better than I have for ages. Even your master's strange words haven't changed that. Maybe it's just 'cos I had a great fuck last night.'

Bottom looked at me sceptically and then settled down into my lap.

I stared into the crystal clear water bubbling over the rocks of the stream. The glistening movement tapped into Francis's voice. For a moment I realised they were the same thing. I visualised a flow of water in the sunlight, made up of the same atoms that formed the vibrationary waves of Francis's voice and the ideas conveyed by it. Should I be trying to understand what he said? Should I be just accepting him in the same way I accepted this stream and the cat on my lap? Perhaps that might allow me to start acknowledging what was happening to me. Maybe I should just start to accede to the strangeness of a world governed by drug-induced altered states, just as Francis had acceded to his voices and the idea of a Phylogenic Memory. And he was right – I had been there. Why would I try to pretend it was any other way? I took a drug and stepped into a different world... and that world was starting to have a positive effect on me. The confusion, fear and horror it could instil were simply learning processes – a therapeutic course that was cleaning me out and curing me.

But its effect lingered. I was no closer to resolving the issue of why the drugs made the *real* world different when their effect should have worn off. My short-term memory was improving, becoming less broken but it still felt as if there was an incomprehensible void within me that was somehow controlling me. At times I recognised it and was able to interact with it but at other times it simply did things to me that I didn't, or couldn't, understand. Maybe that was at the heart of my perception of the world speeding up whilst I stood still. Maybe this was just the latest concept in a litany of weirdness.

What was the Void though? Was it real or just a fabrication of my central nervous system? Was there something controlling it or was I controlling it via my misunderstood subconscious? I shut my eyes tight and attempted to dredge up the remembered awareness of some of the more exotic moments since I'd arrived at the house. I tried to visualise the androgens outside the pub. I couldn't, but what did begin to swell up was the atmosphere of the place. There was a muddy authenticity of period – a moment in time and space captured in every last detail of my environment. It had been more than just the old cars or the shabby unkempt interior of the pub – there was the essence of a past time captured in the memory, just as that past had penetrated the present. For those minutes that I walked down the high street and went into the pub I was encountering that space in a different time than my own. The feeling was overwhelming and unavoidable. I was genuinely there in 1970 or whenever it was supposed to be. But of course that couldn't be so. I wasn't really there. It was simply the drugs making me think so. The same drugs that made me think I fell asleep on the pavement outside the Green Man. The same drugs that were making me click in and out of the everyday even when I didn't think there were any in my system. The same drugs that were creating the impression of the vast fathomless Void that was taking control of my life.

My eyes flickered open as a slight breeze came up and rustled the branches of the willow trees over the stream.

Are you sure about that?

I tensed up; my eyes now wide open. 'Don't start conflating natural sounds with voices,' I said, under my breath to Bottom. But I knew what I'd heard. And as I got up from the stream bank and walked back to the house with Bottom cradled in my arms I realised that they'd been talking directly to me.

I came in through the French doors at the back of the house and made for the library. As I moved through the hallway I heard Francis talking to himself somewhere upstairs, as did Bottom, who wriggled free and shot up the stairs. Once at the library door I paused. The forms of the androgens that I had been unable to visualise at the stream suddenly came to me. Was I imposing this on the memory or were their faces really those of Francis and Syd. I laughed out loud at the thought and muttered an expletive.

'Madness.'

I started and swung round to see Francis with Bottom squatting strangely on his shoulder.

'First sign of madness – talking to yourself.'

'Oh, Francis. I guess you would know.' I regretted the hasty words immediately, but he just smiled and made to go into the library, obliging me to lead the way.

'This is quite a collection is it not.'

My heart was still pumping hard after the surprise and my head swam a little. I wasn't sure if he meant the books or the records. He probably meant both as he first went to pull a few LPs out and then moved over to one of the heavy oak shelves with the ominous looking Latin tomes. He seemed to hover over one shelf in thought for a moment and then he extracted a volume. It was the same one I had taken out on my first visit to the library.

'This is called Boethius's *Consolation of Philosophy*,' he announced.

'Yes.'

'Will you read for me?'

'Erm, I don't read Latin I'm afraid.'

'Oh go on,' he said, handing me the book, open at a page near the end. Bottom grinned at me.

I took the book from him and looked at the page. It was in English.

'I am told you must read a passage,' said Francis, suddenly earnest. 'Go on, I am to listen.'

I scanned the page for a few seconds, my hands shaking

slightly. I wasn't sure if it were a residual of the jolt Francis had given me or the knowledge that once again something beyond my control was taking over. I found the beginning of a paragraph and began to read, my voice thin and flat:

> 'Let us, then, if we can, raise ourselves up to the heights of that supreme intelligence. Once there reason will be able to see that which it cannot see by itself – it will be able to see how that which has no certain occurrence may be seen by a certain and fixed foreknowledge, a knowledge that is not opinion, but the boundless immediacy of the highest form of knowing.'

I flicked a few pages on:

> 'If you wish to consider, then, the foreknowledge or prevision by which the Void discovers all things, it will be more correct to think of it not as a kind of foreknowing of the future, but as the knowledge of a never-ending presence.'

I closed the book then opened it up again to the same page. It was in Latin – indecipherable dead language. I looked to the second section I had read and looked for a word that might mean the Void. I only found *Deus* where the word should have been.

'The Void,' I said, sensing the overwhelming quiet of the room.

'Nothing,' replied Francis, in a whisper that wasn't his own voice. 'Nothing and everything, for all eternity.'

I looked up at him but he was not there. There was just Bottom sleeping contentedly on the Gentleman's chair by the window.

XXIV

Twenty-four is a special number. When Midsummer-Bio *bundle up their magical-collective DNA and introduce the twenty-fourth pair of chromosomes into human cells the*

177

evolution that began with phenethylamine and tryptamine induced altered states during the late 20th century will begin its final stage. It will take over four centuries for humanity to adapt to the new existence and to be ready for complete Collectivity of thought and action. Death will long ago have been eradicated as a concept and replaced with transition. The adoption of the twenty-fourth pair of chromosomes will allow for the final evolutionary step, where collective intelligence finds a physical form in humanity to match the metaphysical. You'll eventually all look like cockroaches, but you won't care about that when you're swimming in the eternal sea of beatitude. The evolution of the twenty-fourth moment will first happen on the twenty-fourth day of the twenty-fourth kalendrical cycle in the year 2424.

The voice was clear and well enunciated but also soft and friendly. I had it in my mind that it was the cockroach girl I had experienced on my trip with Ober who had spoken. But I wasn't sure about that. Neither had I heard it in the normal sense. The voice had seemed to come from... well; it had seemed to come from my stomach. It had vibrated up and down my wound making me feel uncomfortable and slightly sick.

I ran my hand over the bandage. Had I ever worked out if the knife wound was real? I opened my eyes with the thought. For a few seconds I had no idea where I was. It was a bedroom – I was in the bed. The dull lines of window blinds were keeping out most of the morning light.

I sat up with a jolt. Titania was standing at the bottom of the bed in a mini dressing robe that flapped open revealingly.

'Did you enjoy last night?' she asked, mirth on her lips.

'Err, yes, of course. *Last* night?'

She didn't respond but instead slipped out of the robe and began to pull on some clothes at the antique-looking dresser. I stared at her muscular ass. I had no idea what to say. Had I ended up in bed with her for a second night? I had no recollection at all. I sifted through the memories: Francis, the stream, Bottom, *The Consolation of Philosophy*...

'Here you go,' said a fully clothed Titania, offering me a ready-rolled joint. 'You might need it today. We've some guests arriving.'

'Is Francis still here?' I said, taking the joint.

Titania smiled strangely. 'Ah, *Francis*. No, he's not. He might put in an appearance later though... depends how you're doing.'

'How *I'm* doing?'

'Everything depends on how you're doing. We can't have you negotiating too many difficult episodes or... concepts. Your treatment is a finely balanced procedure. You don't need too much exposure to the Francises of this world.'

She pulled her hair back into a bunch and made for the door.

'And don't be lazing in here all day – Ober and I would like a chat to you before the house fills up. Say half an hour, in the kitchen.'

I nodded. She was half out the door then leaned back in.

'Oh, thanks for last night. I like a guy who does as he's told.'

She left, I reddened. But I'd already been through the details of the sex with Titania. I'd already remembered it. I'd put a day between that and now. Hadn't I?

I found my way back to my own bedroom at the other end of the landing, got dressed, lit up the joint and went downstairs.

They were at the big kitchen table, sitting facing each other but not talking at all. I stopped at the door, thinking I might be interrupting something. But Ober must have heard me, or sensed my presence, as he turned and beckoned me in. I sat at the far end of the table taking rather self-conscious tugs at the joint.

'Good morning,' said Ober, 'how are you feeling?'

'Ok I guess. Yes, ok.'

'That's good, because we have some people coming to the house today. There'll be a meeting later on this evening and they will be staying the night.'

'All be gone by tomorrow though,' said Titania.

'Yes,' continued Ober, 'so if you can put up with a twenty-four hour invasion the house will be back to its usual quietude by tomorrow afternoon.'

The word 'twenty-four' swirled around my head for a

moment. It seemed to get mixed up with the inhaled cannabis smoke and travelled into my body, ending up in my stomach where it aggravated the wound. I pulled my thoughts away from it.

'How many?'

'Twenty-four including us.'

I laughed. Titania squinted at me.

'It'll be a tight squeeze. Where will they all sleep?'

'The forecast is for a warm night, so we'll probably sleep outside. Get in touch with nature.'

I looked between Ober and Titania. Their faces were straight, unreadable. 'And what's the meeting about?'

'Well, why don't you come along and find out for yourself,' said Titania, maintaining her squint.

My heart chugged up a gear to think of myself amongst that many people but there was no real fear, no terror of having to be amongst such a crowd as there would have been a few weeks ago.

'I suppose so, if that's ok with you.'

Good good,' said Ober. 'There'll be no reason for any anxiety amongst these people. They're all professionals and know about you and your conditions.'

'Really?'

I didn't know why that made me slightly uncomfortable, but then I'd never really discussed confidentiality with Ober. For all I knew I could be the subject of half a dozen academic papers by now.

'They constitute the collective that own this house... and our other property.'

I suddenly got the impression that Ober was drip-feeding me information. In fact, wasn't this what had been happening since I'd arrived at the house? No, even before that. Maybe he didn't think me mentally stable enough to be given explicit information. It might all be too much for me. But this was a chance to pin him down on some issues. He and Titania didn't seem in much of a hurry to go anywhere.

'So are they all psychiatrists?' I asked, it being the first thing that came into my head.

Titania laughed. 'No they're not.'

'But they are all people who are responsible for a large amount of consciousness,' said Ober, not laughing.

'Eh?'

But he was saying no more. Another drip-feed. I decided to drop the subject and get back to my own issues. 'Will Francis be coming back at all?'

Ober and Titania shared a meaningful glance. I looked from one to another, nervously dragging on the dog-end of the joint.

'Because you should know about our conversations. He seemed to know things. Big things. Big ideas. He sees his schizophrenia as a chance to contact something greater than himself. And then there was the Boethius book in the library. It was in Latin, I know it was in Latin... but then when he was with me I could read it. I could read it in English. And it talked about the Void and a never-ending presence...'

I was gabbling. In my attempt to make sense of things I'd confused the issue. At least I wasn't stuttering. Titania got up and came over to me, then crouched down to my level.

'Francis the Flute is coming from the same place as Syd Barrett my sweet,' she whispers, kissing my forehead and running her fingers through my hair. Her words rebound off something, something far away. They become like a distant memory before she's even finished speaking them. 'Which is not to say they're not real. In some ways they are more real than Ober and me in front of you right now. They are simply parts of the single consciousness to which you now have access. They are part of a never-ending presence.'

I look at her. She gets more beautiful every time I see her. Her shining turquoise eyes hold such empathy, such understanding.

'There are a lot of people contacting the Phylogenic Memory,' says Ober, now beside me as well. He winks: 'Mostly mental cases like you at present. But gradually, progressively, by immutable degrees we'll reach a critical mass – a tipping point.' He grimaces. 'No, let's not use wretched media clichés. Let's think of our own phrases... howsabout, a *pivotal magnitude*... and a *canting juncture*. Yes, good ones. When the pivotal magnitude is reached and we achieve a canting juncture the collective wisdom of the Phylogenic Memory will back up and start working its neurological magic on humanity. Of course, it's going to have to be strictly controlled, and there are going to be some unfortunate patterns of genocide. But once we unlock the *ostium mortis* with the golden key it won't really matter that much. You should be privileged that you are in on things from such an early stage my friend. Skipping around time like a quantum magician.'

I try to speak, but I can't get my tongue to move. Or is it because there are so many thoughts crowding into my head that I can't hold onto any one for more than an instance. Ober picks one out though.

'Why the late 1960s? You keep tapping into that time because it was the first time in history – not prehistory, just history – that a large proportion of society experienced the potential of expanded consciousness. The sixties made a huge phylogenic impact. It all went wrong of course, but it's an important time and you keep drifting there in your altered states because you subconsciously recognise this. And you have a physical contact with it through your childhood – at least only a few years off. You've conflated an important moment in the forwarding of civilisation with the golden memories of a child. It was a proto-period – a necessary time that has helped pave the way for the next stages. It ended in about 1975. Music mirrors the decline – nothing worth listening to after 1975.'

He smiles playfully. I still can't speak. Titania takes me in her arms and holds me close and tight. Her delicate jasmine perfume envelops me. For a moment I'm back on the green hillside with Alice... my Alice or Alice Liddell? I don't know. It doesn't matter. She turns her face to me, she's just a cartoon, an Alice in Wonderland cartoon, but her turquoise eyes are very real.

'Listen to me carefully and remember this,' she says, holding my face in her hands. 'You need to decide whether what they are telling you is true or whether it is a psychiatric experiment. I can't tell you – only you can make the decision.'

I blink against the sun. She grips my face.

'Remember this. *Remember.* Your joints are loaded with

Tryptamines. That's why you're coming here all the time. That's how they can suggest so much to you.'

I sway backwards away from her and my head hits the ground. I turn my face to one side with one eye open. I hear Alice groan in disapproval as through the grass only a few steps away slithers an androgen. He reconstitutes himself as a green pixie, all mischievousness and alienlike, then claps his hands. 'Somes is trues et somes is nots. Those drugsers can brings everyones heres. But ams I reals? Heh heh heh.'

I opened my eyes slowly and reappropriated my surroundings. I moulded myself up against Titania's naked body and pulled the sheets up around my neck. Within a minute I was asleep again.

When I woke up for the second time – or was it the third? – I knew where I was and what had happened. Ober and Titania could choose how they wished to communicate with me: in dreams, in trips, in reality. Did it matter?

I found my way back to my own bedroom at the other end of the landing, got dressed, and prepared myself for the arrival of the Collective.

XXV

I sat in the library for most of the morning, ostensibly reading *Paradise Engineering* but in fact mulling over the conditions of my altered states. Had there been any time since my first trip with Alice Liddell that I hadn't had one type or another of Ober's drugs in me? The image of the cartoon Alice on the hill shifted in front of me as I closed my eyes just as she had done every time I went to light up a joint with some of Ober's cannabis that morning. I was gagging for some but I was determined to stay on top of things for when these people started showing up. But should I have been allowing my actions to be based on the say-so of a cartoon character that I may have contacted during a trip some time ago and then remembered in a dream?

My confusion was near total. But oddly, so was my contentment. I couldn't explain it rationally. My life wasn't my own, my memory was still badly mixing up the recent past,

183

my trips were revealing the unimaginable and the unpalatable, and there was a certain amount of evidence that I was beginning to demonstrate certain symptoms that could be used to diagnose me as schizophrenic. But somehow these things were layered over with... with what? It was like a light – an illumination from an unseen sun. In the same way as all the grottiness and filth in a landscape can be dissipated and dispersed by the ambient colours of a setting summer sun, so my contentment was being enabled amidst the chaos by something I had no name for but which was casting a settled glow over my existence. I was no longer quite as concerned about myself as I had always been. I felt as though I were on the brink of being able to do something useful in life – useful for other people and for society in general. I had no idea what it might be, it was undefined, but I felt *capable* of achieving whatever it was. And that was not a feeling I was used to. I could even look with kindly understanding on my grief and guilt, for mum and Alice... even her, our, unborn child – as if I were judging with tolerance and forbearance the acts of another. Ober might tell me that it was the wisdom of the Phylogenic Memory, taking me over and regenerating me. And maybe he would be right. Was this what was in store for everyone? I had the sudden thought of some of the wasters from the blocks just letting go of all their industrial egos and being nice to one another and everybody else. I chuckled at the imagery.

A scratching sound brought me out of thought. It was Bottom testing his claws out on the oak legs of the Gentleman's chair opposite me.

'So you're still real are you?' I said, tapping my lap.

He started to make his way over to me but then stopped in that melodramatic way cats have when they sense a change or an intrusion in the air. Three seconds later I heard what he had heard: the chugging engine of a vehicle pulling up to the house. As it reached the inner courtyard I recognised it as a motorbike. I didn't know if there was anyone else in the house, so I picked up Bottom and went to the front door. Unless this was a courier, it must be the first of the Collective to arrive. Without a trace of the anxiety that would normally have accompanied me into the hallway I opened the door.

There was a second, just a second, when he took off his helmet that his head seemed to melt away leaving a congestion of oily colours and streaked shapes moving about like wind-blown tree branches dripping storm water. But I blinked and it was gone. Instead there was a little bloke looking faintly ridiculous in all-over leathers that were slightly too big for him.

'How now, spirit,' he announced, offering his hand for a shake. 'I'm Robin. I'll be first to arrive, I always am.'

I put down Bottom and we shook hands. As he retracted his hand his eyes narrowed.

'So here you are in person,' he said, his accent American, maybe Canadian.

'Err, I guess.'

'Mmm, and there's still some in your system. I can feel it. That's good, very good.'

I tried not to pull a face of any sort and beckoned for him to come in. He was very short and dark skinned, Asian perhaps, but it was difficult to tell – there were a lot of different bloodlines mixed up in him. He dumped his rucksack in the hall unceremoniously and then took off his leathers. Two minutes later we were in the library with Bottom purring and rubbing himself against Robin's legs as if he were his long-lost owner.

'I love this record collection,' he said, pulling out vinyls at random and running his hands over the covers. 'It really encapsulates the period... don't you think?'

He had a twitchiness to his manner, as though he should be somewhere else but couldn't help hanging around for just a little while longer. His eyes met mine in question, but instead of waiting for any sort of reply he moved up close to me as if to examine my face. He squinted and seemed a bit put out.

'How much do you understand at present?' he asked, moving back to the record stacks. 'Because I'm not always sure that Ober recognises the need for guidance along the pathway.'

'The pathway?'

185

'Oh, whatever you want to call it. You're ill, mentally ill, right? Ober finds you, fires you up with so many entheogens that you can't help but get better, because you've confronted everything in your trips. But then you find yourself unable to differentiate an altered state from consensus reality.'

Consensus reality – I had the abrupt image of mum speaking the phrase in the car with Alice. Robin stopped speaking and bobbed his head from side to side. It was like he was attempting to extract the thoughts from my head. I got the overriding impression that he was being successful.

'The thing is with you my friend,' he continued, 'is that your altered states of consciousness have too much *reality* in them. Most of our mentally ill pathfinders work with archetypes – big mother goddesses, giants, Persephone, birds of prey picking their bodies apart, that sort of thing. But you've managed to really get under the skin of Time and put yourself in ranges that mimic consensus reality very closely, very closely indeed. The UFO club was a fucking classic man – it may as well have been 1967.'

'So Ober's told you about that?'

'No, I was there.'

'What do you mean, you were there?'

'The Collective monitor you, every step of the way. Or, should I say, have monitored you every step of the way. All your trips have happened. We plugged into them a while back, when you were in hospital. We only needed that first phenethylamine trip with Alice Liddell.'

'I'm not with you Robin.'

'Phylogenic Memory?'

'Right.'

'There's no time there. You only experience a linear-type movement of time during your altered states because you can't quite escape from using your brain. You'll only get out of that when you die. But all of your experiences, past and future as you think of them now, are and were accessible to us because we've manipulated time with our drugs and can join you on your Phylogenic trips.'

I looked at him as though to ask if he were joking. But my stomach muscles were tightening up. He wasn't joking.

'Your invoking the faery... I'm sorry, during that car crash trip with your mum and sis... that gave us the answer to a problem we'd been having trouble with for some time.'

'I'm sorry.'

'A tryptamine compound carrying the second N-methyl group. Your faery gave us the clue we needed. I don't know where you dragged him up from but we took him at his word and synthesised a new tryptamine compound: α, N,N,O-tetramethylserotonin. Turns out it's the magic link. Taken in synergistic conjunction with the phenethylamine 2C-E, at much larger doses than previously attempted, we can direct the action so to speak. We can create reproducible experiences. It's the first step in the next round of human evolution. That's why we're meeting today – to assess results.'

'To assess results,' I repeated, trying to put Robin's quick-fire words into some kind of order. But he'd turned back to the records.

'Anno-Evo... what do you think?' he said, turning around.

'Never heard of them.'

He laughed. 'No... as a name for our new synergy: the *year of evolution*.'

'Yeah, I guess... Robin...'

'Mmm.'

'Can I ask you who you are? And who the others are that are going to turn up today.'

He slotted the record back onto the shelf and narrowed his eyes at me again. 'I'm not too sure how much Ober would want me to tell.'

I shrugged.

'But it probably won't do any harm. I'm a neuro-chemist. That's all I've ever done. I was at a big US university – you'd know it, big money and even bigger pretensions. I was part of a research programme studying the effects of ketamine on glutamatergic neurotransmission in schizophrenics.'

'I don't understand what that means.'

'You don't need to – basically we brought in institutionalised schizos by the truckload pumped them up with ketamine, measured glutamate activity in the brain and observed behaviour. More worthy science with the end objective of synthesising an antipsychotic drug to treat schizophrenia and make countless billions for the pharmaceutical corporation that patents it.

'But I soon found out that I was much more interested in what the schizos were saying than measuring glutamate neurotransmission in their Hippocampi. You give some of these guys a pulse of ketamine and they start talking about allsorts. At first I just thought it was the usual schizophrenic gabblings from the planet Zog, but as I began to run the key words and themes of their transcripts through stat-analysis I began to see patterns in the data. Without the drug there was no pattern, but with it they were telling me something.'

'Telling you what?' I broke in, tense with expectation and picturing Francis the Flute in full flow.

'Telling me that they were being told about the future and that the voices doing the telling were some kind of universal consciousness.'

'But what made you think this was anything apart from madness?'

'The consistency. The people on the programme didn't know each other and the control group of Normals showed no such consistency. Within sixteen weeks I'd run all the transcript data and was looking at a single vision of reality as interpreted by forty-eight institutionalised schizophrenics. It was broken and disjointed of course, but in effect they were all saying that the voices in their heads were generated from the collective unconscious, humanity is about to make an evolutionary shift into collectivism and that after some pretty nasty environmental disasters and some patterned genocide we're all going to be living blissed-out ego-less existences with our brains all hooked up together.'

'And you believed them?'

'Certainly not, but I couldn't ignore that kind of consistency in the data.'

'So what did you do?'

He smiled ruefully. 'Well, I did the only reasonable thing I could do. I bypassed every ethical guideline and regulation set up and monitored by the Institutional Review Board and the university and started testing the schizos with other drugs.'

'Other drugs?'

'PCPs at first, but then LSD, tryptamines and phenethylamines – they're relatively easy to synthesise when you have the labs at your disposal. It was astounding. These people who had been shut away from society, laughed at, feared, shunned, treated worst than animals – they started to... how can I say this, come into focus. It was as if the psychedelics regulated their behaviour but that they were still able to bring over the inherent knowledge of a schizophrenic. And it was always the same: collectivism, break down of the ego, no fear of death, radical social evolution.'

'But I still don't see how you could put much weight on it – schizophrenics taking psychedelics; their brains could have just been programmed to say these things – you might have suggested it to them at some point and got the results you were expecting.'

Robin wagged his finger at me. 'You've been having conversations with Ober my friend – that's good. And absolutely right. I thought so myself. So I decided I needed to get a bit closer to them whilst they were under the influence, get more out of them than just their words, get more... *feeling.*'

'So you took the drugs with them.'

'I certainly did. I started with LSD moved onto mescaline and went on from there. Didn't work at first. I just got blitzed. Good deep fun, but not very productive. It took months for me to realise that it was more than just the drug. I needed to be close to them for me to... to, *contact* them properly.'

'Anaclitic sessions.'

'Indeed. Schizophrenics like it – they're not used to being hugged. The first time was a revelation. You still need the right synergy of drugs but the contact is everything. It enables the joint trip. I was in their alternative reality – not making it up myself, not some subjective hallucination of what I thought might be there, but actually inside their world. Confusing as hell, and you've got to realise that there's a lot of peripheral noise in there but basically you're sharing a reality conveyed by a single consciousness that knows everything.'

He fell back in the gentleman's chair as if exhausted. Bottom shimmied and then jumped on his lap. I remained standing.

'Is that what the Void is?' I asked, aware that I might be showing up my ignorance.

'The Void is everything and nothing,' he said, as if talking to himself. 'If you can get your head around the fact that eternity is absolute nothingness then you start to understand what the Void is.' He closed his eyes and then slowly opened them. 'Quite a difficult concept though... that one.'

'Err, yeah, you could say that.'

'And one that you are only going to begin understanding when you start to break down your ego.'

'I thought the ego was an unfashionable concept these days.'

Robin laughed. 'We don't give a shit whether some up their arse academics with an over-reliance on post-modern conceptualisation think the ego is an outmoded narrative... it exists. Doesn't matter what you call it – it's there in everybody and the only way this world is ever going to become a better place is if we start to break it down so that every cunt and his mate doesn't think that looking after number one is the primary objective of being alive. You've taken the drugs; you know what they do. The reason they work so well on schizophrenics is that they have less ego to break down in the first place. And once we found out how to get into their world the next step was to bring the medication to... to the likes of you – those who are mentally ill with depression, anxiety disorders and the like. Those who have suffered emotional trauma are usually the most receptive.'

'And then?'

'And then we produce it in industrial quantities and let everybody have a go.'

I snorted. 'Oh come on, that's impossible. What are you going to do, drop it through everyone's letterbox as a free sample?'

'Well, we managed to administer it to you without you knowing for quite some time.'

I reddened. 'But that's just me... just me in a house under your control. It's gonna be a bit different surreptitiously dosing up a complex society like ours.'

'That's correct my friend. But there are so many systematically controlled methods of doing it: in the water supply, in food and drink, in medication, in tobacco, in cannabis, in the opiates. You've got to remember that the population in general needs only a tiny but consistent dosage over a period of a few months or years – just enough to take the edge off their normal selfish, materialistic, unthinking patterns of behaviour. Just a sniff of something beyond their usual blank-eyed take on reality. Because what really matters will be the ever-increasing number of people who are taking it of their own volition. Once there are enough of those to cause a pivotal magnitude and a canting juncture then the evolution will be under way... the lumpen proletariat will have just been softened up to allow it to happen.'

I frowned. I'd thought Ober had made those phrases up on the spot yesterday but Robin used them like they were well-worn currency. But then that conversation with Ober probably happened nowhere except my head.

'And are you sure it will make the world a better place?' I said, aware of the earnest, priggish tone in my voice.

'You've seen the future as much as I have. What do you think?'

I didn't really have an answer to that. I recalled the cockroach girl. Her ego-less existence had felt devastatingly euphoric. How could it be wrong? But she was just a vision. She was just an idea of how things could be a very long time from now.

'Kind of,' whispered Robin. 'But it's the most likely evolutionary model we have.'

'So you read minds as well?'

'You mustn't underestimate us my friend. Things *are* going to start changing and we are going to be driving those changes. Nothing is going to stop it.'

'Quis custodiet ipsos custodes?' I said, without really knowing where the words came from. I couldn't remember where I'd heard it but it must have been from Ober. It seemed appropriate. I closed my eyes and saw the Latin phrase turn into English, just like the Boethius. 'Who watches the watchers?'

Robin's eyes flashed with amusement. 'Oh that's very good. I can see why Ober picked you out. Unfortunately, the answer is that we have no one to answer to but the endless

Void. The Phylogenic Memory controls our every move – won't allow us to do anything that isn't right and for the benefit of the evolution. You see, none of us is doing it for ourselves. We've come to the understanding that enlightenment will only be revealed when everything you do is done for the collective good. We're incorruptible.'

His smile was mischievous. It was also infectious – I smiled too.

I walked over to the window overlooking part of the garden and took in the soft midsummer glow holding itself over the grass, flowerbeds and herb garden. It distilled contentment through me. But the presence of Robin held that contentment up – there was something else in the air, something disturbing the mix. I swiveled round to face him again.

'You said you'd already experienced all my trips. You've already been inside them all?'

'Yes, I did.'

'So there are a set number?'

'I suppose you could see it like that.'

'Which means that at some point they finish?'

'That's true.'

'Why do they finish?'

Robin's face took on an inscrutable look. He evidently had no intention of answering. As if sensing the environmental shift Bottom arched his head and squinted at me with his alien feline eyes.

'Could you just tell me... is your name Robin Goodfellow?'

He sunk back into the chair grinning. I closed my eyes.

XXVI

I heard the Collective turn up in pairs and individually during the course of the afternoon. After speaking with Robin I'd had a bit of a relapse and was holed up in my room, afraid of the notion of interacting with these people. I realised my stutter had almost completely vanished but when I thought of them all milling about the house talking high-concept whatever, I was sure that I'd be gibbering my words if I attempted to speak to anyone.

When the longcase clock struck five, as if acting on its cue, Titania knocked on my door and sidled in with Bottom about her feet. She looked as good as always. My first thought was whether she even remembered our night together. My second thought was that she might have remembered but that she probably didn't care.

'You want to come down?' she said, perching on the dresser. 'Everyone's arrived. They'd like to meet you.'

Bottom jumped up on the bed with me and flopped onto my stomach. His purring eased me a tad.

'To be honest Titania, I'm a bit afraid. I haven't been around that many people for a long time. I'm not quite sure I'm ready for it. Would it matter if I just stayed here?'

'Probably not, but I think you'll get a lot out of meeting these people. They're on your side you know.'

Her smile seemed sincere. It was enough to tip my decision. I dressed, smoked a joint – too bad if it were laced, I needed it – and went downstairs to the kitchen, all the time steadying my breathing and holding onto Bottom whose resonant purring acted as a sedative.

Robin was there at the kitchen table, showing something on a laptop to a quartet, two women and two men. They all looked familiar but I couldn't place them.

'Ah here he is,' announced Robin, 'come and have a look at this.'

'Hail mortal,' said the oldest-looking man, a glint in his eye... of course, his turquoise eye. 'Peaseblossom.' He held out his hand.

'Right.' I shook it. 'And I suppose you're Cobweb, Moth and Mustardseed?'

The woman closest to me looked at me over her glasses and grinned. She didn't have Titania's looks but she had the same type of insinuating presence. I thought I'd seen her before but it was probably just the cannabis making me think so. She stepped closer to me and inspected my face as if looking at a painting in a gallery. I was starting to sweat. The joint had kept me calm but this situation was just too new, too unusual for me. I handed her the cat.

'Thanks.'

She ushered me round the table to look at the screen.

On it was a series of hexagons, nodes, lines, letters and numbers. Robin clicked and the shapes became a 3D animation slowly turning around.

'That's the molecular structure of your new Anno-Evo tryptamine compound,' said Robin. 'And this...' he moved the cursor, 'is 2-CE.'

The animated structures revolved around each other and then melded into a single, confused globule with red and blue coloured balls divided by grey hexagonal cases.

'And here's one for you,' said Peaseblossom, handing me a black and white lozenge pill. 'I'm afraid we can't allow you to be a part of tonight without it.'

'Jeez, you don't waste any time do you.'

But my faculties were already beginning to warp and tunnel off with the effect of whatever had been in the joint. I took hold of the pill and looked again at the screen. The globular molecular structure slowly transformed into a human head with dark curly hair, revolving towards me. It was Syd Barrett. His face came full on and then he looked at me, eyes glistening. He winked.

I'm one of them my friend. I'm an androgen – I don't want to say fairy 'cos that might give the wrong impression if you know what I mean. It's not a bad existence... for now anyway. I live in the Phylogenic Memory and advise. And I'm advising you to pay a lot of attention to this lot because they're about to change the world and you may or may not benefit.

I swayed. Syd's voice became lost in static before retuning.

> *Hey ho, never be still*
> *the old original favourite grand*
> *Grasshoppers green Herbarian band*
> *And the tune they play is "In Us Confide".*

There wasn't much point me trying to resist was there? Was there? Where is there? What is where? Where?

I swallowed the big black and white pill.

194

XXVII

What is it about fucking Gloop? I know his presence at the beginning of trips is a red herring and that he's probably just stuck in my subconscious for no other reason than because he's so outrageously disgusting. But I do wish he would just fuck right off.

Currently he's wanking himself off at hammer-drill speed, his right hand a mere blur. Jism is splashing everywhere. There's even the insinuation that it's glopping over my face, which is not pleasant. On he goes, shouting and screaming as he prolongs his orgasm indefinitely. I have no choice but to watch him – it seems that there is something else being made ready for me and that Gloop is the hallucinogenic warm-up act. Finally his dick explodes, literally. Hopefully that means I won't be seeing his hand-shandy act again. But who can tell?

Anyway, this is how it is.

Just in case you haven't realised yet, there is no such thing as Time. It's simply the result of a perception limitation in the human brain. What you think you're going to do tomorrow and what you know you've done yesterday are merely temporary patterns of memory that bear no more relevance to reality than the glimpse of eternity experienced by a dying monkey in the South American rainforest. The perceptions – every single last one of them – all get gathered up into the Phylogenic Memory, but very few actually affect it in any way that alters reality. Think of the question *what is reality?* It's an important if somewhat trite question, but the answer explains why there is no Time and, in fact, why there is no Space either. The answer to the question is *the Void*. The Void is everything and nothing at the same moment, and that moment is eternal. There is no such thing as *you* but for the want of a better word to describe... well, *you*... when *you're* a part of the Void you'll understand infinity, and when you're an infinitely tiny, immeasurable part of the Void squeezed into a life-form's brain you won't.

I have a picture of the drug transforming my brain. It seems to dissolve it. The words are not being spoken by someone else, someone external to me, but they are the product of my own consciousness. And yet that consciousness is slipping away. It is slipping away. I have become we, and we have become everything.

A massive landscape. Watch it devastated by a numberless series of nuclear reactions delivered by huge, matt black, alien-looking ships. We need to act within Time for some things. If we don't we'll just have to give up on the human experiment. These moments in Time are recorded as necessary patterned genocide. In Space they are Africa, the Middle East and Asia Minor. You see, there is a need for control in the movement towards enlightenment – controlled populations of Time-hampered humans. The environmental catastrophes did most of the work – a beautiful example of self-induced destruction – but things need to be rounded up. Nuclear cataclysms are simply the easiest, most reliable option.

We only bother because we find that amidst the numberless universes where Time-locked consciousness develops we can expose the quantum mechanics of nothing and eternity from a non-eternal, egotistical viewpoint. It's useful for us. This viewpoint will always be reconciled amongst the life form unless they first impose destruction on themselves by means of Time-reliant environmental or nuclear devastation. The reconciliation takes the appearance of life forms recognising a collective memory and then finding methods to embrace it and utilise it for their own benefit. Finally the individual becomes part of a collective and the collective prepares for enlightenment. Enlightenment is death and a return to the Void. Take our word for it, we've seen it happen more times than you have numbers.

Mmm, I'm outside. I'm me, but I feel that's about to change. I want it to change because being an individual is despairing. The greedy, selfish obsessive wantiness of it. I need to escape it.

Someone moves into my space and contacts me. Others are party to our interaction.

'Do you think there is any such thing as Truth?' asks the person, although the voice is undifferentiated from my own internal voice. 'Do you think what you've heard is Truth?'

'Truth?'

'A deep reality. Something upon which all opinion and theory is based. Something which is eternal and never changing.'

'I hope so.'

'Why do you hope so?'

'Because otherwise our existence is pointless, chaotic, meaningless.'

'But maybe pointlessness, chaos and meaninglessness are the Truth.'

'What about the Void? Isn't that eternal?'

'Maybe we made that up.'

This scares me. To be given the idea that everything is nothing... but then isn't that the definition of the Void?

'Well done,' says the voice, now a chorus of voices. 'You've learnt something. It's something you and everybody else knows, but something that you'll never grasp until you take the neurological leap that allows you to give your ego the slip. The Void is meaninglessness, chaos, never-ending emptiness. It is without Truth. It is without anything at all. And yet it is everything because it is eternal.'

I'm scrabbling around on the ground. It's night but there is a summer luminescence that coats everything with a deep, dark blue sheen. One eye is open and tracking through the grass stems, coming up close to multi-dextrous insects that reverberate and glisten in the humid air. They sense my consciousness. That's quite an eye opener – they know I exist, but the way they know it is so alien and dramatically different from mine that it blows my mind. Literally. It blows my mind. It now exists outside of its usual constraints, in pieces and fragments.

A fragmented mind. In a million pieces. There can be no proper understanding of what underlies our consensus reality until it is made sense of in a million ways at the same moment. If you can come to an acceptance that you don't

197

really exist as an individual then you're on the path to enlightenment. But paths to enlightenment have never been easy. You are almost certainly going to have to become a schizophrenic first. Not to worry though – before too long you'll be in the majority. And we know what that means in socio-political and cultural terms don't we.

Don't we.

Alice climbed off of me, our sweaty naked bodies dampening the sheets of the bed. She turned away from me and nestled her body against mine as I held her belly and breasts. I kissed her ear.
'I love you.'
'I know.'
'Do you?'
Such predictable routines. But they helped reinforce everything that made up the emotional attachment. I smiled into her thymey black hair knowing she was thinking the same thing.
'Do you think love is truth?'
I was taken aback – she never talked after her 'I know.'
'Um, depends what you mean by truth I guess.'
'An eternal truth. Amidst all the chaos and beliefs and theories maybe love is the underlying truth that makes up the universe... and every universe. Maybe it's the only constant. And maybe it exists everywhere.'
This didn't sound like Alice. I tautened up a bit. I was suddenly aware of movement in the bedroom, like an eddying gust of wind. But the day was still and hot. I pulled my face from her hair.
'Perhaps... but what makes you say there is more than one universe?'
'Because I think that in another one I'm dead and you're mad.'
'What?' I sat up and she turned to face me.
'I saw it, just momentarily, but more clearly than I can explain. The Void isn't emptiness or nothingness – it is love. That's what eternity is. You can't explain it or understand it using space and time because all it is is fathomless love.

Never ending, never beginning love. And what you and I have my sweet brother is just an infinitesimal droplet of it. But it's special and it's real and its cultural unacceptability is irrelevant. We're touching the Void.'

A droplet of her sweat falls onto my face. I turn over but there is nothing but blackness. There is no one there. I dissipate again. I am we.

We meditate within the canopied clearing, gathering up the phylogenic memories necessary for our current purposes. A distant resonant memory infiltrates the continuum. It is of the time of individuality, so many centuries ago in consensus Time. These memories don't often come to the surface – they have such limited value for us. Our bodies twitch nervously at the alien thoughts – it makes our antennae buzz with a strange static.

The depression, the helplessness, the loneliness – they are an astounding memory. They are long forgotten in everyday, physical reality but cast a long shadow over the Phylogenic Memory, even though they're repressed most of the time.

There is an individual (we smile and weep at this) trapped in a cycle of despair and guilt, too weak and alone to escape his own limitations. His inability to connect to the collective consciousness is frightening. He is so alone. He is almost connected to one... one of his family (we all grin and grimace at this) but they are prevented by some unfathomable social coding. But now he's being freed. It's a tortuous process but eventually he is opened up and manages to escape his confines of wretched individuality. The way his ego (we gasp and recoil at this) attempts to hold on is unnerving but eventually he makes it with the help of some proto-collective making use of some early, primitive types of psychoactive drugs. He is freed and released. He learns that Time can be transcended but that the human brain and nervous system temporarily prevent it by localising all concepts of reality.

And why are we gathering this memory? Oh, it is because he is here. He has dissipated amongst us and is experiencing our collectivity just as we experience his individuality. Maybe the psychoactives aren't so primitive after all (we nod and groom our legs at this). But he can't quite shake off the last vestiges of ego-control. It means that he loses his battle to stay amongst us and is briefly materialised as an Old World individual in our midst. It is only a moment though. We speak to him and tell him he must leave. Then he is gone and we realise that he has just about reached the end of his journey in that life. We bow our heads and recognise his transition through physical death as we would one of our own component parts (we weep and celebrate at this).

'The seventh phase is Samadhi, enlightenment, a breaking of the cycle of physical life and death, a realisation that nothing is everything and that the Void contains an infinity of Love. It is an acceptance of non-existence, an accession of utter dispersal, a concession that the Void is all there is. Only then will you be healed. Only then will all the pain and suffering end. Only then will the human experiment be over.'
    Ober crouches down and lobs a stone into the glistening turquoise pool. Its impact sends out gentle concentric circles to the edges of the pool, which come to the banks and dissipate into nothing. The water smoothes and I slowly descend into it. It enfolds me and lowers me into another place, another type of being. I have no sight and I hear nothing but I can feel her embrace, her oneness with me. I am we.

We are here to guide you through the next part. Just remember that nothing is ever as it seems… especially when you're coming down off Anno-Evo. Just keep listening to our voices in your head.

XXVIII

'Why was I able to read the Boethius?' I asked, my voice rebounding off the walls and echoing around the drawing room. I wasn't sure why that was important, but it was. 'I know it's in Latin, but I could read it. I understood it.'

'People like Boethius make a strong imprint on the Phylogenic Memory.' The voice may have been Ober's – I wasn't sure. 'Their genius is there to be tapped into when needed: "the boundless immediacy of the highest form of knowing" – you were merely enabled by the altered state you were in to extract some information, some idea that was of use to you.'

'And the same goes for Syd too I guess.'

'You guess right. The drugs just help you to access places that are normally closed. Sometimes they are called the past or the future. Sometimes they are called another reality. But they'll always help you to grow in understanding, in awareness, in knowing, in acceptance.'

I thought I had my eyes open but everything just kept collapsing in on itself. I would move my eyeballs and walls, floors, furniture, even the air itself dissolved then reformed for a moment before breaking up again into a million electric black molecules swarming around me. I could sense the presence of others in the room, human I thought but I wasn't sure.

'Things start here,' the voice said again, in a slightly different tone. 'We are entering the first preliminaries of the evolution of the human species. And you have helped us my friend. We have needed your disorders to guide us... to help us test out some theoretical and technical imponderables. You have been only one of many but you have been many in one.'

I tried to move. I floated but I couldn't propel myself any distance. I made a concerted effort to open my eyes and fix the room around me. I did. But it was useless – they were all androgynous faeries, moving about me stealthily and observing me with big black eyes... black eyes alternating with turquoise flashes. Their limbs contracted and shifted in a jerky slow motion. I'd seen all this before. Bastards. Why were they doing this to me?

'Why are you doing this to me?'

You don't need to know. You've gotten all the information you need really. But we want to let you know that things are about to get a little strange from now onwards. Don't worry though, it's all planned. It's all known. It's all part of the grand strategy.

I looked at my stomach. I was clothed but I could see my naked torso. In a few moments the knife wound gradually shrunk into a shrivelled clump before disappearing completely in a puff of static air, leaving smooth pale skin.

I closed my eyes. Syd and Francis appeared before me and then melded into one person who slowly turned into Alice. She reached out and touched my hand. I felt her nails run down the tops of my fingers and then her lips against my own.

'Love,' she whispered, her voice dripping like a mountain stream. 'It's the only truth.'

Sit tight, this won't take long.

There is an enormous clattering noise and a scattering of the beings around me. My vision reforms and I can focus on the door. Quince is there, Mr Quince. There are others with him. He looks younger, meaner, fitter. No tweed suit and pipe now. Shit, he's got a gun. They've all got fucking guns. For a while time grinds to a halt and they are all suspended in animation, entering the door in some kind of formation with Quince flanked by two bullet-proof vested marksmen armed to the teeth and wild-eyed. I relax into the moment of stillness and smile at the comic grimacing of the men stuck coming through the door. I kind of get the feeling that if I wanted to I could just get up and walk out the door and there would be nothing they could do about it. But I don't. What would be the point? I've been told that it's all part of the grand plan.

I examine Quince more closely. This *is* a younger him. The man I had met was an older him at some point in the past... my perception of the past. He'd just gotten mixed up in there in order to fit into a time period that meant something important to me. I laugh, Consensus Time reasserts itself and the SWAT team, or whatever the fuck they're called, come spilling into the room.

Quince ignores me and moves swiftly to the window where he quickly grapples Ober to the ground. On the other side of the room Titania is being held on the floor by one of the armed men. He's sitting on top of her and groping her tits, unable to resist making the most of the situation in his testosterone fuelled state. She is smirking.

The Collective are pinned down without resistance. It doesn't seem like much of a grand plan to me.

Well, you only have a limited insight. This is just what had to happen now. There are always reasons for things sweetie. Now brace yourself, your reality tunnel is about to change.

Something snapped in my brain. It was like an elastic band, a giant elastic band, had been pulled taut and then snapped violently inside my head. I saw it, heard it and felt it. As I came round from the twanging in my head I found myself outside of the house, handcuffed and being manoeuvred towards one of the cars parked up outside. I was completely straight. I couldn't believe I'd come down off the drug so instantaneously. Maybe that was how Anno-Evo worked.

The humid night air clung to me as my head was pushed down and I was shoved into the back seat. The luminous orange lights on the console wavered for an instant but there was no doubting the stark reality of the situation. I was under arrest.

Peaseblossom was shouldered through the other door to land next to me. He looked at me. At first I thought he was scared. But then I squinted into the gloom and saw in his eyes... I saw in his eyes *excitement*.

Exordium.

XXIX

We weren't taken to a police cell as I had expected; they had evidently organised for us to be dispatched to a special location. It seemed to take about an hour to get there, during which time we sat in silence watching the obsidian, silhouetted landscape pass by outside. I was afraid. First, because I'd never been arrested before – an achievement in itself living on the blocks – and second because I just couldn't believe how quickly and completely I'd come down off Anno-Evo. I kept expecting the two coppers in the front to turn into something non-human and for Peaseblossom to transform into a cockroach, or at the very least Syd Barrett. But they didn't. No voices in my head either. I was straight and we just drove through the summer night.

Our destination was a heavily gated holding centre of some sort. It looked military. My heart started galloping and I even sensed myself stuttering in my internal monologue. I turned to Peaseblossom for the first time.

'What's happening to us?' I whispered, surprising myself with the stutter-free question.

'It's pretty obvious isn't it?' he replied, loud enough to ensure the two coppers heard. 'The Establishment is attempting to crack down on a subversive organisation. They'd probably justify it as drug-funded terrorism if it needed to be made public.' He looked at me and smiled. 'But it won't go public.'

I tried to ask what he meant but we came to a sudden halt in front of a concrete, windowless block and were swiftly taken out of the car by two suited men who had been waiting for us. As we were led into the building I saw a couple more cars come through the gates behind us, which were then shut by armed personnel in flak jackets. I'd not noticed them until then.

My legs wobbled as I walked. What the fuck was going to happen to us? What did he mean, "it won't go public"? My pumping heart started to quiver and palpitate and my eyes were beginning to tear up. I kept telling myself that I would soon be discovered as an innocent party in this... well, innocent-ish – I was sure they'd test my blood and find it running high on class-A substances. But it would be obvious that I wasn't part of the Collective and whatever dissident underground movement was being cracked down on. Wouldn't it?

Don't worry. Enjoy the experience.

Instinctively, I stopped walking to listen to the voices. My guard dragged me on and into the building, tightening his grip on my arm.

Once inside I was separated from Peaseblossom and taken down three flights of stairs, lit only by red emergency lights. A big, heavy metal door was unlocked and, without a word, my handcuffs were removed and I was shoved into a dark room. The door clattered shut behind me and was locked.

For a moment I stood still, opening and closing my eyes in an attempt to adjust them to the darkness. But it was useless – there was no light. The room was blacked out completely. I put my arms out in front of me and shuffled forward. After about six paces I sensed something before me that I presumed was a wall. Gingerly, I stretched out my arm and touched whatever it was. I recoiled immediately. It was soft. I shuffled forward again and reached out both arms. It felt like a cushion, a fabric cushion. I started to run the palms of my hands and my fingers over the soft, spongy wall. I followed it around, ten paces, corner, six paces, corner, ten paces, corner, six paces, corner. The walls were padded, completely padded.

Clumsily I moved into a corner, sat down and rested my back against the padding. There was utter silence. If it hadn't been for the touch of the fabric on my fingertips the sensory deprivation would have been complete. I attempted to ease and steady my breathing but my mind would go wandering and when it came back to my breathing it was shallow and restless. I was shaking too, mostly from fear but also from the chilled, slightly damp air. It was already starting to make me feel clammy. I imagined mould spores growing on the mattress-like padding and my chest started to contract and wheeze with psychosomatic predictability.

I quickly lost track of time. I tried to convince myself that it was existing as normal outside the cell and that I would rejoin it when I was released. But in the soundless blackness this idea was no more than a theory. How did I know that anything else would ever exist again?

After an unknown amount of time I fell asleep. I dreamt that Bottom squeezed into the cell and that he began talking to me telepathically.

'You're in the shit now mate,' he said, his cockney accent

mixed up with a purr. 'When you wake up from this dream you're gonna have no idea how much time has passed. You won't know whether anyone will ever let you out or if you're just gonna have to die in darkness on your own.'

'Right, thanks.'

'That's alright.'

'And how do I know this is a dream?'

'How do you know your entire life isn't a dream?'

'Empirical evidence,' I said, as he jumped onto my lap. 'I have a set of memories that tell me that I was born, grew up and have now landed myself in a blacked-out lunatic cell. It's happened. That's my life. I remember it.'

'But don't you remember dreams as well?'

'Yes, but I know they're dreams. I know they're fantasies conjured up by my out of control subconscious. They don't belong in the real world. I don't get them mixed up with reality.'

'Mmm, interesting theory. What about psychedelic drugs? Do they just stimulate your subconscious too?'

I drifted slightly, as if the floor were moving. I didn't know what to say. The dream was making Bottom take on an authoritative persona. I was beginning to feel weak and sick.

'I don't know. I think... I think they're able to take me somewhere else.'

'So where's that somewhere else? Do you think your physical body goes there?'

'No, no of course not.'

'Then what does go there?'

'My mind, my soul.'

I was getting flustered. I knew I was sounding like a dimwit but there was a weight pressing down on my head that was stifling my thoughts and making me inarticulate.

'So you're telling me that trips are different from dreams, but you don't quite know why.'

'Kind of.'

'What if I were to tell you that you that your entire life has been created out of someone else's imagination and what you usually think of as concrete reality is simply the way that entity's imagination creates your world. In the same way as the weirdness of this dream is typically dreamlike to you so the "concrete reality" of your everyday life is typical of the imagination of our hypothetical entity. When you die you'll just become a memory of said entity. But what you think of as dreams and trip experiences are momentary escapes from the entity's imagination that allow you to see deep reality. Only then do you see how things really are.'

'Bottom.'

'Yeah.'

'Why don't you fuck off.'

'Righto.'

I woke up with a jolt. For a second I thought I felt Bottom on my lap still, but some arm waving assured me he wasn't. I touched the padded wall. Nothing. I couldn't feel it. I pressed my fingers into my legs. Nothing. I couldn't feel a thing. I ran my fingers over my face. But I didn't know if it was my face or not because neither my fingertips nor my face registered the touch. I attempted to compose my breathing and to work out whether this was still a dream. It had to be. My sensory deprivation was total. That was impossible. I couldn't even work out if I had a body because I couldn't feel anything beyond a vague presence of something wrapped around my thoughts.

Do you think this is what it's like when you die?

'I hope not. There is nothing but my mind. What is it supposed to do?'

Maybe it just exists. Maybe this Void is the deep reality and all it can do is make different realities from its own imagination. Infinite different realities. That's all there is.

'What about love? I've been told that the Void is pure love and that that is the only constant. That is the only deep reality. Eternal love permeating everything, everywhere, forever. And once we recognise this we achieve enlightenment and rejoin the Void.'

Who told you?

'You did… no, I did. No, I wasn't told at all. It is just the truth. The simple truth.'

XXX

Days of nothingness. At least I think these are days. I don't know. All I have are my internal thoughts and even they seem to be degrading, becoming less vivid and less frequent. But then I can't judge frequency because the concept of time has atrophied. My only contact with my own physicality is my thirst, which is unbearable. In fact it's starting to take over all my thoughts. Everything is falling out of my mind leaving nothing but the overwhelming need to rehydrate.

I can no longer tell if I'm conscious or not. There is simply nothing. After a period – days, weeks, aeons, who knows – even the thirst starts to become nothing more than a numb pain. But the location of the pain is unknown to me. Gradually it shrinks and shuffles off somewhere else, somewhere external to me. And in its place… in its place is an inluminous, soundless, fathomless, formless Void.

I am the Void. I don't exist.

XXXI

Or don't I? Ober appeared in phases. Those phases were past and future and also the infinitesimally small moment that represents the present. But it's useless to attempt to describe this in terms of temporality – because as we all know time is simply a construct we have made in order to make sense of life and death.

Anyway, he came along in parts. At one point he explained to me that he'd lied to me about the drugs I'd taken. In fact I'd always been on Anno-Evo, in ever increasing dosages until I had reached the threshold that had taken me here. He also told me that Robin Goodfellow had not synthesised the compound from the advice of my faery after the car crash but that he'd actually retrieved the appropriate plant from the faerieland of an altered state and synthesised it from that. I wasn't sure I believed that, but then what do I know?

Anyway, Ober was only in my mind, where else could he be? But he seemed pretty real. He told me that the Collective had got everything they needed from me and that I had been healed. When I asked him (please understand that all communication with Ober is intuitive and non-sensory) about the raid on the house he just laughed and suggested that I'd witnessed something akin to a play. The Collective were simply assessing the ability, commitment and level of infiltration of various political and military high-ranking personnel. The result was always known but the procedures had to be acted out in the real time of consensus reality. Quince and his men were just puppets, and were now undergoing some extremely heavy-dose entheogenic sessions to realign their personality and perceptions. He also ticked me off for letting Quince in the house to bug the rooms, but only in a light-hearted way.

Apparently half the reservoirs of Western Europe were already permeated with Anno-Evo, which was relatively easy to produce in industrial quantities. Lots of people were starting to hear lots of voices and the Collective were very satisfied in the level of control they were able to maintain. Things were happening quickly.

And so why was I still in my padded cell? If it was a padded cell.

'You're in it because you are mad my friend,' said Ober, in my mind.

'But you said I was healed.'

'Well, when I say mad what I mean is that you've been inducted. It's an inverse madness if you like. You've been healed from the madness of mortality. It's good. You'll live the rest of your life with a bicameral brain. You'll be someone who has touched the Void and realised that eternity is non-existence and that it is filled up with Love. Instead of depression, misery, hate, lust, obsessiveness, selfishness, greed, ambition and fear your existence will be an extension of the nothingness of the Void... pure Love. You won't care about anything else. You're going to be living in a very different world to the one that you've known my friend.'

'I'm afraid we had to finish off the chemical changes in

your brain with this sensory deprivation. It's quite standard practice. Helps you to be reborn.'

'Reborn?'

'You're dead my friend.'

There was a stirring in my heart. It was the first time I'd felt anything since... since before I could remember.

'Don't worry, you'll be the same person, same brain. You were only dead for a while. But life on planet earth is going to be different for you from now onwards. And don't forget – this is extremely important: *we can do anything we like with Time. Once we reach the canting juncture we can impose the changes on any moment in time. Everything you've been told about how long the fundamental social changes will take was just a mask to make the timescales seem more believable.* Good luck, and thanks for your help. Without you and others like you we would never have worked out how to reach where we are going.'

A lucid image of Ober formed for a moment in my mind then quickly fizzled into other forms: Titania (my cock stirred at her image, I must have been regaining my senses), Robin, Francis, Syd... Bottom. They congealed together for a moment and then faded amidst a static-filled wipe across. Mum's face appeared in an amorphous, vague way before disappearing into blackness.

I fell into a deep, dreamless sleep.

XXXII

It was always easy to accept the places that Anno-Evo took you. The increased dosages I'd been recommended recently from my local Custodian simply magnified the lucidness of the Experience. But I have to admit that this last one was something else. The complexity and characterisation of the Experience reached new levels. I wondered if perhaps there had been a development of the compound, whether the Collective were working towards the Samadhic Progression more quickly than had been expected.

I leant on the parapet and gazed over the blocks. I'd always loved this time of year when the ivy, clematis and honeysuckle covered the concrete buildings to create a scented greenery with bursts of mauve and yellow colour. The sun was dipping in the April sky and the whole co-operative was bathed in its subdued purple haze. The bubbling fountains in the courtyard below caught some light reflected from windows above so that they glimmered red and orange. The peace of the place was profound. It was never something I took for granted. And after my last Anno-Evo experience it seemed even more important. That was probably the lesson I had needed to learn: what could have been.

Don't forget that Time is malleable and that without consistent progression towards the seventh phase we could still be in danger of slipping back into egoisis. You need to stay alert... stay connected.

I allowed my Instructor's voice to fade and then closed my eyes. I always found it easier to make the connection without visual disturbances. After about a minute I began to hear the telltale static disturbance you get just before a connection, and I started to visualise her.

'What are you up to?' I thought. 'You feel so happy.'

'I'm always happy aren't I,' replied Alice, sounding mischievous. *'We've just finished yoga. The children are about to drink their water so we're going to stay with them until they're safe.'*

'Hurry back. I love you.'

'I know. See you tonight.'

I zoned back into myself and drifted back inside. The claustrophobic interiors of the last Experience hung as a residual memory and so the open plan space was comforting. Knowing I shared everything with the co-operative warmed me inside. I idled for several minutes just taking in the openness of the level and watching people mill about, pleased to feel the ever-present connection with my compatriots.

Eventually, I sat down at the sounding-board, plugged myself in and began to let my thoughts go. I visualised my Experience from the beginning and then allowed it to wash over me and those who were recording it. I knew they'd have missed quite a lot of it originally but the sounding board usually consolidated everything for the Phylogenic.

It was slow getting started – I had been meaning to call in a technician to look at it for a while now – but soon I felt the whirr, click, thump of the neuroloading unit and I settled down to let them empty me out.

Whilst that was happening I asked one of the compatriots to put some music into my head. She connected with me for a moment and then hit the neurotransmitter. My memory activated the song and made me believe I was listening to it: 1973 – *Neurosis Teurosis*, Syd Barrett and the Pink Floyd Sound. Fabulous stuff.

I settled into the chair and closed my eyes. The imagery in my consciousness swelled in the usual way and I relived the trip as a disjointed but coherent virtual cognition. Could I have been given access to an alternative history on this trip? I'd heard others in the co-operative talk about some of the strange places large doses of Anno-Evo had been taking them recently. They had spoken of it being like our world but different in many ways. But this had been my first experience of it. It was as if the 1975 Canting Juncture had never happened. I laughed out loud at this, which made the sounding board buzz and vibrate. I settled back down.

The residuals of Alice disturbed me. I wasn't used to being disturbed or upset during neuroloading and I stiffened up enough to cause a crackling interference in the process.

Relax sweet one. Just know that what you experienced was only how it could have been. You were only there to pick up some observational fragments from an alternative reality. It never really happened in the sense that what you are doing now is happening. Relax.

I did relax. This particular Instructor's voice was always so calm and reflective. Her voice coincided with the virtual cognition of Titania seducing me. The sound of her whispering in my ear was relived with penetrating clarity. But it quickly dissipated and I was immediately neuroloading one of the trips within the trip on... what was it? DMT. Pure DMT!

212

How primitive was that. But it certainly did do a job on me. I sank into the womb of the Neolithic long barrow as if it were happening to me again and allowed the deeply satisfying nurture of the Great Mother to engulf me and feed my consciousness. When I came to lay outside of the barrow, reborn and with new life, I became confused by the tenderness of my own mother's touch and words. How bizarre -- to know your own mother. The cognition quickly skipped to the car journey and crash.

And that's why the Collective disbanded familial units. Once that was done things became easier... society blossomed.

The anger was shocking. How could anything like the Love between Alice and me ever be wrong?

Quite. But that's what happens to people when they allow their egos to gain control and substitute all those negative emotions for Love.

And then there was the sequencing of the seven phases of humanity, shown me by Ober. I had quickly realised that Ober was a real person from the Collective, who had probably followed me into the trip as a guide, someone to create structure and to ensure I had useful experiences. His ushering me into the sixth phase was particularly beautiful. Of course, we all knew this was where we were heading, Anno-Evo had allowed us to see it often enough, but to have it shown to me in virtual cognition of a trip within a trip was profoundly moving. To experience and interaction with the *Homo-Cryptocerci* as if from the perspective of an old-human was illuminating whilst at the same time sad. How sorry I felt for those before the Pivotal Magnitude. How lonely they were. How alone with themselves, unaware of what awaited them.

But as my tears welled with sympathetic union there was an odd noise from the sounding board. It was a clanking deep inside the machine, a clanging of metal. It was like heavy metal doors being slammed shut in the distance. Then, suddenly, the lights started going out. First the ambient lights that always moved like globules of coloured oil on the board faded and then the lights in the building went out. But the lights hadn't been on. It was still daytime. The early evening light had bathed the room. That meant the sun had gone out.

And that meant something bad.

XXXIII

I shuffled around in the darkness trying not to let my face touch the damp padded wall. I was shaking all over. I'd been there. I knew I had been there in that world and now for some reason I was back in the padded cell. The loss was overwhelming. All the connections were gone. They had been ripped from me like epidurals from a patient in hospital. I was alone again.

Alone.

The voice in my head made me freeze. I hardly dared breathe.

Alone again or. Maybe there are multiverses and you've been given so many mind-altering drugs that you don't know which one you're supposed to be in any more. Or maybe you are actually in more than one place at the same time. If you knew the first thing about quantum physics – which you don't because you're too stupid – you'd realise that the sub-atomic world does not adhere to what you think of as reality. Particles are in many places all at the same time, moving backwards and forwards in time, existing in fuck knows how many dimensions... and you are, after all, just a very big mass of particles. Mind you, it's all just theory. At the moment there is no doubting your current predicament. Do you think it's real?

'I don't know. Can you help me? Can you please help me?' I didn't know to what or to whom I was talking. There was no answer anyway. A single tear blobbed out of my eye, down my cheek and dropped onto my hand. Instinctively I put it into my mouth and tasted the saltiness. It felt very real. This wasn't a dream or a bad trip. I was alone in the blacked-out cell. I slumped my head and began to cry.

Time passed; at least I think it passed. But I was now questioning all my presumptions. Maybe this was it. This was death. I'd overdosed and died and this was it: nothingness without time or space. And yet my senses came and went. I would feel nothing, sense nothing but my own consciousness, but then imperceptibly this would change and I would begin to smell the dampness and feel the ground and padded walls. I would never see anything in the blackness but my own voice seemed to make a sound in my ears.

'If anyone is listening to me... I'm frightened. I don't think I deserve to be treated like this. Why am I being treated this way?'

My voice sounded odd but I was sure that it was real. But then it echoed around inside my head and my senses of touch and smell became muted, making me think that I must have just imagined my own voice.

You have no voice here. When you next use it remember that it's just a figment of the Phylogenic imagination. Ready?

I woke up abruptly, heart beating hard, rubbing my eyes at the new light.

A million bright ambassadors of morning.

I quickly stood up and looked around for the origination of the voice. Of course, there was nobody there. I squinted at the relative brightness of the room. The bright ambassadors were indeed streaming through a window high up in the wall of an innocuous, pastel-painted room, which was small but comfortably furnished with a single bed, armchair and desk. Through an open door I could see an en-suite bathroom in semi-darkness. I rubbed my eyes again. The memory of the blackened padded cell reverberated but was being swiftly drowned out by what I saw in front of me. I went to the wall underneath the window and touched it: plasterboard, dry plasterboard. I moved to the main door and turned the handle. It was locked. That brought a prickle down my back but the relief of having apparently escaped the blackened cell outweighed the anxiety of being in a locked room.

Then I remembered the dream of another world of which I had been a part: the ivy-clad, honeysuckle-scented blocks, the big open room, the sounding board. The spatial and temporal authenticity of the experience came with the memory and hit my like an onrushing neurological train. I dropped into the armchair. That had not been a dream. It had happened to me.

Correct.

The voice fizzled away. There were footsteps outside the door, the lock clicked and a woman came in. I froze in the chair, my muscles contracting throughout my body. My head was involuntarily nodding in spasm.

'How are we this morning,' she said with studied nonchalance.

She was young but was trying to make herself look older with Laura Ashley frock, scraped back hair, horn-rimmed glasses and old-fashioned briefcase. I attempted to say something but I just ended up gulping as the spasm in my head spread to my throat. She looked at me with the slightest of quizzical frowns.

'Do you remember me? I'm Helena.'

I stared at her. My blankness must have been a clear answer.

'Don't worry. It doesn't matter. I'm your assigned psychiatrist whilst you're at the centre.'

'Really?' I said, my spasmodic gulping clearing for a moment. 'You look too young. Where's Ob-b-ber?'

It shouldn't have but the stutter surprised me. Helena's expression was inscrutable. She didn't reply but perched herself on the edge of the bed, opened up her briefcase and placed a notebook on her lap.

'We need to go through a few things to update your initial assessment. We need to know just where you're at.'

I had relaxed a touch. The gulping seemed to have abated. I couldn't be sure but she seemed nervous. It helped me keep control. 'Can I ask you some questions first,' I said, pleased to lose the stutter.

Rather stiffly she nodded assent.

'Where am I?'

'You're at a psychiatric centre.'

'And how long have I been here?'

'A few weeks.'

It was pretty clear I wasn't going to be learning much from my questions, so I decided I might as well ask some big ones. 'What year is it?'

She laughed and wrote something in her notebook but didn't even look like giving an answer.

'Was I brought here after the raid on the house?'

'I think that perhaps we need to leave these questions till a bit later. We need to know a few more things about your condition first, whilst you are... please.'

I felt an obligation to compliance. It outweighed the urge to either ask more questions (whilst I was what?) or to get up, walk out the door and see what she would do. As that last thought went through my brain I realised she'd been using 'we' not 'I'.

'The first thing we need to know is what you remember about the last few days. I'm going to ask a series of questions and I'd like you to answer them as succinctly as possible... that's as *simply* as possible.'

'Yeah thanks.'

She reddened a fraction and straightened her back. 'Do you remember being taken from the house where you were staying?'

'Yes.'

'By who?'

'The police I guess. Mr Quince, Peter Quince was with them.'

She nodded and made notes. 'And what do you remember about your time in the house?'

'That's not really a question I can answer *succinctly*.'

She blushed properly this time, which made me feel guilty so I started off on a waffley resume of what I remembered. But I soon realised that she'd stopped taking notes and was looking at me over her glasses. I stopped, glad that I hadn't gone into too much detail.

'I think I need to tell you at this point,' she said, poshening up her voice a little, 'that you have had several acute psychotic episodes brought on as a functional cause of your schizophrenia.'

'My schizophrenia?'

'In fact you've been suffering from a series of psychotic episodes since you came to us. This is the first time we've had you in anything like a lucid state.'

I was instantly on edge. 'If that's t-t-true why would you be coming in here alone?'

Her eyes flickered towards the door. I followed them with a lurch of my head and saw the tiny CCTV above the door.

'Oh.'

'Everything is recorded, sound and vision. We do have orderlies should things... well, you know. Sorry, I should have explained this.'

Her nervousness was having a calming effect on me.

'Am I your first patient Helena?' I asked, attempting to convey some goodwill humour that might calm her down.

She averted her eyes for a moment, took off her glasses and then brought her eyes back to meet me. They were bright and turquoise. The rush of blood through my lungs was enough to cause me to gasp out loud. She didn't seem to notice and carried on talking, now with a recaptured degree of authority.

'These psychotic episodes are typical for a person suffering from schizophrenia, although in your case they seem to have been particularly acute episodes. You've had a succession of complex multi-sensory hallucinations and primary delusions. The easiest way to think about it is to imagine that you have been experiencing waking reality through your dreaming brain. Your perception and conception of the real world have been processed by the right hemisphere of your brain to a much greater extent than a—'

'—A normal person.'

'A person without schizophrenia.'

'So you are telling me that I've been living a dream for the past however many months.'

'Only during your psychotic episodes.'

I sunk back into the armchair to consider this. What had

they gotten out of me during my psychotic episodes? Was the blackened padded cell one of the episodes? And how could I differentiate these episodes of deluded hallucinations from reality? I thought of Ober and Titania, of everything that had happened to me in the blocks and at the house. I thought of Alice.

If we shadows have offended,
Think but this, and all is mended,
That you have but slumber'd here
While these visions did appear.

The voice was Robin's; I recognised it instantly. In the doorway, accompanying the voice just for a split second, a small androgen slithered over the threshold and grinned at me before vaporising into nothing. I stared at the empty space with my mouth hanging open.

'Are you ok?' asked Helena, her voice echoing slightly.

'Yes I'm ok. I'm ok.'

But without realising it I had pressed my fingers to my temples and was rocking backwards and forwards in the chair. It probably didn't look overly impressive.

'Because we're in no hurry. We just want the best for you.'

'Do you?'

'Yes.'

'Are the voices going to go away?'

She cocked her head to one side and pursed her lips. 'We have a lot of medicinal and therapeutic tools at our disposal to help you. I'm not suggesting it will be easy, or quick, but we have a good record of treating your type of psychosis. I think there is a good chance of you recovering and living a normal life.'

I attempted to ignore the ghastliness of what a "normal life" might entail and tried to decide if she were lying or not. She was obviously trotting out standard psycho-speak for nutters but there was something not quite right about her tone. But then how could I even be sure what her tone was – I'd just been hearing some character from my potentially non-existent past quoting poetry at me at the same time as seeing a fairy materialise in the doorway of my cell in a loony bin. And she had turquoise eyes.

'But we do need to get some details of your life history if at all possible. We've not been able to gain access to your medical records for various reasons and you don't have any close family, am I right?'

'That's right. No close family.'

'But we do know that you were detained under section four of the Mental Health Act at the end of last year and then released under a supervised discharge. And that's about it… can you tell us anything else?'

'Who authorised the discharge?'

A fragment of a smile crossed her lips for the first time. 'Do you not remember?'

'Yes, but surely you know. You don't need me to tell you.'

'As I have said, there's a bit of a hole in your medical records. You're life history is a bit of a mystery after that sectioning. All *we* know is that you were discharged. We had hoped talking about it might jog your memory a little.'

We stared at each other in silence for a minute. I realised she was probably trying out an arsenal of psychological tricks on me but I couldn't be sure what she was really getting at. After the minute I decided I might as well come clean.

'Ok. Ober, Professor Oberon Liddell, discharged me. I had a whole raft of anxiety disorders and depression and he treated me with a course of psychedelic drugs: LSD at first then phenethylamines, tryptamines – they were given to me in ever-increasing dosages. I was taken to their house in the country after an injury and I was treated there. It worked. They got rid of my stutter, dissolved the anxiety and cured the depression. The only thing is, I've spent most of my time during the last eight months in an altered state of consciousness and now I'm having trouble deciding whether this world is as real as the other world that I know exists. Is that enough?'

Helena looked at me through another half smile. 'And for what reason was Professor Liddell treating you at the house?'

'I just told you.'

'Was there not another reason for you being there?'

'Well… the house was owned by a Collective. They had

certain ideas, certain plans. The whole thing about the entheogenic drugs was that they could change our consciousness for the better. They could help evolve humanity into a more co-operative collective intelligence. They took you to another reality and you could bring back the wisdom and knowledge found there. They'd just developed a super drug called Anno-Evo... although come to think of it Ober told me that had been the drug from the start... he told me that when I was in the padded cell...'

Helena was looking at me over the top of her glasses again. My fingers were still pressing against my temples. I quickly removed them and looked at the floor.

'Go on,' she said, gently.

'I can't tell you all the things I've experienced. I know it just makes me sound like a nutcase. But it *was* real. That alternative world was real in a way fundamentally different than this reality but it exists every bit as much as this.' I motioned around me at the room. 'And you know what? They all had turquoise eyes – just like you.'

'I don't have turquoise eyes,' she replied, as if she'd expected to be told she did.

I leaned forward in the chair and stared at her. She took her glasses off for me.

'They're actually two slightly different colours due to an accident when I was a child.'

One grey, one deep blue, just like Ober's. Was this some kind of message? Was I being contacted, or maybe even tested?

'People with your acute condition will often attribute uniformity to groups of people they believe to be in control of their lives. This often takes the form of a colour or even a smell. It's actually quite a classic delusional symptom amongst psychotic pat—' She trailed off, coughed and flicked through her notebook ostentatiously. 'But this is something we can work through later. For now I think the first thing we need get a handle on is what drugs you remember being administered to you. Do you remember or know their names?'

I went through the list of what I could remember. Helena tried to maintain a dispassionate professionalism but I could see her eyes widening as I rattled off the catalogue of psychedelics. At the end I closed my eyes and tried to remember the chemical name for the compound that needed to be mixed with 2C-E to make Anno-Evo. I attempted to visualise the fairy in the road but the name wouldn't come to me.

'It doesn't matter,' said Helena, evidently wanting to move on.

'Yes it does,' I said, sharply. 'Anno-Evo will change humanity forever. It will allow people to see that death is not real and that our consciousnesses are linked to a single Phylogenic Memory that stores every thought, action, sensation... everything from this world and all the others. Imagine what it's like to tap into that.'

'Well, you tell me what it's like.'

I sat back in the armchair suddenly aware that I was probably conforming to psychotic type. The abrupt desire to be alone washed over me.

'I'm sorry Helena, but would it be possible for you to leave me alone now.'

'Of course. But I'll come back a little later if that's ok.' She got up and made to leave but turned at the door. 'We're confident that these lucid spells will become the norm, but we do need to keep you under quite close supervision for the foreseeable future. I'll see you in a little while.'

I stood up, got my breathing under control and looked out of the window at the patch of blue sky with wispy clouds passing over it.

What she plans for you needs to be seen as a threat. This is just a remnant of the world you need to escape. It's a vestige of memory that you've slipped into. It isn't real. But don't worry – we'll get you out.

'When?'

Real soon my friend. Real soon.

XXXIV

Helena didn't come back. I sat wide awake throughout the night until the dreary grey light of dawn confirmed that I'd been left alone for the best part of a day. I remembered the dawns that I had experienced from Alice's bedroom – we always slept in her bedroom – and how they would make me low. It was the time I always felt most guilty for what we were doing. She would never be awake, it would just be me and the dismal softness cast over the room by the dawn dullness.

But where did that exist? Where were those moments lodged? Were they just perceptual memories stored in my temporal lobe ready to die with me? Or were they already a part of Ober's Phylogenic Memory, feeding in to the collective wisdom of humanity? And if they were what good were they doing?

They don't need to be doing any good *my friend. They just exist and inform. They form the outer surface of the Void. They constitute the meaning of life. They help us to understand Love.*

The voice was Ober's. But it was from a dream. I woke up with momentary hypnopompic imagery and sounds swirling through my head, and found myself back in the blackened padded cell. I felt around me, recoiling again from the dampness of the walls and floor. But this time I could hear things that definitely weren't in my head. They seemed to be rebounding off the walls or surfaces of some huge cavernous space around me – like the dripping of water at first but then more like distant human voices, broken into half syllables and echoing into one another. I tensed up and strained to hear what they were and to judge where they were coming from. I knew I was in the cell but the blackness appeared to stretch out for an immeasurable distance. And the distance was both space and time. From out of both came a figure. I couldn't see it but I sensed its presence. It contained everyone and no one at the same time. For a moment it filled me with what I recognised as an acute depression. But I soon realised that depression was only a part of what it was. Everything and nothing. Nothing. I allowed myself to fall into its vast nothingness.

And now I'm following Helena down a dimly lit corridor that smells of cheap air-freshener. Or maybe that's her deodorant or perfume. She is silent and will not make eye contact when she looks behind her to make sure I'm still following her. We come to a door at the end of the corridor; she opens it, ushers me in without speaking and closes it behind me.

Ober sits behind a strange looking table made up of globular, oily lights. Titania stands behind him, arms folded.

'Sit down my friend,' he says, nodding towards a chair.

I sit down. The table is a sounding-board – I suddenly recognise it.

'It's time for you to come with us,' says Titania. 'Time to escape all this.'

'Of course you don't have to,' says Ober. 'But you'll be much happier joining us than you will if you stay here.'

'Alice is waiting for you,' says Titania, with a glimmer. 'It is a place where Love is exerting its influence on humanity in many and glorious ways. It's all worked out as well as we had expected... better probably.'

She has her usual air of witchiness about her with a smile that makes me smile. But I feel suddenly ill with stomach cramps and a headache and I can't remember why I am here. I look at Ober, mutely questioning.

'This is just a memory of a world that never was,' he says, motioning around him. 'We just needed to get back to a time when human consciousness first shifted from one phase to another. And we needed you for that. We needed your psychosis. Others were helpful, but you provided the key. You found us Anno-Evo. And once we had that we could go back with you and plant it in humanity. Remember that night in the UFO club?'

'That was a trip.'

Ober laughs. 'No, that was the moment it happened. 27 January 1967. That was the moment we transferred one world to another. Think of the quantum particle that is in many places at the same instant. Well, turns out it's more than theory -- that's how it all works – the universe, infinity and everything. Only sometimes the particle meets itself and shakes hands. In this case it met to the sound of Syd Barrett and Pink Floyd. We swapped Anno-Evo for LSD and the counterculture won. From thereon in the Collective has made constant progress. We rule the world now my friend. Well, most of it.'

'But—'

'You've been crossing backwards and forwards from this reality to the other since we met. But now this one has become degraded and you are starting to realise it's not real. You'll come round tomorrow and recognise it for what it is.'

'Just a dream,' says Titania. 'A Phylogenic dream.'

I look from her to Ober and back again. My headache is thumping at the sides of my skull and my stomach cramps are getting worst. I'm starting to feel as if I might be sick. It prevents me from concentrating on what they're saying.

Titania pulls a tiny wooden box out of her pocket and places it on the sounding board. Ober opens the lid and takes out a big lozenge-shaped pill. It changes its colour, chameleon-like, with the sounding board's moving globules of multicolour lights but I can make out the embossed writing on it: *Anno-Evo 24-x*.

'We're pulling out all the stops for you my friend,' says Ober. 'This is brand new. It's the most deeply effective tool we have at our disposal. It will speed up the evolution. The compound's been synthesised from a secret Faerieland orchid. We had to spend a lot of time in elf-infested lands to negotiate its transference.'

He grins and gestures for me to take it. The physical pain of my cramping stomach is becoming almost unbearable. I can't think straight. Am I supposed to trust them? Are they real?

'Are you real?'

'As real as anything else.'

I pick up the pill, feeling a tug of memory from the sounding board as I do so. It is the memory of Alice and her love. It sinks into me, authentic and vital, and starts to dissolve the pain in my head and stomach. I look at the pill for a moment, allowing the multicoloured swirling to settle into a calm, watery turquoise. I look back up at Ober and then Titania who winks and smiles her smile.

I close my eyes and swallow the pill.

Terminus et Exordium

Imagine if you were able to share the consciousness of every person in the world who happened to be falling in love at a given moment, altogether at the same time. You would be invaded and overwhelmed. The ecstasy of the individuals would translate beyond the personal sense of worth and happiness brought about by the descent into love and would become a universal recognition of what fills the Void. And the recognition would come with a sense of the deepest reality. Your collectivity has gone beyond ideas and theories and has come to the bottom of things. It is no longer opinion or perception. It just is.

I took Alice by the hand and led her over the stile and onto the footpath that wound through the woodland. The blossoming of life was everywhere. Bluebells carpeted the ground and oak, lime and beech announced the return of vitality to the world with their shimmering new greenery. Above us the clear turquoise sky showed in patches through the upper reaches of the woodland canopy and in the distance, at the end of the sinuous course of the path, the white light of a clearing formed a circular, sunlit halo.

As we got closer to the end of the path I realised that summer had arrived and the dense vegetation was crowding over the sunken footpath to form a kind of tunnel made up of trunks, leaves and branches. The brightness of the clearing ahead was in stark contrast to the deep greens and browns all around me and I squinted into it.

We stopped and I turned to Alice. She took my face in her hands and kissed me gently.

'Are you ready?' she asked, running her fingers through my thin, white hair.

'I think so.'

I stroked her temples. Her hair was as white as mine but

despite all the years her face always seemed smooth and soft to the touch. It was only the temples that showed the signs of her age, muted wrinkles delineating her eyes. I held on to her tightly and buried my face into her thyme-scented hair.

'I love you.'

'I know.'

I don't need to walk any further. The light comes to me. When it reaches me I remember it. It's where we all belong, where we all come from and where we all return. It is the Void. It is nothing and it is everything. It is love and it is death.

I am dead.